Jessica Seeker
and the
Ghost Walkers

NANCY ELLEN BROOK

 FriesenPress

Suite 300 - 990 Fort St
Victoria, BC, Canada, V8V 3K2
www.friesenpress.com

ISBN
978-1-4602-7377-7 (Hardcover)
978-1-4602-7378-4 (Paperback)
978-1-4602-7379-1 (eBook)

1. Fiction, Native American & Aboriginal

Distributed to the trade by The Ingram Book Company

Dedicated to the memory of

Arnold Bainbridge.

Journey well, my beloved.

Special Thanks

special thanks to all of you who have given me your friendship, love, generosity of spirit, support, guidance, and when required, a friendly boot in the butt to keep me moving. I love you all. Without you, this book may never have been written.

Dale and Lynda Harney, Mary Rankin, Ron Lazlock, Gail Shepherd, Linda and Peter Spahr, Lydia Mallette, Fuchsia (Lois) Holubitsky, Norm and Marg Blaskovits, Marilyn Scott, Michael Aherne, Deborah Wood, Harvey Popowich, Steve Moore, Connie Parker and Danny Carr, Dr. Ann Wilson, Rocky Hendrickson and Cathy Sitwell.

I also thank all the wonderful folks at FriesenPress. Their expertise and skill helped me make a lifelong dream come true.

Until next time. Journey well, everyone!

PART I

THE MEDICINE WOMAN AND THE WOLF

Chapter One

ife was draining out of me. These men were doing the one thing I hadn't been able to do for myself—killing me. I just wished it didn't hurt so much.

The cheap whiskey, black pearl, and skunk I'd had earlier in the evening were beginning to wear off. And now, every time the truck bounced over another pothole in the road, there was pain. Lots of pain mixed with the stench of a mildewed tarpaulin that covered my naked body.

But it didn't matter anymore. It was almost over. I could sense death reaching for me.

I felt the truck slide in the gravel. I heard stones pinging against its undercarriage as it came to a stop. The truck doors were opened and then slammed shut. I could hear the men's work boots crunching on the gravel as they walked toward the back of the truck and then the aching creak of the tailgate as they opened it. Someone reached under the stinking tarp and grabbed my bare ankles.

"She was quite the little fighter. I like 'em spunky," one of the men said. He sounded like the man who had the crooked nose from too many bar fights. His breath stank from a mixture of garlic and beer.

I could feel sharp objects grabbing and clawing at me, shredding the skin on my back as the men dragged me toward the tailgate. The pain stretched and seemed to moan of its own accord, but not a sound escaped through my swollen and bloodied lips. My eyelids were heavy and sealed shut with dried tears and blood. My face was throbbing with pain.

As the smelly tarp fell off, a rush of cold night air passed over me, but I wasn't able to shiver. My body was limp and unresponsive to any demand I made of it.

"Shame she's such a mess," said the man with the crooked nose and garlic breath. "Nice head of long red hair though. She ain't too tall or short, neither. Just the right fit if you know what I mean."

I could feel him running his hand over my body as he spoke. "Liked those green eyes of 'ers, too."

"Think she's dead?" another voice asked.

This voice sounded like it belonged to the man who had punched me in the face and ripped off my panties. He had me first and hurt me the worst. Big, hairy, rough hands. He stank of stale beer and rancid sweat. They had said that we were going to a party at their bush trailer. I should have known I was the party.

I tried to open my eyes but they wouldn't respond. It didn't matter—I'd seen them as they took their turns with me. I didn't need to see them again. I didn't moan or groan as they slid me out of the truck. I just prayed silently for the peace, numbness, and nothingness of death.

Damn it hurt.

The men's voices bounced back and forth.

"If she's dead, it's your fault you stupid bastard. Why'd ya have to go and beat 'er up like that?"

"Ah, fuck off!"

"How's about we have one more round with her. I've still got a hard-on."

Then another voice, much younger than the rest, said, "Rodger, you're a sick bastard."

The other men laughed. It was the laughter of booze and lust.

"I wasn't being funny. I meant it," said the younger voice.

I remembered a young voice and the boy who was attached to it. My eyes weren't completely swollen shut when he had entered the room and I saw his young pimple pocked face.

He was the only one who had not touched me. He was more frightened than he was drunk or aroused.

"Kid, someday you'll stop being a wimp," said the man with the whiskey breath. "And you can start tonight."

The laughing had stopped.

"Leave the kid alone. Let's just get done with this and leave."

Two of the men lifted me off the tailgate and dumped me onto the ground.

How I wished for death. To finally be free of pain, suffering, and living. *Death, why won't you come for me?* I thought. I begged for it to come, but it didn't.

Although he hadn't spoken yet, there was another man there. I knew he was there because I could smell his sickly sweet cologne. My eyes were too swollen by the time he got hold of me, but I didn't need to know what he looked like. It was probably better that way.

Each man grabbed one leg or one arm and lifted me up.

They yanked me so savagely that my shoulders popped out of their joints with a snap. Pain. Searing pain.

I wanted to scream but I couldn't. My throat was too dry to create a sound, and my lips were welded together with blood.

The popping sound of my shoulders dislocating seemed to surprise one of the men.

"Fuck. She's fallin' apart!"

"Let's just toss her in the ditch and get the hell out of here."

The men carried me down what seemed like a short incline, and dropped me on my back in a shallow pool of foul-smelling ditch water.

The water was refreshingly cold and the pain subsided for a moment.

One man spat on me. I could feel the warmth of his saliva landing on my naked belly. It felt strangely pleasant. Then, I heard them walking way. Their voices traveled off on the wind as they left me to die, lying in the garbage and filth of the ditch.

"Think anyone saw us leave the bar with her?" asked the young voice.

"Don't worry kid. Nobody was paying any attention to us."

"Nobody's gonna care about 'er anyway."

"Yah, she's a whorin' dopehead. Nobody gives a fuck about that kind of bitch. Ain't nobody gonna know she's gone."

"Hell, we've done the world a favor."

Someone laughed. The truck doors slammed shut. I could hear gravel being hurled into the air as the truck sped away.

There was only me now. Naked and lying in a few inches of putrid water while being serenaded by the sounds of chirping crickets and croaking frogs.

I couldn't open my eyes to see the stars, but I knew they were there. Shining. Eternal. Without judgment...forever shining.

Alone. Waiting. Death was coming. Beautiful, dreamless death. The nightmares and visions that plagued me for so long would finally stop. Peace. The gentle darkness of peace. I felt something I had never felt in life. I felt joy.

It was over. I relaxed and just listened. Is this what they meant by being in the moment? It was rather pleasant.

Crickets chirped. Frogs croaked. Time passed slowly.

Then, as though there were an echo from miles away, a voice—a wheezing, croaking female voice—spoke to me.

"Your time has not yet come. The Mothers say you have important work to do and much to learn."

I felt someone lift my head, wipe my lips clean, pry them open, and then pour a liquid into my mouth.

"Swallow. This will take the pain away."

The liquid had the fragrance of rotten eggs, the consistency of maple syrup, and the taste of vomit. For a moment I thought this was my right of passage into hell. I had to swallow or choke. I swallowed.

As the pain started to slip away, two bony hands made me sit up and then they wrapped a blanket around my shoulders. The blanket was warm and felt like it was woven from rope. It had the aroma of something I'd smelled before. I remembered. It was sweetgrass...for a moment I remembered a sweetgrass ceremony one of my foster parents had taken me to. That was a different time, a long way away from where I was now.

I tried to move my arms to push the bony hands away but my arms didn't work.

I felt the hands searching under the rough blanket until they arrived at my shoulders.

There was a wheeze and a cough, and the croaking female voice said, "The sooner I do this, the better it will heal. It'll hurt a little."

I tried opening my eyes and mouth so I could see and curse this woman, and tell her that she was disturbing my death plans. My swollen eyelids refused to part. I couldn't coax my vocal cords into making any sound other than a moan.

I thought I could hear a dog panting, but I wasn't sure.

Then suddenly those two bony hands were back at their mischief. They slipped the rough blanket away from my arms, grabbed my left arm and yanked on it. There was a slight popping sound and then a deep, sharp pain raced through my shoulder, down my back, and up into my head all at the same time. I felt myself moan, but I couldn't hear it.

"Good. One down and one to go," the voice said. "You're tough for such a small package. I've seen grown men faint when I relocated their shoulders."

Then she repeated the procedure on my right arm.

On the inside I was screaming. But on the outside, there was no sound at all.

"Done."

Damn. I was still alive. The pain didn't matter, just the fact that I was still alive pissed me off.

It had been so peaceful before she arrived, just me and those shining stars I couldn't see, and a serenade of chirping crickets and croaking frogs.

She dragged me out of the water, resting me on a dry patch of what felt like long grass.

"Wolf. Protect her," she said. She wheezed and coughed. She seemed to take a moment to catch her breath and said, "Girl. You stay here. I'll be back."

Strange how things strike a person as funny at a time like this, but I wanted to laugh at her for giving me that order. I couldn't have gotten up and walked away, even if the Lottery had told me they'd give me a couple million dollars to move.

I heard her walking away. More correctly, I didn't hear her footfalls…I just heard a gentle swish in the grass as she left me. Maybe she was just a ghost, sent to make my last few moments of life a little more miserable. *Yes, why should dying be any easier than living had been?* But at least there was no more pain.

I don't know how long she was gone. I either fell asleep or passed out. I only remember waking to something poking me in the forehead and the croaking wheezing voice was talking to me again.

"Okay, girl. I'm just going to roll you onto this little contraption here. It's a travois, but I call it a donkey powered hammock," she said, as though that little tidbit of information was important to me. Then she spoke quietly to her helper. "Wolf, go keep Jojo steady and calm. He's restless tonight."

I thought I heard a dog pant again.

The old woman wheezed and coughed while she rolled me over until I was lying face up in her strange contraption.

I could feel something soft under me. It had the scent of leather but felt like soft, fine spun silk. After she arranged my body for moment, she placed the rough warm blanket over me tucking it around the length of my body. Then I felt her tie something across my chest and legs.

I heard the animal she called Jojo, make a snorting sound. The woman uttered a few words I didn't understand and my hammock began to move forward. I was suspended but I was also being dragged along the ground.

The contraption bumped along but there was no pain. I could feel the sleep of death trying to claim me. Good. Maybe at last it was all coming to an end.

At least I could hope for the end. But suddenly, I had that old feeling that someone was watching me, and wondered if the feeling would follow me in death the same way it had followed me in life.

Chapter Two

I awoke to something poking me in the forehead. I heard a wheeze and a cough. In an instant I knew it was that annoying woman.

I hurt everywhere. I tried to open my eyes but they wouldn't budge. Something was holding my eyelids shut.

Strange odors surrounded me. There was the sharp scent of sweetgrass, herbs, and what seemed to be spices— ginger and cloves, along with a lot of aromas I had never smelled before. Most of them stank. And some of those disgusting fragrances were close to my nose.

I heard the woman cough and wheeze, and felt her bony fingers poking at me as she checked and replaced my bandages. She rolled me over onto my side and checked my back. She replaced more bandages and then rolled me flat again.

Pain. Lots and lots of pain.

"Please leave me alone. Let me die in peace," I heard my own voice say.

"Drink this," the croaking voice said.

I didn't really believe there was a hell. I always felt that in the end we were all just worm bait, and there was nothing after life. At least that's what I hoped. But at this moment, I was seriously reevaluating that point of view.

"Drink. It will make the pain go away."

I instantly remembered the odor of rotten eggs, but before I could offer up a decent defense, the liquid was being forced between my lips and down my throat. I had to swallow or choke. Once again, I swallowed.

The pain started to disappear quickly, as though it were being pulled away from me by an invisible hand.

Sleep rapidly followed.

This procedure was repeated many times. How many times and for how long, I don't know. It was mixed with feedings of a warm, salty, bitter tasting fluid the croaking voice called thistle soup.

I finally awoke to something being removed from my eyes, and one of the very unpleasant odors I had experienced so close to my nose—was gone.

"Open your eyes, child," the croaking voice said. "Do it slowly. I've covered the window, but it may still seem too bright for you."

She was right, when I opened my eyes the light flooded in and for a moment I saw flashes and flutters of white sparks.

"It might be helpful to squint a bit," she advised.

Squinting helped. Things began to take shape, as my eyes adjusted to the light. I slowly scanned the room.

It was a small room with a door that opened into a hallway. The walls of the room were maple wallboard. Early sixties basement-family-room-décor. There was a vintage black and white picture on the wall beside the doorway. In the picture was an old woman with braids and a beaded headband. She wore what appeared to be a white leather dress with intricate beadwork. A large black bird was perched on her shoulder. A high backed wooden chair sat under the picture.

On the wall beside the bed was a large dream catcher with brightly colored stones woven into it. The only window in the room was covered with an old, yellowing, loosely woven fabric. Bright sunlight streamed through the moth holes and rips.

When I looked down at the bed, I finally saw the rough blanket that had covered me since the old woman had found me in the ditch. It was a crudely hand woven blanket with a huge golden stylized sun symbol in the center.

I looked at the end of the bed. I saw movement. Suddenly, a large figure began to rise up. I wasn't sure that my eyes were working properly, but the figure was materializing into a giant dog's head. As I focused on it, I realized the dog actually looked like a large silvery-white wolf. It was panting and staring at me with blue-green eyes.

"Is that a bloody wolf?" I asked.

"There are a couple of things you need to understand. Never call my wolf bloody. He's a sensitive creature of Mother Earth and he is my Totem Protector. And he is also yours until you find your own. He requires your respect. He has sat at your bedside ever since you came here. It would be good manners for you to thank him for his protection."

"Holy shit," I said, and I couldn't take my eyes off of him. This creature of Mother Earth was a white giant, possibly even bigger than a giant. His head alone was almost as large as my entire body.

"There's nothing holy about shit. And I would prefer that you used more respectful language in my house. Please, thank Wolf," the croaking voice said.

I finally pulled my eyes away from the wolf and looked at the woman I had only known as a croaky wheezing voice.

She looked to be about two hundred years old. Her wrinkles were deeper than ruts in a wet mud road. Her eyes were a watery brown color flecked with bits of emerald green. Her mat of grey hair was parted in the middle and braided into two long braids that hung down past her waist. And tying it all together was a brightly beaded headband with tiny images of a white dog or I suspect...a wolf.

She wore an old, oversized red plaid shirt, a quilted black vest, and a pair of old blue jeans with holes in the knees.

"Well, Wolf Lady let's get one more thing straight," I said, trying to look her directly in the eyes, because her appearance really did hurt my eyes, "You should have let me die in the ditch. I'm not 'thanking' that animal for anything that saved my life. Why couldn't you mind your own business?" My voice was getting stronger.

The wolf let a slow rumbling growl slip through his curling lips.

"I know, Wolf. She's a rather feisty little thing isn't she? And girl, it wasn't your time to die yet," she said busying herself with removing and replacing the stinky bandages that littered my body. And just for the record, they stank worse when they were fresh.

I tried to push her bony, gnarled hands away, but my arms failed to work and the pain in my shoulders was unbearable. It took everything I had to keep from screaming. Instead I said, "And who the hell are you to tell anyone anything?"

"Mouth."

"What?"

"Mouth. Watch your mouth."

"Now listen here—"

"No. You listen. Our Mothers guided me to you the night I found you in the ditch. They have told me you have an important destiny and you have been sent to us for your training. I don't argue with the wisdom of Our Mothers. And you shouldn't either."

"Our Mothers? Wolves? Frig. I've landed in Oz and you're the Wicked Witch."

"I suppose there are some who would call me a witch. But, back to your mouth. Frig is better, but it still isn't acceptable. You must learn to communicate without all the colorful expletives."

I couldn't help myself, I laughed. This old wizened-up woman dressed like a fossilized remnant from some second rate cowboy movie was saying "colorful expletives."

"Laughter is good. Means you're feeling better. What's your name?"

"Ask '*our mother.*' She seems to know everything."

"It's Our Mothers. Plural. And they don't know everything. But until such time as you wish to tell me your name," the old woman raised her left eyebrow, "I'll call you Toadstool."

"What?"

"Now. Let's see how your shoulders are doing. I've been moving them for you while you slept, but that's not as good as you moving them yourself."

She put her bony hand on my arm and began lifting it. I fought back, or at least, I tried to fight back. But it was too painful. I finally had to let her lift my arm.

"Good, Toadstool." she said, giving me a nod of approval. "It'll take a bit of time before you'll have full use of your arms, but this is good progress. Here. Drink. This will help cleanse your body of all the toxic waste you've been dumping in it. It'll help control the cravings for a...fix."

And before I could stop her, she was sticking a spoonful of the rotten egg liquid into my mouth. I tried to spit it out. A few drops flew out, but most of it went down my throat.

"Damn."

"Mouth."

The wolf growled. Clearly the wolf was annoyed.

"Hmm. Yes, Wolf. I think you're right. Toadstool will be an interesting student."

"You can't feed me that shit and keep me here against my will."

"Mouth," the old woman said and got up from the bed. She was at the doorway with a speed and grace that would have been difficult for a twenty year old woman, let alone one that looked like she had at least two hundred years on her scrawny chassis.

"Now, sleep Toadstool. Journey well," she said.

"I'm not a friggin' toadstool."

"Mouth. Wolf, let's go. We have some patients to see," she wheezed, coughed, and started to exit but stopped. She turned to look at me, "I'm Mother Wolf." Then she was gone.

The next time I woke, the old woman was cleaning my wounds and adding new dressings. These dressings didn't seem to stink as much as the others. Maybe I was just getting used to the smell. And maybe it was my imagination, but there seemed to be a slight hint of mint in the air.

"Feeling better today, Toadstool?" she asked, and then she smiled showing a distinct lack of teeth in her mouth. In fact it looked like she was completely toothless.

"My friggin' name is Jessica."

"Well, Jessica, I can hear that your mouth isn't working any better."

She sponged the wound on my leg and placed a clean thick dressing on it. There seemed to be some plant material and other things wrapped in the dressing. Luckily I couldn't examine it too closely, but it appeared as though there was something moving in it.

The old woman looked at me as if she knew what I was thinking, "Maggots. You have a small but stubborn infection and a lot of dead skin around the wound. The maggots will clean it up in a jiffy."

"When can I leave?" I could feel shivers crawl up my spine as she tied the dressing, or poultices as she called them, to my leg. I felt the maggots wiggle against my skin. I wanted to throw-up.

"You're free to leave anytime. You're my patient and my student. Not my prisoner," she examined the dressing for a moment before she spoke again, "However, there is a man here who would like to speak to you."

The old woman pulled the sun symbol blanket over me and tucked it around my chest.

"A man to see me?" I asked, trying to get up but the pain in my shoulders, back, and legs stopped me.

"Yes." She called out, "Constable Tom. She's ready."

"Constable Tom. What the hell?"

"Mouth," her face folded up into one giant annoyed wrinkle, and she sounded like an aggravated school teacher, "Jessica."

There was no time left for discussion. Constable Tom, a tall, well-muscled, tawny-skinned man dressed in a police uniform, was already entering the room.

"Now, Tom. She's still as weak as a newborn kitten, but as scrappy as a bobcat with mange. You go easy with her. Don't mind her mouth."

With deference to the old woman, the tall, tawny-skinned, policeman said, "Yes, Mother Wolf."

Mother Wolf turned her attention to me, "When the Constable is done, I have some nice hot thistle soup for you, young lady."

"Yum. Saving the maggot casserole for dinner?" I asked.

The old woman laughed and then said, "No, I was planning a nice earth worm meatloaf and a salamander salad for this evening's meal."

The frightening part was that I didn't know whether she was joking or telling the truth. Then, as usual, the old woman moved so silently and quickly that she seemed to just evaporate from the room. Constable Tom and I were alone.

"Hello, I'm Tom." He gave me one of those emotionless, but polite smiles.

"Yah. I've got that much already. What do you want?"

"Well, Mother Wolf has told me about finding you. In fact I helped her put you into this bed," he smiled again.

"How nice. Thanks for the lift and the visit. Bye now."

"I have a young man in custody who confessed to what was done to you." His voice was deep and smooth. He appeared to be unaffected by my invitation to leave.

"Nothing happened. I just had a nasty fall. So, I guess there isn't much else to talk about."

Constable Tom, in one smooth motion took off his police hat, picked up the high backed wooden chair by the door, and gently placed it beside the bed. He relaxed into the chair. It creaked.

He said, "Three of the men that...ah...assisted you in your fall...are dead. Seems ol' Rodger had too much to drink. He ran his truck off Pearson's Bluff that same night. Only young Eric walked away. He had a good long gash on his chest, but he survived. The others didn't."

"And your point is?" I was surprised I felt so little emotion for the dead men. But, I was relieved the young boy was alive. To me, he was innocent of any real crime. He hadn't touched me, and in a strange way, I felt sorry for him.

"I'd like to have your side of the story."

"This Eric, he's...what? Eighteen...nineteen?"

"He's seventeen."

"Well, he had nothing to do with anything. You can let him go. Interview is over. Don't let the door hit you in the ass, when you leave."

Constable Tom gave the doorway a quick glance and grimaced, before he spoke again.

"Mother Wolf saved your life. She's a first rate Shaman, Medicine Woman, and healer. You owe her respect. And you could show respect by not using language that offends her," he said. He crossed his arms over his chest and leaned back in the chair. "You would have died of shock or exposure if Mother Wolf hadn't found you that night." He said with such respect and deference it sounded as though he was speaking about a goddess and not a wizened up two hundred year old crone with stinky poultices.

"I was happy to die out there. But Wolf Lady had to interfere. Thanks for the visit and the advice. We are done."

If I could have moved, I would have leapt out of the bed and been on my way, but the pain and stiffness was keeping me pinned down.

Constable Tom raised his left eyebrow. He had dark brown searching eyes. He had the kind of eyes that look right into a person's soul and sees whether they're lying or telling the truth.

He said nothing for a moment. He just stared at me, then got up, "I'll need your name to finish my report."

"The old wolf woman calls me Toadstool. I think that's good enough."

"I can arrest you for obstruction of justice."

"Then arrest me."

He placed his police hat on his head, adjusted it, and looked at me for a long moment. Then he picked up the chair and once again with one smooth movement, replaced it to its original spot by the door.

"If you change your mind and you want to talk, just let Mother Wolf know."

"I won't change my mind," I said.

He stared at me, "The boy will go free."

"And that's a bloody problem for—who?"

He shook his head, "I can see Mother Wolf has her hands full with you."

I would like to say that Constable Tom walked out of my room, but I don't think Constable Tom walked anywhere. It was more like he strolled out of my room. Tall and proud.

Constable Tom didn't return to interview me again, and the old wolf woman didn't mention him again or anything else about the night she found me.

After Constable Tom's visit, the old woman was set in healer mode and put everything she had into getting me well, which included stinking poultices, numerous repetitions of "mouth" and an unending supply of annoyed wrinkled faces. She had much more success with healing my body than she had fixing my 'sick' mouth.

The old woman constantly put fresh dressings on my wounds. And although I stank like a walking outhouse, I was left with almost no scars. I suppose that if I wasn't going to die soon, the lack of scars was something to be thankful for.

There were weeks that lead to months of painful exercise for my shoulders. But my shoulders healed and were stronger than they had ever been.

I thought many times about being robbed of death. I thought about leaving the old woman, but I had nowhere to go and surprisingly, for the first time ever, I didn't really want to run. The old woman's pain vomit formula seemed to help me overcome my cravings for alcohol, but once in a while I did have a craving to get high. Just one little hit of black pearl or TNT was always haunting me. On those occasions, I would take a walk in the woods.

I felt safe in this place. No one expected me to be anything more or less. They accepted me. No one asked me questions about my past. All of them wanted me to feel better, and they were glad I was helping Mother Wolf.

During the months I spent recovering at the old woman's four-room-cabin-clinic, I began to meet the people who came to her for healing potions and stinking poultices. She made sure she introduced me to every one of them. All of her patients welcomed me to the Pinewood Reserve as though it were the greatest location on the planet. Many of the old woman's patients brought gifts, everything from home baked pies to clothes for me.

And always, they gave her tobacco carefully wrapped in a little bundle. When I asked about the tobacco, the old wolf woman explained that the tobacco was an old custom, a gift of respect for her skills, services, and position as their Shaman and Medicine Woman. She used the tobacco in her ceremonies and in some of her medicinal preparations.

Most of the patient-chat was about families, weather, hunting or fishing, and sometimes politics. Most of the talk was of little interest to me, until one day one of the wolf woman's more talkative patients told me Mother Wolf was a city doctor. "A real, honest-to-goodness MD."

That was a surprise because the old woman seldom used anything that resembled modern medicine, other than a few sutures, a scalpel occasionally, sterile latex gloves always, and when pressed, a Band-Aid™.

"Don't believe in all that fancy mumbo-jumbo," she said. She always added the statement that 'Our Mothers know more about natural medicine and healing than all the specialists in the world.' I have to admit that when she talked with 'Our Mothers' it was a little creepy, because the Mothers were all dead.

On the other hand, the illnesses she couldn't handle in her little cabin-clinic, things like brain surgery and the like, she would send those patients to the city to see the right doctor for the job. "Modern medicine does have its place," she would occasionally and grudgingly admit.

And again, to my surprise, many of the city doctors sent her their patients for arthritis and migraine treatments. The remedies the old woman usually prescribed consisted of special herbs, teas, and those stinking poultices.

But for me, life in the cabin-clinic was quiet and simple. I'd never experienced that before. The city and all of my troubles seemed very far away. As though none of it had existed and my past was extinguished. I had lost my cell phone when the men attacked me and I actually didn't miss it all that much. Just as well, because the old wolf lady didn't have a great deal in the way of technology around. She claimed it was all a distraction and, for the most part, served no useful purpose.

On the other hand, I enjoyed the long walks in the woods that surrounded the dilapidated cabin-clinic. I enjoyed the warm, wet, earthy aroma of the forest. The sounds of birds chirping and the sight of squirrels scampering about calmed and amused me.

The old woman took me for long hikes on many of her trails and taught me about the medicines the forest provided, and how to honor the trees, plants, and animals that lived there. We always asked the trees and plants for their permission to harvest what we needed. We always thanked them and honored their spirits with a small sprinkling of tobacco.

Even Wolf had stopped growling at me, and accompanied me on many of my solitary walks along the forest paths. I think he even started to like me. I guess that's because I cleaned up my mouth a little, and I started calling the old woman, Mother Wolf, plus I finally thanked him for protecting and looking after me. I have to admit I felt safe with him at my side. I even made friends with Jojo, the donkey. I discovered he had a weakness for apples and pears. A secret I never shared with Mother Wolf. She always wondered how I managed to get him to do things he stubbornly wouldn't do for her.

Life was comfortable, easy, and safe at the cabin-clinic.

The nightmares that had haunted my sleep every night for the last ten years had gone away, and all of my haunting and frightening visions from the past had stopped. I had peace for the first time. Mother Wolf said the dream catcher over my bed captured the bad visions and nightmares in its web and protected me. She also added that 'Our Mothers' were protecting me. On several occasions she tried to explain the ancestry of the Mothers and how they related to her and to me, but most of the time I wasn't listening. I found all of the storytelling to be a lot of old-timer superstitious stuff. It didn't mean much to me.

Even with all the protection, I still had some visions from time to time. But they weren't frightening visions. Sometimes I would wake in the middle of the night and know one of the women was going into labour. Sometimes, I would know an emergency was coming to the cabin-clinic and I knew what the emergency was. Sometimes, I could see what was making a patient sick before the patient arrived at the cabin-clinic, but the old frightening nightmares of the past and the feeling that someone was watching me were gone.

On the other hand, maybe at long last, the past was over. For the first time, I dared to hope my life could be better and I was finally free. I began to hope and think that maybe I could have a new home here.

I began to help Mother Wolf prepare potions. Mother Wolf called them "medicinal drinks or teas". I also learned how to make all those stinky poultices. She taught me the secrets for natural medicine. I paid her back by not swearing—most of the time. She let me help her with stitching up wounds, birthing babies, and prescribing medicinal herbs. During all of it, I only fainted four times.

There always seemed to be urgency in her desire to teach me everything she knew. She consulted Our Mothers frequently when I failed to grasp the teachings and floundered into a string of those colorful expletives. Mother Wolf's face would fold into large angry wrinkles and she would squeeze out "Mouth" from somewhere deep in the middle of the folds. When I minded my mouth, she was the most patient and kindest of teachers.

My favourite work was helping her with her midwife duties on the reserve. It was a special kind of magic that happened when I saw a woman give birth to her child. First there was the pain and then there was the joy. The day I saw my first child born, I felt something new growing inside me. I tried to identify it. Although I had never truly felt it before, I think it was hope. For a moment while I held a newborn in my arms, I dared to imagine that I could have a normal life, one with a husband and family.

I began to dare to hope that my life could change and it would be possible to find happiness. Maybe. Just maybe.

Life in the cabin-clinic wasn't a burden to me. Gradually, with each day, I woke up feeling happy to be alive and helping people. As much as I hated to admit it, and as silly as I sounded to myself, I began to think that maybe Mother Wolf and her people were helping me heal my soul.

From time to time, I'd think about my other life and returning to the city. Sometimes I missed the modern conveniences of having internet, cell phone, television, and hot water on tap. But as I stayed with Mother Wolf, I realized there was nothing in the city for me other than a few clothes and a tiny, barren basement apartment.

As for a job, I'd been fired from my piss-ant position as a fast-food kitchen helper because I'd come into work drunk and high. I'd have to go back to being a hooker to make a living.

I didn't really have any friends. I kept to myself.

So basically, there was no one and nothing I missed. No one would be looking for me other than my landlord who wanted my rent payment. And even he wouldn't look long. He'd just take my clothes out of the closet and put them in a box, throw it in some corner somewhere, and rent the apartment again.

There would be no family missing me or looking for me. According to my foster papers, my mother was Métis and only sixteen years old when she gave birth to me. My father was identified as 'being of Irish descent' and nothing more. I was born out of wedlock and my parents abandoned me. I was put into the foster system and that's where I stayed until I ran away. I disappeared from the government's radar until I was arrested at eighteen for shoplifting and later for prostitution. From then until now, at twenty-two years old, being arrested for a variety of offences was the norm for me.

All-in-all, the cabin-clinic was the best home I'd ever known, and Mother Wolf, Wolf, and Jojo had become the only real family I'd ever had. I was at peace here.

But for me, good things never seem to last.

One night, at twilight just before darkness set in, that feeling of something watching me returned. Something that was just out of reach and just out of sight. Lurking in the shadows. Watching. Waiting. Biding its time. Nothing made the feeling go away.

***

Eight months passed. Mother Wolf suddenly came to me early one morning before dawn. She woke me and sat down on the edge of my bed. She stroked my head and looked at me with sad eyes. For the first time since I'd known her, she seemed shaken. She wasn't her calm, composed, and commanding self.

She held out a braided white rawhide necklace in her hand. On it was a small white leather pouch. She called it a medicine bag.

"Jessica, you will need to wear this always. It contains protective herbs and spirit medicine. You will need it very soon. Wear it when you sleep and when you're awake, even when you bathe," she said as she placed it over my head and settled it around my neck.

It felt warm against my skin. Suspicious of the things I'd seen Mother Wolf use in her treatments and poultices, I waited a moment to make sure nothing wiggled inside the small white bag. Nothing moved. The medicine bag had the scent of lavender and leather. A comforting aroma.

"What is this for?" I asked.

"I made this medicine bag especially for you. It'll help to protect you against what is coming," she said.

For the first time since I had known her, I saw what seemed to be fear in her watery old brown eyes.

"What is coming?" I asked.

Mother Wolf raised her hand in a gesture that meant she wouldn't answer any more questions. It was her habit and her way. She had once explained to me that this was the Shaman's way of teaching. The student would know what they needed to know when they needed to know it. It was her way but it was a habit that annoyed the hell out of me. But these months with her had taught me not to push against the raised hand. It never did me any good. The information exchange was over. Not even the threat of a nuclear explosion would change her mind once the hand was raised.

"Tomorrow, we'll go to Vision Quest Mount," she said as she stroked my head, "There is still so much for me to teach you but there isn't time now. Go back to sleep, child. You will need your rest."

"But—"

She raised her hand again, to stop any further questioning.

"Sleep...how can I friggin' sleep after you've said what you've said?"

Her face rolled into one annoyed giant wrinkle, "Mouth...after all you've learned and healed, you still have such a sick mouth."

She wheezed, coughed, stood, and left my room, but she didn't move as quickly or as quietly. I thought I heard her moccasins shuffling slightly on the floor. I touched the Medicine Bag to make sure I wasn't dreaming. It was there. I wasn't dreaming.

I shivered. There it was again. The old haunting feeling like someone was watching me.

Sleep? Such a silly request. How could I sleep after Mother Wolf's ominous visit? I closed my eyes.

Chapter Three

I awoke hours later to the sun streaming in through the holes in the yellowing old fabric that covered the window. Mother Wolf was calling my name. I checked and the necklace with the white Medicine Bag was still around my neck.

I felt strangely uneasy.

I sat up in bed and was immediately greeted by the light scent of burning sweetgrass and the strong, fresh aroma of brewed coffee. Ah, coffee. It was one of the few luxuries that Mother Wolf allowed. There was also a faint fragrance of mint in the air.

"Jessica," Mother Wolf called to me from the kitchen, "I've laid out a dress for you. It would please and honor me greatly, if you would wear it today."

I looked over at the old wooden high back chair next to the doorway. Draped over the back of the chair was a white leather dress. I looked at the picture above the chair—a picture I had seen every day since Mother Wolf had taken me in. In the picture, an old woman wore a white dress with embroidered animals on it, and perched on the old woman's shoulder was a big black bird. Mother Wolf had told me the bird was a raven.

The picture had always fascinated me, because the old woman's eyes seemed to follow me when I moved around the room.

I looked back at the dress and realized it was similar to the one she was wearing. When I looked back to the picture again, I remembered Mother Wolf had called the woman one of Our Mothers—she was Mother Raven. She was also Mother Wolf's actual mother.

As I lay in bed looking at the picture and the dress, I wondered if this could really be the same dress. But how could this be the same dress? The dress appeared to be brand new.

Not possible.

Just an overactive imagination, I told myself. Then I got out of bed and approached the dress. I picked it up with both hands.

I had expected the dress to be heavy, being made of leather and covered with beadwork. But it was lighter than a cotton shirt, and was so fine and soft it draped gently over my hands and hung in soft folds. I touched it to my face and it seemed to caress me. It felt alive, warm, and strangely...loving. It almost seemed to be magical.

The dress was beautiful with all of its colorful beaded designs of an owl, a badger, a raven, and other animals. There were insects as well—a butterfly, a dragonfly, and a spider. And twisting among all the animals and insects was a snake with large rust-red diamonds on its back.

And complementing all the animals and the dress's intricate design was a white leather fringe that circled the bodice, ran along the arms, and trimmed the hem. The dress was spectacular and elegant all at once.

It was a garment fit for a princess, and certainly meant for someone far more worthy of it than myself.

I heard the shuffling of Mother Wolf's moccasins on the floor, and looked up as she arrived at my door. Again, I noticed that she looked worried, and it was unusual that I could hear her footsteps.

"Do you like the dress?" she asked.

"This is the most beautiful thing I've ever seen."

"Good. Then I hope you'll wear it. You'll need to get showered and dressed right away. There is much to do."

"This dress is too good for me."

"That may be true. But it is yours nonetheless. I'd be pleased if you would wear it," she looked at her watch. Her watch, electricity, plumbing, and her coffee maker were the four modern things she allowed in her life.

"It's almost noon, and we have to get to Vision Quest Mount before five o'clock and sundown."

Mother Wolf didn't wait for me to ask any questions, she just put up her hand, and left without saying anything more.

I showered, then towel-dried my hair. There were no blow dryers or curling irons. I noticed I'd forgotten to remove the new white Medicine Bag from around my neck, but it had miraculously shed the shower water and was dry.

I brushed and braided my hair, tying it off with a strap of red leather that matched my hair color perfectly.

The red leather strap was a gift one of Mother Wolf's patients had given me after I had helped deliver her baby, and it had become one of my most treasured possessions.

When I went back to my room, I carefully lifted the dress and looked at the beaded animals, I realized the detail of the creatures was so fine they seemed to come alive and look at me. My imagination was working overtime.

I searched the dress for a zipper or buttons, but there was nothing. Finally, I pulled the dress over my head. It slid down my body, caressing me with its warm softness as it flowed over the length of me. And like magic, the dress fell into place molding itself to my body. It was as though it had been made to fit my precise measurements. It simply snuggled into every contour of my body, stopping only when the fringe on the hem floated just below my knees.

I was barefoot when I walked out of my room and into the small kitchen that doubled as an examining room. Mother Wolf was busy collecting and assembling parcels of herbs and potions. She had a deep-in-thought-frown on her face. The look she usually had when she was assembling special ingredients for serious occasions.

She stuffed a blanket and some bundles into a saddlebag she had put over Wolf's back, when she looked up and saw me. She put both of her bony gnarled hands over her mouth. For a moment, I thought she might cry.

When she lowered her hands, she finally said, "Oh, child," a term of affection she only used on me when she was pleased with me, or when she wanted me to do something I didn't want to do. "All the Mothers have worn this dress throughout the years, but I'm sure none of us have ever looked as beautiful and as regal as you look wearing it today."

Even Wolf, wagged his tail in approval.

"All the Mothers have worn this dress over the years? How could that be, this dress looks like new!"

"You must have felt its medicine or magic as some have called it." She looked down at my bare feet and gasped, "Oh dear, I've forgotten the moccasins!"

She left the kitchen and went into her room. I could hear her wheeze and cough as she opened several drawers. A few moments later she returned with a pair of long legged white leather moccasins that were beaded with scenes of mountains, trees, lakes, meadows, and clouds. They were every bit as detailed, elegant, and as beautiful as the dress.

She quickly handed me the moccasins and said, "Put them on. We must hurry."

She finished putting packets of herbs and colored crystal stones onto a piece of white leather and rolled it all into a bundle.

While she finished packing Wolf's saddlebag, I slipped my feet into the long legged soft white moccasins. And, just like the dress had molded itself to my body, the moccasins molded themselves to my feet. They fit so well it was difficult to tell where my own skin ended and where the moccasins began.

"I think that's everything we'll need," Mother Wolf said.

I didn't want to take my eyes away from the moccasins but I did, and watched as Mother Wolf finished wrapping the last leather bundle so skillfully that there was a long loop of twisted red leather flowing out the end of it when she was through. She placed the loop over her arm and slid the bundle up to her shoulder until it hung over her back like a backpack.

Then she looked over at me. She smiled a large toothless smile of satisfaction. This was truly a rare occasion. I could count the times on one hand, when she had smiled at me that way.

"Our Mothers, tell me they are very pleased. Very pleased indeed." She stuffed a travel mug of coffee in my right hand and a bran muffin in my left. "You'll have to eat on the way, because we have to leave now. Let's get a move on. It's a long and difficult trail, and we have to be at the mount before sundown."

She opened the kitchen door and was about to leave, when she stopped, turned, and looked at me. She raised her left eyebrow.

"Jessica." She rarely called me Jessica. She frequently called me Toadstool. "Many things will be happening to you on the Mount today. It's a sacred place and out of respect for Our Mothers, watch your mouth. Please."

"Of course I'll watch my mouth. What do you think I am...a barbarian?"

"Sometimes, Toadstool, you leave me wondering."

Then she said a couple of phrases I couldn't understand, but I felt it was some kind of prayer. And I had a feeling the prayer was directed at me and my mouth. When she finished, she beckoned for Wolf and me to follow her.

She led us to a patch of brush and shrubs at the edge of the forest. She pushed the branches and foliage aside revealing a narrow path. If Mother Wolf hadn't led me to the entrance, I would have never found it.

She took the empty coffee mug from me and tucked it into Wolf's saddle-bag, wiped a couple of bran muffin crumbs from my face, and led us into the secret pathway.

As we made our way along the path, I noticed that she hadn't been exaggerating about the hike. The trail was twisting and uphill most of the way. I had to dodge branches and step over ankle-spraining roots. The ground was uneven and riddled with rocks large and small. But my moccasins seemed to make me more sure-footed than I was used to, and nothing poked through the soft soles. It was as though something was guiding my steps and floating my feet on a cushion of air.

Mother Wolf stopped several times to rest for a moment gathering her strength and breath. She seemed much weaker than usual. She was pale but her cheeks were red. Normally on our walks through the forest trails she'd stop and point out medicinal herbs and plants. She'd explain how to prepare them as a poultice, skin cream, or tea. This time there was none of that. She didn't speak at all and would hold up her hand to me when I wanted to speak.

We arrived at a clearing in the forest. There was a hill with a rocky outcrop in the center of the clearing. Mother Wolf announced that this was Vision Quest Mount, and she had only one hour to make the site ready before dark. She told me I was not allowed to ask any questions, and all would be revealed "in due course." Then she coughed and wheezed.

I noticed that she looked more frail and older, if it were possible. Her cough seemed to be much worse and more frequent during the last few days. I began to worry. But I was distracted from those thoughts, when I saw that there was a shallow grave-like hole situated in the middle of a rock circle.

"What's this for?" I asked, pointing to the shallow hole.

"All in due course, child. Just sit up there, and if you must speak, please watch your mouth." She pointed to the small rocky outcrop at the top of the mount. "In fact being respectfully silent right now would be an excellent path to follow." She made a sitting motion and then made a zipping motion over her mouth.

"But that looks like a grave," I said.

Mother Wolf's whole face turned into the annoyed giant wrinkle. I made the zipping motion over my mouth, turned and headed for the outcrop of rock that she had pointed to.

She took the saddlebags off Wolf's back and began to unpack. There were blankets, pouches of herbs, a small round flat drum, along with other odds and ends.

While I watched, the sun moved lower in the sky and with the coming twilight came the feeling that something or someone was watching and waiting. The feeling grew stronger than it had ever been. I had the feeling something was lurking just out of sight and it was drawing closer and closer to me.

PART II

THE VISION QUEST

Chapter Four

Mother Wolf set to work without another word to me. She walked around the stone circle and shallow grave first clockwise and then counter clockwise sprinkling tobacco along her path. Wolf walked alongside her, stopping occasionally to sniff the air. He howled once, and from the forest came answering howls.

From time to time, Mother Wolf would stop her preparations and have a chat with someone. That someone was invisible to me. Over the months I had lived with her, I had become used to this behavior and I knew she was communicating with Our Mothers. It had been her habit to spend evenings sitting in a rocking chair on the porch of the cabin-clinic and have deep discussions with Our Mothers. Sometimes I could understand what was being discussed, but I could only hear her side of the conversation. It was always a little spooky to watch and listen. It would have been easy to consider her insane, having a discussion with the air, but I respected her and her knowledge. When she didn't want me to know what she was talking about she'd switch to the old language of the ancestors, and I would simply leave.

After Mother Wolf finished circling the shallow grave, she proceeded to set up the single small drum she had unpacked from Wolf's saddlebag. The drum was about four inches thick and about twelve inches across and had been carved from the trunk of a pine tree. It was covered with a thin skin of white rawhide.

Around the drum, she created a circle of tobacco and crystal stones of various colors. Wolf was at her side. From the forest there was a wolf howl and Wolf answered back. Although the evening was warm, I felt a chill pass through me.

When Mother Wolf was satisfied with the circle around the drum, she returned to the shallow grave. She placed a variety of herbs, plants, and leaves on the bottom of the grave chanting words I didn't understand, interspersed with serious discussions with Our Mothers in the ancient language of the ancestors. When Mother Wolf finished with the bottom covering of herbs and leaves, she covered everything with a long narrow blanket of beaded rawhide. The hide had the same designs as my dress and moccasins.

From where I sat, looking down from the outcrop at the top of the mount, the creatures on the hide appeared to be moving. I remembered that Mother Wolf had said the dress had special medicine or magic, I wondered if the blanket was the same, and if it also had magic. I wondered too, about what the magic was. What did Mother Wolf mean when she said *'medicine or magic'*?

I called to her, "Mother Wolf. What kind of magic does my dress have?"

Mother Wolf paused for a moment checking her work, and consulting her unseen Mothers, and then shouted back to me, "It contains the spirit medicine of all those who wore it before you." She raised her hand, indicating I would understand when I needed to know. No more questions.

She finished up her tasks by gathering and assembling bundles of long and short branches, stacking them beside the shallow hole. Next to the bundles of branches she laid out a rawhide blanket. A white wolf's head was beaded on the blanket and its large blue-green eyes stared up at me, as though they were watching me. I tried to look away from the wolf's eyes but couldn't. I felt as though the wolf on the blanket was trying to speak to me, but I couldn't understand the words it spoke inside my head. It spoke in the words Mother Wolf spoke when she talked with Our Mothers in the ancestor's language.

Mother Wolf prepared a small fire between the shelf where I was sitting and the shallow hole she had just finished outfitting. When the flames were strong enough to support it, she threw some herbs and strange objects into the growing blaze. For a moment the fire snapped, popped, and flamed brightly with the colors of the rainbow and then settled into oranges and reds matching the colors of the sunset.

Then there was silence. Not only in my head but all around me. No birds. No wind. No thoughts. Nothing. Just silence. The sunset was a thin red-orange streak across the horizon. Night was falling.

Wolf was walking around the wolf blanket, when he suddenly broke the silence with a howl. The howl made goosebumps rise on my arms. I felt a chill deep in the marrow of my bones.

The sunset was gone, when Mother Wolf beckoned me to come to the side of the shallow hole. I walked slowly towards her. She motioned for me to step into the hole.

"What the fr—" I stopped instantly, when she gave me the wrinkled-annoyed-face look. "Okay. But I need to know what is going on here."

"You, my child, are going on your first Vision Quest," she said as though that were explanation enough.

"Vision Quest?"

"Yes. Child, you need to find your Totem. I'm sorry I didn't prepare you better for this day, but unfortunately my time has run shorter than I thought it would," she said, then coughed and wheezed.

She had an expression of dreaminess about her. The look she often had when she was talking with Our Mothers.

"Mother Wolf, I need to know more. This looks like a grave. A very special grave, I'll give you that, but still a grave."

"Please, Jessica. There is nothing that can harm you here. We are all watching over you. But you must get in, the sun has set," she said, and tugged at my arm with urgency. "Please, you must trust me. I have never harmed you and I never will. I protect you with all that I have at my command, including my life."

Wolf added his plea with a mournful howl. Mother Wolf and Wolf seemed to be getting agitated and fretful. I was frightened by their behavior because both of them had always seemed relaxed, unshakeable, and always in control.

Again, I felt as though someone was lurking in the shadows near the forest. Watching. Waiting. Like a hungry cat waiting patiently just outside a mouse-hole. I knew I was the mouse and I felt as though I was getting way too close to the opening of the hole.

Mother Wolf tugged urgently on my arm, and her watery ancient eyes pleaded with me to obey.

I could also feel the shallow hole calling to me with the same strange words the wolf blanket had spoken to me. Then as though something possessed my body, I finally stepped into the hole without wanting to do so. As soon as I stepped onto the blanket that lined the grave-like hole, calmness engulfed me.

"Kneel, Jessica Seeker," Mother Wolf said, and her voice carried a power that was impossible to resist. For just a fraction of a second, I wondered how long she had known my last name. She had never used it before today. The thought just flashed through my mind, but didn't stay. In its place I felt an overwhelming need to kneel. I knelt.

Even with the beading, the blanket lining the grave felt soft against my knees. There was a faint fragrance of mint, sage, and lavender floating in the air. My calmness deepened, as though this were a natural course of events.

Everything would be all right. I thought and hoped.

Wolf sat down beside Mother Wolf. He looked at me with his deep blue-green eyes. I noted that his beautiful silvery white coat was glistening. His fur never seemed to get dirty. He could walk through a mud puddle but his feet would come out sparkling white. *More magic*...the thought drifted through my mind.

Then I noticed Mother Wolf pressing a small black vial into my right hand.

"Place two drops on your tongue. Less, and you'll not arrive where you need to be. More...and you'll die," she pulled the stopper out of the vial, "Do this now. Time grows short."

Suddenly the calmness left me. I could feel fear gathering in me again and knotting my stomach.

"I can't do this." The words and the fear came rushing out of me. "I'm not a member of your tribe. I don't have a drop of your people's blood in me. This isn't my place."

"The Mothers say you are one of us. That's all that is required."

I could hear humming off in the distance. My desire to argue with Mother Wolf evaporated.

"Touch the vial to your tongue twice," she said as she raised my right hand and the vial to my lips. "Two drops. No more."

I did as I was told. Mother Wolf removed the vial from my hand, placed the cork in it, and put the vial in the small white medicine bag that hung on the braided white rawhide necklace around my neck.

I was beginning to feel sleepy. I could feel Mother Wolf guiding me to lie down. The sun was gone. The only light came from the campfire. Mother

Wolf coughed and wheezed as she took tree branches from the bundles beside the grave, and placed them across the top.

She laid the Wolf blanket over the branches and the light of the fire disappeared. Everything went dark. I tried to call out to her. I tried to sit up. My voice and body didn't respond.

I heard a drum beating and chanting off in the distance. There was a flash of light, a door seemed to open in front of me, and I was sucked through it.

Suddenly, I was standing in front of the Sheffield house. It was one of the largest houses in the small town of Wheaton. Other than in my nightmares, I hadn't seen the house in more than ten years, but now it loomed in front of me, the same as it had on that rainy night over a decade ago. As real and as frightening as it had been back then.

The outside light above the door was on. It backlit the columnar supports, the flower baskets that hung from the columns, and the white fence that enclosed the porch. Small gardens and well pruned shrubs dotted the front yard. Normally, this house was the envy of the neighborhood, but tonight it frightened me and all of the town's people as well.

The front yard was bathed in the red and blue flashing lights of two police cars parked on the street in front of the house. All of the lights were reflected in the wet street and sidewalk.

Rain pelted my face. The nightmare was back…in surround sound and 3D high definition.

But this time the nightmare was different. I was truly living inside the dream. As the rain hit my face, it also soaked through my clothes. I shivered. I could feel the pebbles on the road under my bare feet. I looked down and I saw a small bare-footed girl standing beside me. She was me when I was twelve years old. She was crying.

I could taste her tears as they flowed into her mouth. I could feel all the fear and horror she felt. I tried to reach out to comfort her. I touched her shoulder but it was clear by the lack of any reaction, that she couldn't feel me, hear me, or see me.

She was crying and pleading for Constable Duggan to listen to her, "This isn't the right person. I saw the name, Robert Sheffield, in my visions but this isn't him," my twelve-year-old-child-self said as I watched the police lead the man to a police car.

Constable Duggan bent down, holding out his raincoat to shelter me from the pouring rain. "Jessica, you shouldn't have come here. This is no place for you."

I could feel my child-self's stomach churning and a wave of nausea hit me at the same time it hit her. I could feel my younger self gathering strength and resisting the urge to throw up, "But you have to listen. If you do this something really bad is going to happen," my child-self pleaded.

"Didn't you tell us where to find the missing necklace, shoes, and ring? Didn't you say we'd find them in Robert Sheffield's house?" Constable Duggan asked.

"Yes. But that doesn't mean he's the one. It's someone else," my child-self said and shivered.

I shouted at the Constable, "Listen to her." But again it was clear that he, too, couldn't hear or see me.

"You've been a big help to us Jessica. We know what we're doing. Go home," Constable Duggan said, turning me around and pointing me in the direction of my foster parents' house. "Go home you'll catch your death of cold out here dressed in pajamas and no rain coat. Go, Jessica." He gave me a slight push to propel me on my way.

My child-self left. Her red hair hung in sopping wet ringlets down her back. I felt her shiver in the cold, but I stayed behind, there was nothing I could do to comfort her.

I watched the scene play out in front of me.

One of the constables was holding Mrs. Sheffield by the arm. She strained against the constable's grip. She reached for her husband, trying to join him. She was screaming, "Please. Please. Don't take my husband away. He never killed those little girls. He could never do anything so horrible. Please!" She gave up the protest and sagged to her knees, weeping as the constables placed Mr. Sheffield in the police car.

I was glad my child-self had not seen this. It would have made the unbearable even more unbearable. As that thought crossed my mind, I saw a young boy standing in the doorway. Watching as the police cars drove away. He didn't seem to react to any of what was happening. He just watched with his pale hazel eyes.

As I noticed his eyes, I could feel the darkness I had felt so often since that night. It was like the darkness around me was alive and waiting for an opportunity to pounce on me like a hungry predator. I shivered and I knew I wasn't reacting to the cold and rain.

Then I found myself wishing with all my heart that the next nightmare wouldn't happen. But my heart knew it would.

I wished I had been like any other normal kid. I wished I didn't have visions. I hated those visions as much as I hated the nightmares. They always brought me trouble.

Whenever I shared my visions, trouble soon followed. In every foster home I'd been placed in, I would have visions of the future. I would share my revelations with the adults, and at first they wouldn't believe me.

But when the prophecies came true, they would finally believe. After that happened a few times they'd become frightened of me. Next, the social worker would be at the front door, and my foster parents would apologize for sending me away saying they didn't think it was a good idea for me to be around the other children. "The children are afraid of you," they would always say.

But I knew the truth. I could see it in their eyes every time. They were the ones who were afraid of me.

Then the routine would start all over again. I'd be sent to a psychologist and tested. I was relabeled every time with a different diagnosis, from hyperactive to depression, to attention-seeking, to whatever was the diagnosis de jour.

The pattern would repeat itself in Wheaton, the way it always did, but this time it would change slightly—this time the whole town would be frightened of me and turn against me. And this time I would promise myself that I would never share my visions with anyone again. No matter what happened. I kept my promise. Wheaton was the last time anyone would know about what I saw or dreamt.

As I remembered my vow, I felt myself getting dizzy, and the scene in front of me with the rain, the boy with the light hazel eyes, and the Sheffield house vanished in a bright light. Again, it felt as though I was sucked through another door. This time I arrived at the Sheffield house in the sunshine of a cool fall afternoon.

The rest of the nightmare was about to play out—again.

I remembered the day. It had been three days since Robert Sheffield had been arrested. And on this cool fall day he had finally been released from custody. He had been released because as the police questioned him, they had discovered that he had been out of town when one of the girls had disappeared. He had no explanation for the ring, shoe, or necklace they had found in his house. But after checking his alibi they couldn't hold him any longer. He was free, but still under suspicion.

I remembered how my visions had called my child-self to the house that day. I had been napping and had awoken with a fear for Mr. Sheffield. In my dreams, I had seen what he was trying to do and I felt I had to stop him.

And now, I stood beside my child-self on the front sidewalk outside the house.

I could feel all the emotions my child-self was feeling. Fear, confusion, and the need to do something. To stop what was about to happen.

I ran with my child-self to the porch, climbed the steps, and stood at the front door with her. She rang the doorbell. No answer.

She opened the screen door and then tried the handle on the inside door. It was unlocked. As she opened the door, I put my hand on her shoulder, trying to stop her from entering. "Stop," I shouted to my child-self. But she didn't respond.

The nightmare was repeating and I couldn't stop it.

I was beside her as she went into the house and called out for Mr. Sheffield. There was no answer. I stood beside her in the hallway in front of the basement door. She opened it. I tried once more to stop her, but I was still a ghost she couldn't see or hear.

She went down the stairs. I followed her. I remembered my child-self had already seen this play out in her vision. We both knew what she was going to find. We both hoped we didn't find it. But we did.

As we approached the bottom of the basement stairs, there was a foul odor—the stench of the old oil furnace mixed with the stink of a dirty diaper. She called out to Mr. Sheffield. But there was no answer.

The entire basement was dark, except for a lighted area behind a wall that separated the laundry room from the shelving and storage in the rest of the basement. My child-self and I walked toward the lighted area.

We turned the corner and we both screamed.

Hanging from an open floor joist in the basement ceiling was Robert Sheffield. His face was purple and bloated. His neck strained against the rope that connected him with the basement's ceiling joist.

BANG.

We both jumped and screamed again.

It was just the old oil furnace thumping on. But the fright had scared my child-self so badly that she ran screaming up the basement stairway.

I remained behind knowing I couldn't help her. I knew the nightmare would play out the way it always did. The neighbors would hear her screaming. They would call the police. The police would find Mr. Sheffield.

But this time, I wanted to know more, and this was my chance. I looked around the area. I found the note the town rumors had talked about. The note had told his wife and son that he was sorry for what he'd put them through and he was innocent. Although, he had not killed or taken those young girls, he couldn't live with the shame of being accused of such a heinous crime. The town would never accept him again. There would always be a shadow of doubt hanging over him. His life, as he knew it, was ruined. And he didn't want to cause his family anymore pain. "You will all be better off without me," he wrote

I had heard about the note, now I knew exactly what it said. During the month after his death, I heard people whispering about how Robert Sheffield had suffered bouts of depression. And as our next door neighbors whispered to my foster parents about Mr. Sheffield's bouts of depression, they added, "I suppose this was too big a bout, and he lost." But in the end, the whole town blamed my visions, and ultimately, me for his death. It was my fault that he'd been arrested and accused of killing one girl and responsible for the disappearance of one other girl.

My foster parents and the town would make sure that I wouldn't be staying in Wheaton for much longer. The social worker would come for me a month later. There would be another foster home in another town and then another town, and in a few years I would run away from my last foster home.

In the time before Mr. Sheffield's arrest, I had a vision about one of the girls and I told the police about my vision. It was the first of my visions the police finally believed. But it was too late, she was dead. I didn't have visions of the other girl.

After the police found the girl where my vision had directed them to look, they believed me when I told them about the other visions that located the necklace, the shoe, and the ring...or at least they followed up the leads the visions provided. But after they found the girls' missing things at the

Sheffield house and arrested Mr. Sheffield, I didn't get any more visions, until his suicide.

In the end, Wheaton's second missing girl was never found. And the two girls became unsolved mysteries. And after time passed without the mysteries being solved, or more girls going missing, the whole thing became a dark secret the people of Wheaton never spoke about. And a month after Mr. Sheffield's suicide, I was about to become a dark secret, too.

My foster parents were worried about my safety and probably with good reason because the whole town was becoming afraid of me. In less than a month I had gone from hero to villain. Some of the kids at school called me a witch and at one point a group of them tried to stone me. They might have killed me if a teacher hadn't stopped them. I spent two days in hospital and had to have twenty-eight stitches to sew my wounds back together.

But now, I stood in the Sheffield's basement trying to make sense of this old living nightmare. I tried to clear my head as I stared at Mr. Sheffield hanging lifeless in front of me at the end of a rope. I could feel myself getting dizzy again. Then I noticed the stool Mr. Sheffield had stood on in order to tie the rope to the ceiling joist. It was turned over and lying against the far wall, as though it had been kicked away with great force. He must have had a lot of difficulty kicking the stool so far away while he hung from the joist. As I wondered about Mr. Sheffield kicking the stool away, I felt as though someone was watching me. I looked around but saw no one.

A bright light flashed, a door opened, and I was sucked through.

Chapter Five

At first I was afraid to look around. I kept my eyes closed, wondering if this was a new nightmare. There had only been two nightmares in the past. I feared that a third and more horrifying nightmare might be added. In my life of twenty-two years, I had had the opportunity to witness much horror in my visions and in real life. I had the ability to attract a lot of bad stuff and I feared all that bad stuff would start to play back for me. I couldn't bear that.

Reluctantly I opened my eyes and before me there was a beautiful garden with flowers in shapes and configurations that ranged from a simple daisy to something as complex and strange as a Bird of Paradise. For some of the flowers, there was no worldly comparison. All the flowers were vibrant iridescent colors that changed as they reflected the soft glowing white light that seemed to fill the entire sky.

There were fragrances of herbs and spices in the air. Sage, heather, cinnamon, and ginger. I felt peace here. A profound soothing peace. I breathed in deeply. The air tasted sweet, and as my lungs filled with warm moist air, I felt the peace grow deeper. I liked this place. I could feel love and joy filling me up. It was all around me. In the air. In the flowers. In the earth itself. I knew in an instant that I never wanted to leave. I wanted to lie down in the fragrant beautiful flowers and rest here forever.

With that thought pleasantly bouncing around in my head, I suddenly heard a cough, a wheeze, and a croaking voice.

Mother Wolf said, "Welcome, my child."

I turned and saw the old wizened up body and face of Mother Wolf. She was wearing her favorite work clothes—the old red plaid shirt, black vest, and blue jeans with the holes in the knees. Then, right before my eyes, she began to transform. Her hair grew darker changing from the matted grey braids to a flowing mane of deep black, shining hair that seemed to move in a wind I couldn't feel. Her watery brown eyes with emerald green flecks grew stronger, brighter, and more penetrating. The wrinkles on her face dissolved into firm tawny skin. Her entire body transformed into a beautiful young woman, who looked to be about thirty-years-old wearing the same dress as the one I was wearing.

"Who are you?" I asked, "And where the frigg am I?"

"Mouth," she said. Her eyes twinkled and she smiled. Her once toothless mouth was now filled with perfectly formed pearl white teeth.

"Mother Wolf?" I blinked several times to make sure my eyes were working properly, "Holy shit, this can't be you. You're beautiful and...young."

"Jessica. My child. What am I going to do with you and your mouth?" her voice was mellow and soft. Her eyes flashed with a mixture of mischief and good humor. "It's good to see that you finally made your way here. I was getting a little worried."

"And where exactly is **Here**?"

"This is the home of Our Mothers. And now, it's also my home."

"Holy-crappolie-oli, this is Our Mothers' place? It's fantastic. I'm friggin' staying here, too," I said. I took in a big breath and began to spin around. Suddenly I was filled with joy and began to laugh like a child. The more I twirled the more I laughed. I wanted to run, sing, and laugh some more.

"Jessica Seeker, you will watch your mouth and that's final!" And right before my eyes Mother Wolf's young face instantly transformed into that annoyed giant and ancient wrinkle. The light that had filled the sky dimmed and there was a huge crack of thunder. Every flower in the garden snapped shut. I saw a few of them yank themselves back into the ground. I felt like I'd been given the ultimatum every child fears, the big *or else* by someone who was capable of carrying out an *or else* that was beyond unthinkable.

"Just forgot myself," I said.

Mother Wolf's face was frozen in the annoyed wrinkled state, and I could swear that some of the flowers close to me were trembling. And the sky grew a little darker.

"Okay. Okay. I'm sorry. I won't do that again. I'm on my best behavior," I said. But nothing changed. "What?"

She said nothing, and now I was sure I could feel the ground rumble under my feet. The sky grew even darker, and most of the flowers began a rapid retreat underground.

"All right. Here it is. My final offer. I will not use 'colorful expletives' like that again the rest of my life," I said, and tried to form a convincing smile on my face.

For a moment nothing happened. But I considered that to be a positive sign because the ground didn't open up and swallow me. Then just above the giant wrinkle, Mother Wolf lifted her left eyebrow.

"For the rest of your life? Somehow I find that hard to believe, but it's a start," Mother Wolf said. The light and flowers came back. And Mother Wolf's face transformed from the giant annoyed wrinkle back to the thirty-something-smooth-and-tawny-face. The beautiful garden with its exotic flowers transformed along with the sky, as quickly as Mother Wolf transformed. It was warm, beautiful, and awe-inspiring once again.

Mother Wolf walked towards me, raising her hand, and offering it to me. Her hand was no longer thin, bony, and gnarled. Instead it was smooth, long fingered, and firm. She took my hand and began leading me through the garden. As we moved forward, the thick beds of flowers moved out of our way forming a path in front of us. And as we went deeper into the garden I noticed that there were brightly colored trees and shrubs scattered across the landscape. Then a bird, striped in indigo and white, flew past.

As we walked further, animals of all sorts, shapes, sizes, and colors popped up, popped out, ran past, or flew by to have a look at us.

During our walk, we were silent. I was afraid to speak fearing I would somehow cause this beautiful and peaceful dream to end.

At the edge of the garden, a giant meadow stretched out before us. It was full of color; tiger lilies, buttercups, shooting stars, and wild roses.

Mother Wolf stopped and I stopped alongside her. She began to hum. I could hear the sound of a drum beating. Then the whole garden was joining in with humming, chirping, squeaking, and other sounds I had never heard before. It was a beautiful symphony of sounds and rhythms. Hypnotic and soothing.

And as the music played, women began to appear on the meadow in front of us. The women were dressed in the same white rawhide dress I was wearing. Some of the dresses had only a few animals embroidered on them while others had almost as many animals as Mother Wolf's and my dress. In all, there were eleven women. All of them young, appearing to be in their thirties. They were all humming different notes.

The music faded away when Mother Wolf and the eleven women stopped humming.

And then, as though it was the most normal thing in the world, Mother Wolf said in her new soft young voice, "Our Mothers, this is Jessica Seeker."

All the women, in unison, slightly bowed their heads to me. And as though that were a cue for more action, animals began appearing around, beside, and on the women.

Mother Wolf turned to me, "And their Totem Protectors also offer their greetings. All of Our Mothers would like to speak with you."

First Mother Wolf introduced me to Mother Raven. As Mother Raven took my hand in hers, I noticed the raven that was embroidered on my dress moved slightly. I could feel it move more than I could see it move.

"Mother Raven, I know you from the picture Mother Wolf has of you. But, you look much younger than your picture," I said.

Mother Raven smiled, and seemed to examine my face and then looked straight into my eyes, "Do you like the dress?"

"The dress is beautiful. Mother Wolf says it has medicine...magic," I said.

"Mother Wolf is correct. It was made with spirit medicine and therefore it has a magic of sorts. The dress contains the spirits of all those who have worn it and passed before you. Just as each of us has the powers of those who passed before us, and when your Totem Protector finds you, your Totem's powers, and medicine will be added to ours and to the dress. You will need all that power and more, when your tests come," Mother Raven said.

"What tests?" I asked.

Mother Raven's soft brown eyes, that had been happy and searching mine just moments before, suddenly grew sad.

"Do not worry my child. You will learn much before your tests come. But, know this. You are the strongest of us all. You have so much power at your command, because you will have the most difficult tests. Always remember, we are with you. We and our Totems watch over you. We cannot see whether you will succeed in your trials, but we will follow with you." Mother Raven squeezed my hand with a tenderness and love I had never felt before. The raven on her shoulder bobbed its head, as though it understood what she said, and agreed with her.

Before I could ask her more questions, Mother Raven simply raised her hand in the gesture I knew all too well. The gesture that said I should not ask any more questions and all would be revealed to me as I needed to know it.

Before I could object to Mother Raven's raised hand, another woman glided toward me. I felt the snake wriggle on my dress as she approached.

"Mother Diamondback," Mother Wolf respectfully announced.

Mother Diamondback had only one creature on her dress, a huge embroidered snake with rust-red diamonds on its back. The embroidered snake coiled around her. The snake's tail started at the hem of Mother Diamondback's dress and wrapped around until its head rested on her shoulder. A living snake, with rust-red diamonds on its back, was coiled around Mother Diamondback's neck and right arm.

As Mother Diamondback took my right hand in both of her hands, the snake on her arm inched forward and rested its head on my hand. Not only did I have a dislike for snakes, but I downright feared them. And as I recalled, diamondback snakes were highly venomous, with exceptional long sharp fangs. Having this creature lay its large head on my hand, at the very least, was uncomfortable.

Mother Diamondback chuckled. Her eyes flashed with mischief, and with her left hand she pushed a strand of her black hair off of her young face.

"Do not be afraid my child. He wanted to touch you and welcome you. He likes your green eyes. He says they look like mine. He likes the color of your hair because it matches the diamonds on his skin. He has a bit of vanity. That's what makes him so loveable," she said as she stroked the snake with great affection, and continued, "My snake and I saved our tribe many times from illness, bad water, and many other poisons. With the help of my Totem Protector, I have the power of transmutation. We can change poison from bad to good. I was the first Mother. Mother Wolf is the twelfth and you are the thirteenth. You now have my power and the powers of us all. Welcome, child," Mother Diamondback said.

Her snake nuzzled my hand like an affectionate pet. I had never touched a snake before. I thought they were cold and slimy, but this one felt soft and as smooth as fine silk. Its touch was pleasant. In spite of myself, I was beginning to like this snake.

"Take care, child. We all love you and protect you. We shall all be your teachers for as long as you need us," Mother Diamondback said. Her snake raised its head, looked at me, and then recoiled up Mother Diamondback's arm. She released my hand.

Each of the remaining women greeted me in the same way, welcoming and reassuring me of their love and protection. Mother Badger, Mother Wolverine, Mother Skunk, Mother Dragon Fly, Mother Butterfly, Mother Spirit Bear, Mother Owl, and Mother Gopher introduced themselves. None of them seemed to want to talk about the tests and trials that lie ahead, all that is, except for Mother Spider. She was the last to greet me. Her dress was missing a wolf and a raven, but had all the other creatures on it. She was the mother of Mother Raven, and grandmother to Mother Wolf.

On her shoulder stood the biggest, blackest, and ugliest spider I'd ever seen. Spiders were right at the top of my don't-want-to-have-anything-to-do-with list, they were possibly even higher on the list than snakes. I preferred furry, huggable, and kissable little creatures, along with the odd Rottweiler, but snakes and spiders—that's definitely a big...no. So when Mother Spider's Totem Protector raced down her arm and ran up mine and then peeked into my ear, I was not a happy camper.

"Oh, that's so wonderful," Mother Spider said, sounding like a cheerleader at a home game rooting for her team. "He usually doesn't take to people so easily. Clearly you are the right person, and he likes you."

"Right person. For what?" I grimaced as the spider poked one of his big hairy legs into my ear.

"Spider spins webs and can see things others can't see. Spider can trap things others cannot see or trap. I have his power. I guide the Mothers and inform them of potential future events, or I should say, as much of the future as I can see on Spider's life-web of possibilities. That's how we found you. And you are perfect. Your Totem Protector will be perfect for you, too. You will love him," Mother Spider said, sounding less like a cheerleader, and more like a motivational speaker.

Cheerleaders and motivational speakers were right under snakes and spiders on my dislike list. But I thought she might tell me more than the other Mothers had. And her spider was distracting me less as he climbed down my arm and ran up hers.

"Mother Spider, thank you for your welcome and protection," I said, using every ounce of charm I could find, "All the Mothers have warned me about the evil, the tests, and the trials that lie ahead, but none of them have told me what these trials would be. And what the evil is. Could you tell me more?" I was expecting the hand in the air gesture, but to my surprise she began to answer me.

"Trouble is stalking you, child. You've felt the darkness and coldness of the trouble that follows you. And...you are being watched. You already know that, too...you've felt it many times, lurking just out of sight but watching you. The trouble and the Watcher will appear when it is their time. Trouble will challenge you and will be dangerous. The Watcher, on the other hand, may interfere as he has sometimes done with us in the past. Ultimately, your life and the lives of others will be in peril," Mother Spider said in a casual easy tone as though she were telling me it was going to rain, and then her tone changed to cheerleader again, "But do not worry my child, we are with you. We love you and we will protect you with all that is at our command."

"Will I win against this 'trouble and the Watcher'?" I asked.

"There is much I know child. But there is much I can't predict or see. Your successful completion of the trials and tests that lie before you, are things I can't completely see or predict. And sometimes, I'm blocked and can't see into the web of life. Our powers and abilities are complex. But these are your trials. Your lessons. Your choices and decisions will affect the outcome. I can't predict what you'll do. You have free will. You have a great opportunity to learn and live, and then you'll be able to pass this knowledge to the Mother that follows behind you, that is of course, if you survive the trials," Mother Spider said, and then raised her hand.

Question and answer period was over.

I thought Mother Wolf was annoying, but now I had twelve Mothers on my case. Enough was enough.

"That does it. I'm sick of the hand in the air. I'm fed up with all the half answers. And this trouble and Watcher shit, can stuff itself up its own ass. I'm not doing any tests or trials. It's over. Done. Fini! You got that?" I shouted at them, and without seeing her, I knew Mother Wolf's face had twisted into that annoyed giant wrinkle, but I didn't care.

I'd had enough. I was pissed off and terrified. All of this was too much for me. I didn't want any tests or trials. I didn't want people's lives depending on me. I wasn't a hero. And I didn't want to be a hero. It sounded like these woman were expecting way too much. I was a street-smart woman; even a hard-ass by some people's standards, but all of this was way beyond me.

The Mothers didn't speak. The air was heavy.

"I'm sorry ladies, but I'm not the one. I'm the wrong person. Pick someone else."

Then from behind the entire group of Mothers, I heard Mother Badger's thick gravelly voice say, "Child. You will be challenged and tested, whether you want to be or not. It is better to be challenged and have our help, than to go on your own. A wise woman would consider her odds better to win with our help than to possibly lose and even die without it."

All was silent. Not a chirp. Not a squeak. Nothing. Just one word lingered in the air, "Mouth."

All the Mothers and their Totems gathered around Mother Wolf and me. A wolf howled. I noticed that Mother Wolf was without her companion. She was never without Wolf. The wolf howled again and the earth beneath my feet rumbled.

"Where's Wolf?" I asked as the group of Mothers gathered around me in a circle.

All the Mothers, except for Mother Wolf, began chanting.

"Wolf will remain with you for a little while longer. He wants to stay with you and protect you while you and your totem learn to work together. There will be a lot of danger, and during your transition in becoming a Mother, you will be most vulnerable. Wolf will be able to help you. He thinks you're a difficult student but he likes you anyway. Trust him. I'm so sorry I didn't have enough time to train you in all of our ways. But remember, all of Our Mothers will be with you. It is time for you to return." Mother Wolf began to chant with the others.

"Didn't you hear me? I'm not doing—" I didn't have time to finish.

The flash of light came, the door opened, and I was sucked through. I could feel myself lying in the shallow grave. I opened my eyes and there was only darkness. I was cold. I shivered. Somewhere nearby a wolf howled.

Chapter Six

In the darkness and cold, my first thought after all the strangeness I had just been through, was whether or not this was the danger Our Mothers had warned me about.

I raised my hands in front of me and touched something rough above me. It was the branches Mother Wolf had used to cover the hole. Then the branches started moving as though something was pulling at them. I heard panting.

"Wolf," I whispered.

There was a whimper.

"Wolf," I spoke louder.

More branches were being tugged out. It was Wolf and he was trying to help me escape. I started pushing more branches away, and he managed to pull the blanket off.

The sun was rising. The sky was filled with the pink and red light of dawn. As I finally managed to get my bearings, I reckoned the night had passed and this was the next day.

As I sat up, Wolf looked at me, whimpered and trotted off up toward the top of Vision Quest Mount where I had heard Mother Wolf drumming.

I climbed out of the shallow grave and followed Wolf, rehearsing everything I was going to say to her, colorful expletives included. This time she was going to listen to me.

But as I approached the top of the Mount, I saw Mother Wolf lying on the ground. Her hands were folded across her chest. Her drum was at her side. Beside the drum was the saddlebag she had placed on Wolf's back the day before. It was packed with all her paraphernalia except for the blankets she had used in and on the grave. On top of the saddle bag, as neatly wrapped as it had been the day before, was her white rawhide bundle with the red leather strap looped as a handle.

I reached down and poked her on the forehead the way she had been so fond of doing to me and called her name. But there was no response.

"Mother Wolf," I said and tried to lift her hand. But her hand was cold and stiff. Wolf sat down beside her.

"I think she's dead," I whispered to Wolf. He whimpered again and sniffed her forehead.

I didn't know what to do. My mind raced. I felt agony. "Damn," I said, and somehow I expected the giant annoyed wrinkle to form on her face. But it didn't. For the first time since I was twelve years old, I began to cry. They were tears of anger. Tears of sadness, of regret, of love. Tears of loss.

Wolf sniffed my face and tears, and then sniffed Mother Wolf's hand. He whimpered and turned his attention to the forest path we had walked the day before. He howled.

I looked at the entrance to the path. Tears blurred my vision and although the sun was rising, it was dark inside the path. I couldn't see anything. There were the sounds of underbrush being crunched underfoot but I couldn't see anyone.

Wolf barked and stood up. I heard a donkey bray. Wolf barked again and wagged his tail. At that moment I saw Jojo, the donkey, pulling the travois and led by a tall man dressed in a buckskin jacket, exiting the path. They walked up the Mount.

I wiped my eyes. No one sees me cry.

As Jojo and the man leading him came closer, I saw the man was Constable Tom. I hadn't seen him since he'd come to get my statement, but I recognized him even without his uniform. He was a tall, square-shouldered, and muscular man that moved in a smooth, powerful, and almost swagger-ing motion.

As he came closer, he called out, "Toadstool. Is that you?"

I stood and called out to him, "Hurry. Mother Wolf needs help. I think she might be dead."

"That's why I'm here," he said, as though he was saying a simple 'good morning,' and with long sure strides, he climbed the Mount. "When she came to me in my dreams last night, she told me to arrive at sunrise. She thought you would be a little freaked out and she didn't want you to be alone."

"She told you she'd be dead?"

"Yes." He knelt down beside Mother Wolf and checked her pulse. "She had cancer. Most everyone knew."

"I didn't."

"Because, she didn't want you to know."

"She didn't want me to know. What the frigg!" I said, and for a split second I thought I saw Mother Wolf in front of me with that giant annoyed face wrinkle. "Go ahead. Wrinkle your face as much as you want old woman. But I've had enough of your secrets, your hand in the air, and all of this shit. I'm done with you. You hear me? I'm done."

The night's events weighed on me, dragging me to my knees. My dress was soft beneath me and I could feel it tighten slightly. I could hear Our Mothers humming the way they had the first time I met them. Vision Quest Mount was alive with the sounds of creatures chirping, birds singing, and wolves howling. It wasn't just sounds. It was the most beautiful symphony of music I'd ever heard.

Then I noticed that Constable Tom was pulling on my arms and lifting me to my feet. He didn't seem to hear the music.

"Do you hear that?" I asked.

"Hear what?"

"The music. The animals...singing."

"Singing?"

"You don't hear it do you?"

"I hear some birds singing, and there's some wolves howling in the trees over there. But singing? Music? No I don't hear it."

"He can't hear us, child. The music is just for you. We wanted you to know we're here with you." Mother Wolf whispered in my mind with her new, soft, young voice. "Look up in the sky, there is someone who wants to meet you."

As I looked up, I heard a long, screaming screech. A large bird was circling above me and descending. The left sleeve of my dress began to grow and extended itself down my arm and stopped at my wrist. Then without my conscious thought, my dress constricted and expanded, helping to raise my left arm up until it was even with my shoulder.

I instantly knew the bird was a male Bald Eagle, and somehow, I could sense his thoughts. His thoughts were high pitched like a screech combined with steam escaping from a tea kettle on the stove. Those sounds became words inside my head.

He asked, "*Land. Arm. Yes?*"

Instinctively, I thought back to him, "*Yes.*"

He replied with his name, but it was unpronounceable with a human voice. I thought back to him copying the sound the best I could in my mind as "*Screech.*"

His answering thought back to me was, "*Screech. Good.*"

I could feel more than hear that he was pleased I had tried to pronounce his name. He was happy to let me call him Screech.

Then he screeched and thought to me, the color red. He liked my red hair and was going to call me by that color. "*Red*".

Screech landed on my outstretched arm. My arm dropped slightly as I adjusted to his landing. My arm dropping unbalanced him, and I could see his long talons dig into my sleeve as he righted himself.

I could feel the pressure of his grasp, but his sharp talons didn't puncture the leather of my sleeve. It was as though the dress was responding to him. The leather stiffened and thickened, adding extra support for his weight and protection from his talons.

"*Hurt Red?*" Screech thought to me.

"*No.*" I thought back to him.

He turned his huge white head and looked at me with his yellow-green eyes, "*Screech friend. No hurt Red. Love Red. Red love Screech.*"

I thought back to him, "*I never tell a guy I love him on a first date.*"

"*No love Screech?*"

I could feel the depth of Screech's hurt. He didn't understand. I supposed humor didn't translate well into Bald Eagle talk.

"*Screech. You are beautiful,*"

"*Red love Screech. Yes?*" He asked as he lowered his magnificent white head.

"*Red loves Screech. Yes,*" I found myself thinking to him, unable to bare the pain he was feeling.

Immediately, Screech moved up my arm and laid his beautiful white head against mine, "*Red love Screech. Good.*"

In front of me a glowing mist formed and out of the mist Mother Wolf materialized. Her appearance startled me. I stepped back. Seeing her appear was more than a little spooky, but in a way, I was glad she was still with me.

I wondered what kind of potion had been in the vial she had given me the night before, because this was the wildest high I'd ever been on. A talking eagle on my arm and a ghost in front of me. Damn!

"Hello, Toadstool. Don't be frightened. You, Wolf, and your eagle are the only ones who can see me."

She was smiling. She looked young and radiant. Then Mother Raven appeared followed by Mother Diamondback, Mother Spider and all the rest. All the Mothers had their Totems with them. It was a noisy moment as the Totems welcomed Screech with grunts, growls, and other animal sounds, and he greeted them back with screeches. Then there was silence.

"Child, your Vision Quest is complete. Your Totem Protector has found you. And what a magnificent Protector he is. He is the most powerful of all the Totems," Mother Wolf said.

Screech puffed the white feathers on his head and nodded to her. She smiled at him.

"Welcome Mother Eagle," all the mothers said in unison.

Then Screech turned his large white head toward me. His yellow-green, searching, eyes stared into mine, "*Red. Fly.*"

He launched himself into the air, and as he flew upward, I was part of him. I could see through his eyes. I felt what he felt. He was in my mind showing me, feeling me, and letting me fly with him.

The earth was rapidly falling away. As Screech soared, I saw myself standing on the mount with Wolf, Jojo, Constable Tom, and the body of Mother Wolf. I was one with Screech and we flew on. The air rushed past my face. The scenery changed below us. From great heights and with the keen eyes of an eagle, I saw a rabbit scurry into the forest. And for a moment I felt a twinge of hunger.

"*Screech hungry. Not hunt. Fly Red,*" Screech thought to me.

He seemed ashamed that I had felt his hunger, and I realized I felt his thoughts more than I understood him. His hunger hadn't disturbed me. His desire to eat the rabbit felt as natural to me as eating breakfast.

"*Red understands. Red needs food. Screech needs food,*" I thought to him.

"*Screech hunt rabbit. Feed Red. Yes?*" Screech thought, and soared higher with a freedom and joy I had never felt before. I was really beginning to love my Bald Eagle.

"*Maybe I'll have a rabbit later,*" I thought back to him, enjoying the wind in our faces and effortlessness of his flight. The world below no longer had a grip on me. I was soaring with my eagle, free of gravity and all that imprisoned me on earth.

I saw deer grazing in a meadow. I saw the river running through the forest. I could hear the power of the wind as it rushed past us. I could smell the freshness of the air with a faint hint of pine. It was freedom on a grander scale than I had ever imagined.

Then Screech thought to me, "*Fly forever. Yes.*"

"*Yes. Forever,*" I thought back to him, wishing we could fly forever, but I suddenly thought about Mother Wolf and Tom back on the ground.

"*Mother Wolf. Yes,*" Screech thought to me, and turned gracefully in the air.

Screech returned and landed on the ledge at the top of the mount, where I had sat the day before and watched Mother Wolf prepare the site. Screech blinked and I could no longer see through his eyes. He left my mind.

Mother Wolf and the rest of the Mothers gathered around the ledge nodding their approval.

"We are all one," Our Mothers said in unison and then vanished.

I felt a pulling and tugging sensation across the bodice of my dress, as though a hand were fiddling with it. I looked down and saw an Eagle being embroidered across the front. It was as though an invisible hand was rapidly tying beads together and fastening them to my dress at lightning speed.

The bright beads rapidly revealed an eagle with its white head in the center of my chest, and its strong wings rested on my breasts. It was the most magnificent creature on the dress. I looked at my eagle sitting on the outcrop.

"It is almost as beautiful as you," I said out loud.

Screech thought back to me, "*Red beautiful. Screech hungry. Rabbit good. Fish good. Hunt now.*"

Screech leapt into the air and then soared. I could feel and see his last thought. He was seeing himself swooping down on the rabbit and then catching a fish.

I heard Constable Tom clear his throat.

I looked at him until I could bring everything into focus again.

"Did you see them?" I asked.

"Ah...who?" he said, like a gambler who doesn't want you to know the cards he's holding.

"Our Mothers...the eagle. Everything." I tugged at the eagle embroidered on the bodice of my dress.

"Ah...well...Mother Eagle," he began with the same kind of reverence he had used when he spoke to Mother Wolf, "I have learned over the years, that Shaman business is Shaman business, and I tend to hold with that."

"And what the hell is that supposed to mean?"

I could see him grimace at the cuss, "Mother Eagle," he nodded to the eagle embroidered on my chest, and continued, "Shamans see the world differently than the rest of us, and I respect that. I never question it. I learned that from my parents and my parents learned that from their parents. Mother Raven is my great grandmother. Mother Wolf is my grandmother. Respect for Shamans run deep in my family."

"So you're related to Mother Wolf."

"Yes."

"That's why she asked you to come here?"

"Maybe. I know she didn't want you to be alone. But I don't know why... she specifically asked me."

"You don't know why she asked you?"

"She asked me because she asked me. It was her request for whatever reasons Shamans make requests. I don't question a Shaman's motivation, judgment, or requests."

He walked over and took the blanket from the bottom of the shallow grave, and then picked up the wolf blanket that had covered the grave. He came back to Mother Wolf's body and said some words I didn't understand. Then he looked at me, "I asked her to watch over me from her place with the ancestors."

"Tell him we'll all watch over him." Mother Wolf's soft young voice echoed in my head.

"She says to tell you they'll all watch over you," I said it before I realized I had said it aloud.

Constable Tom nodded as though this was completely normal, placed the narrow grave blanket on the travois, and then lifted Mother Wolf's thin, frail body as though he was lifting a precious child. He placed her on the travois she liked to call the donkey powered hammock. He covered her with the leather blanket embroidered with the wolf. He went to the saddlebag on the donkey's back and pulled out the hand woven blanket with the sun burst on it and tucked it around her body and then tied the leather straps around her chest and legs, fastening her to the travois.

Constable Tom helped me gather up Mother Wolf's things. He placed the white leather roll tied with the red strap on the travois beside her. Then he gathered up Wolf's saddlebag and draped it over Wolf's back and strapped it down.

I picked up the drum that had been beside Mother Wolf and carried it.

For a moment Screech reconnected with me, thinking, "**Home. Yes.**"

For a moment I could see the top of the forest through his eyes and then I fell back to seeing the world from my perspective. *"**Home. Yes.**"* I guess this was home...for now.

I had lost my desire to argue with the Mothers about my future, destiny, trials, or tests. I was worn out. And I didn't want to think anymore.

Wolf nuzzled my arm and whimpered. Then he smelled the drum. Without thinking about it, I lifted the drum and started tapping it. I could feel its vibration strumming through my body. I could hear Our Mothers chanting softly along with the beat.

Tom led Jojo down the mount and onto the forest path Mother Wolf and I had taken the day before. Wolf and I fell in behind. We made the trek back to the cabin-clinic without uttering a word. Our Mothers chanted and the forest was filled with music and I tapped on the drum keeping the beat. Off in the distance I heard my eagle screech.

Softly inside my head, I heard the silky young voice of Mother Wolf say, "Child, there is so much we have to teach you. There is so little time. Trouble is coming for you. Great evil pursues you. It will have to wait. But you must still stay alert, Mother Eagle."

Then the voices of all the Mothers joined her saying, "We are here. We love you. We will never leave you."

My eagle screeched again in the distance. And suddenly, I could feel someone, or was it something, watching and waiting just out of my range of vision. "Is this the evil I can feel and not see? The thing I have to watch for?" I thought to the Mothers.

The Mothers were silent.

I thought specifically to Mother Wolf, "Now see, that's what really pisses me off. All these riddles. No answers."

I continued to beat the drum and the music of the forest continued.

Two words reverberated in my head, "Patience" and "Mouth."

Chapter Seven

When we arrived at the cabin-clinic, there were cars parked in the yard and five women were standing outside the cabin-clinic waiting for us to arrive. I had met all the women over the course of my stay with Mother Wolf. They were patients Mother Wolf had treated with her assortment of stinky poultices, herbs, and other remedies.

An older woman, an elder Mother Wolf called Swan and a young pregnant woman, called Sky, approached me. Swan handed me a package that was neatly tied with a strand of rawhide. It had the scent of rawhide mixed with the aroma of fresh tobacco. She bowed her head slightly and then spoke quietly with great reverence.

"Mother Wolf came to us in our dreams last night," Swan said, "She asked us to help. It's a great honor she has given us."

"Mother Wolf was radiant with her long black hair and beautiful dress. She was so young," Sky said, and then stepped forward staring at the embroidered eagle on my dress, "Your dress looks like hers. Except it didn't have the eagle on it. She said your Totem Protector would be on your dress. It's a Bald Eagle. It's a brave and wonderful Totem that has chosen to be your Protector. It has strong medicine. Welcome, Mother Eagle."

Sky raised her hand and she seemed to want to touch the head of the eagle on my dress, but Swan gently pushed her hand away before she reached me. Sky quickly withdrew.

"Sorry, Mother Eagle. It's so beautiful. I forgot myself," Sky said, bashfully backing away from me.

"Sky is young and impulsive, Mother Eagle. She didn't mean to offend you," Swan explained.

"Offend me. How?"

Swan looked surprised, "She was about to touch you without your permission."

Sky had stopped backing up and was looking at the ground. I could almost feel the heat of the blush that was filling her face.

I stepped toward her, took her hand and raised it to my chest, resting it on the eagle's embroidered head, "It's okay. The picture of my eagle is almost as beautiful as he is. I give you my permission to touch his picture or me any time you like."

Sky lifted her head. Her brown eyes were warm with tears forming in them, "Thank you, Mother Eagle. I don't deserve such an honor."

I felt a sensation of warmth flow over me. It was a strange and foreign feeling. I didn't let people get close to me. It was a wonderful feeling. Then another feeling overcame me. I wanted to hug this young woman. I didn't hug anyone. But before I could stop myself, I was embracing Sky. It felt good.

When I released Sky, I looked at the other women and they were smiling.

Swan said, "Thank you, Mother Eagle. We...the other women elders who have come here...have much to do to prepare Mother Wolf for her journey. But you should probably rest. You've had a long night."

Swan was right, I felt very tired and it had been a long night. My life had changed in an instant and I couldn't control it. I didn't know what was expected of me or what to do. I didn't want anyone to expect anything of me. I wanted to run. Where would I run? I didn't know. I just wanted to escape. I didn't want to be Mother Eagle. I didn't want people to depend on me. I certainly didn't want to be Mother anything or anyone. I was a loner. Detached. No expectations. No commitments. I just wanted to be me, Jessica Seeker.

I thought about wanting to be Jessica Seeker and realized I didn't want to be her either. Jessica Seeker was a foul-mouthed druggie. Most of the time, she was a prostitute to earn money, and the rest of the time she was running away from herself, her nightmares, and her visions. *Oh God, I wanted to just be free of everything.* I envied Mother Wolf. She had found the sweet relief of death and I was still alive.

Alive, damn it! Alive in a life I had never chosen or wanted. Why wouldn't life let me escape? Why did it hold me here with such zeal?

In the distance I could hear my eagle shriek, and for a moment I was soaring with him. The land was green and the rivers were blue. Animals scurried on the ground. Birds sang in the trees. I could hear my eagle in my head, he said, "**Red. Screech. Fly together. Fly forever.**"

I heard myself answer the eagle in my head, in a human voice, mine, "**But I don't want to fly forever.**"

"**Screech love Red. Red fly forever,**" Then as suddenly as I had been flying with Screech, I was back again on earth with Sky at my side.

Sky took my arm and started to lead me away, "Mother Eagle, I've made a bath for you. I've put lavender and mint in it. I heated the water, so it's nice and hot. Come. I'll help you. You must be exhausted."

And frightened, I wanted to add. But of course I would never admit to anyone that I was frightened. I went with her. My whole body suddenly felt tired and weak.

Constable Tom stepped in front of us, "Mother Eagle, I need to speak with you for a moment." He turned and walked away. After a few steps he stopped and turned back to look at me. I suspected he was waiting for me to follow.

"It seems you have unfinished business," Sky released me and joined the other women who were lifting Mother Wolf from her donkey powered hammock.

Wolf watched them.

I turned away and walked over to Constable Tom as the women carried Mother Wolf into the house. Out of the corner of my eye, I saw Wolf look at me. He hesitated for only a moment and then he followed the women inside the house.

As I reached Constable Tom, he began to walk again. I fell in step beside him. Sky was right. I was exhausted. Bone-crushing tired. I had to will my feet to move. Even with my feet clad in the magic of my moccasins, I felt clumsy beside Constable Tom as he took his slow, long, even, strides forward. When we had put a considerable distance between ourselves and Mother Wolf's cabin-clinic, Constable Tom stopped.

"Constable," I said, "Thank you for coming up to the mount to get me and Mother Wolf."

"You're welcome, but if you don't mind Mother Eagle, I'd like you to call me Tom. Like Mother Wolf did," he said in his deep, smooth voice.

"Well, Tom, what did you want to talk about?"

"Mother Wolf wanted me to give this to you," he said, as he reached into his rawhide jacket, pulled out a large brown envelope, and handed it to me, "There's a letter for you from Mother Wolf. It also has the papers for the house and land. The cabin and the clinic are yours as long as you use them to help our people."

"You mean your people." I avoided taking the envelope from him.

"No. I mean what I say. I mean our people. You are our healer... our Shaman."

"Just like that?"

"Just like that."

"What if I bugger off and leave you all?"

"You won't. And...with respect...it doesn't suit your high status to use that kind of language."

I expected to see his face fold into a giant wrinkle like Mother Wolf's always did, but instead he gave me a smile. It wasn't his formal polite smile—this one had warmth in it.

"I don't want the clinic or the cabin."

"Do what you like, but at least take this. Read her letter. You may change your mind."

Like the Mothers he didn't seem to get it, and I wasn't going to tell him... but I was afraid. I wasn't a doctor like Mother Wolf. I didn't have her knowledge. I didn't even know what a Shaman was or did. In my way of thinking, I was a poor choice for any of it. What had the Mothers been thinking when they chose me? Even on the best day of my life—I wasn't Mother material.

"I won't change my mind. I don't want the responsibility of the clinic or the commitment of being a Shaman. I don't do responsibility and commitment. So I'm sure as hell not taking that envelope."

"Mother Eagle, I know you've been through a lot in the last few hours. I won't pretend to know how you may feel. And it's not my intetntion to argue with a Shaman, but it would be kind of you to relieve me of this burden. I'm simply a courier charged with the task of giving you an envelope. Please, take it."

"What happens if I don't take it?"

"Then I will have failed in fulfilling Mother Wolf's final request. I don't know what will happen." He lowered his hand with the envelope in it.

I heard the mellow young voice of Mother Wolf in my head as she intervened on Tom's behalf, "Child, you try the patience of all those who care about you. Just take the envelope from him. Make your choices later. Argue with me later. But don't torture this poor man."

I felt someone poke me in my back. I looked around expecting to see Mother Wolf behind me, but it was Wolf. I hadn't noticed him joining us. He was as silent in his comings and goings as Mother Wolf had been. But there was nothing Wolf or Mother Wolf could do to make me take the envelope.

I heard my eagle screech. I looked up and he was right over head. I could feel him in my mind. I heard Wolf whimper and I looked down just in time to see him lean his giant head forward, gently taking the envelope from Tom's hand.

Before either one of us could react, Wolf was padding off toward the house with the envelope tucked securely in his mouth.

Then I heard Screech in my mind with his voice sounding like escaping steam from a kettle, "***Wolf good Protector. Wolf love Screech. Screech love Wolf.***"

"***Can you talk to Wolf?***"

"***Yes.***"

"***Did you tell him to take the envelope?***"

"***No.***" He left my mind. I had the strange feeling that it was his way of putting up a hand the way Mother Wolf did when she didn't want to answer any more questions.

Tom said, "I guess it's settled. You'll have to work things out with Wolf and Mother Wolf."

"It isn't bad enough I have twelve Mothers on my case, I now have to deal with the friggin' animal kingdom, too. This Shaman shit sucks!"

Tom's face became pale. The muscles in his jaw seemed to tighten and twitch.

Mother Wolf appeared in front of me. She was surrounded by a red glow. She was no longer the young beautiful woman, but was a very angry old woman whose face was knotted into the biggest giant wrinkle of anger she had ever given me.

"MOUTH. SHOW RESPECT TO OUR TOTEMS AND US!" Her voice boomed in my head. I instantly had a throbbing headache.

"It's the Shaman-shit thing...isn't it?" I asked out loud to Tom and Mother Wolf, while I rubbed my throbbing temples and forehead.

"Yah." He watched me massage my head. The color was slowly returning to his face, "I don't get involved much with Shaman business as I've said, but I do know that making them angry can be rather painful. You don't insult the Mothers or their Totems. And judging by the pain you're having, I think you've just discovered that. Trust me they can do worse."

Weariness and pain were overtaking me. I'd had enough. I wanted sleep. Deep, dreamless, life infusing sleep—and something to stop the headache.

I heard my eagle screeching over head, and through the pounding pain I heard his thoughts, "**Stop. Wolf tell Mother. No hurt. Stop.**" His tone was fierce. The pain eased off, but it didn't go away completely.

I felt my legs buckle under me and I almost crumbled to the ground, but Tom caught me in his arms.

***

I awoke in the cabin-clinic's bathroom. I was lying in a warm tub of water. The aroma of lavender and mint filled the air. There was also the spicey pungent odor of burning sweetgrass and sage. I had a mild throbbing pain in my head.

Sky was sitting on a small stool beside the tub. Her eyes were closed and she was humming as she stroked her pregnant belly.

I felt a cool breeze coming through the window above me. I looked up at the window and saw Screech perched on the ledge. He was staring at me.

"**Red. Hurt?**" he thought to me.

"**Not hurt. Mothers were teaching Red respect,**" I could feel Screech didn't understand, so I added, "**Mothers gave Red a flying lesson.**" I created an image in my mind, showing him a baby eagle being pushed out of a nest for its first flight.

"**Flying...lesson. Yes.**" Screech bobbed his head in understanding.

"**I suppose I needed the lesson. But, I get angry when they won't tell me anything. Too many secrets. Why do the Mothers keep so many things from me?**"

"**Mothers protect. No scare Red.**"

"**Scare me? About what?**"

"**Ghost Walkers. Between.**"

"**Ghost Walkers? What are Ghost Walkers? And what is the Between?**"

He shook his head and closed his eyes. I could feel him in my mind, and it felt like he was reluctant to answer me.

Finally he thought to me, *"Ghost Walkers. Not dead. Not alive. Lost Between. Between bad place. Dark. Screech go Between."* He paused for a moment and fluffed his feathers, *"Screech tired. Screech sleep."*

Screech left my mind. It was clear that our discussion was over as he tucked his head deep into his shoulder.

From what the Mothers had told me, their Totem Protectors shared powers with them. Could my eagle go into the Beteen? Was going into the Between Screech's power? And what the hell was the Between and who were the Ghost Walkers? There was so much I didn't know and I wasn't altogether sure I wanted to learn. But I had to admit I was curious.

I turned my attention back to Sky. She had stopped rubbing her pregnant belly and was no longer humming. She was looking at me.

"Talking with your eagle." She sounded as though it was an every day occurrence for people to talk to animals.

I supposed she was used to the ways of Shamans, the same as Tom was used to them.

"Yes," I answered. "He was worried about me."

"Tell me about it. He smashed through the screen door when he thought we weren't going to let him in. Since then we've opened all the windows and doors." Sky rubbed her belly as she continued, "He's a beautiful Totem. Strong and walks between worlds."

"Walks between worlds? What does that mean? And what are Ghost Walkers? What is the Between?"

The questions tumbled out of mouth and I couldn't stop them. I must have sounded foolish to her. But I needed to know more. I eased myself out of the tub and reached for the bath towel on the rack.

Sky got up from her stool and stepped away from the tub moving closer to the door. She turned her back to me, affording me some privacy as I toweled myself dry.

"I'm sorry, Mother Eagle, but I've been told to stay with you. I can't leave you alone. And he won't let me leave." She kept her face turned away, twisted her body slightly, pointed in Screech's direction and added, "Your eagle makes a huge ruckus and flies at me when I try to go. His wings pack quite a wallop. Do you want me to leave?"

"It's okay. I'm not shy," I said, thinking about how many times I'd been naked in front of strangers. Granted, I was usually drunk or high or both, and didn't remember much of it, but naked was my usual state of attire. And I was determined to get some answers. "So what's with Ghost Walkers and the Between?"

"Is there anything else you need, Mother Eagle?" Sky avoided my question.

"Yes, I need to know what you meant about the eagle being between worlds."

Sky was quiet for a moment, and then said, "Eagle is the messenger between our world and the world of the ancestors. He has the power to be in both places at the same time. With an eagle as your Totem, you will be able to do the same. The eagle's medicine is strong," Sky said, with her back still turned to me.

I grabbed the robe hanging on the hook beside the tub and put it on.

"So eagles can be dead and alive at the same time?" I wrapped the belt of the robe around me and tied it off.

"Yes. Eagle takes the spirits to the heavens. He can talk with the Ghost Walkers who are Between—" Sky suddenly stopped, turned to look at me, and appeared to be unwilling to say more.

"He talks to Ghost Walkers?"

"I think it is best to ask him." Sky's face turned blush-red, "He is your Totem, he will teach you. I'm sorry. I've spoken when I should've remained silent."

Once again there was a crazy urge to hug Sky and comfort her, so I hugged her. I let her go after patting her on the back several times. She relaxed, and I liked that I could give her comfort.

"It's okay Sky. There's too many rules. I don't know them all, and I'm having a hard time keeping track of them. But don't worry. I'm sure Screech—"

Sky jumped. She covered her ears, and hopped around on the floor as though she were dancing on hot coals.

"What now?" I was completely confused.

Suddenly, Screech was awake on his window perch, screeching in my head, "***Red. Need Screech. Screech protect.***"

Sky was shaking, "Mother Eagle, you shrieked...like an eagle. I'm sorry, I don't speak eagle."

I realized I had vocalized my Totem's name but I'd done it out loud, and it must have come out as an ear-piercing shriek. This time I carefully concentrated on the word Screech, and then said, "I'm sorry, his name is—"

"Oh no, Mother Eagle, don't tell me his name. That is a sacred thing, shared between him and you only. He is simply Eagle to us." Sky looked over at Screech who was bobbing up and down on the window ledge. I followed her gaze and saw Screech's talons slicing deep ridges in the wooden sill.

"*Another flying lesson,*" I thought to him and he relaxed.

"Sky. Thank you for my bath. It was wonderful, I needed it. But now, I'd like to get some sleep," I said tucking my arm under and around her forearm.

We walked down the short hallway to my bedroom. The door was closed. I heard chanting and drumming. There was a strong spicy aroma of burning sweetgrass and sage. I wanted to open the door, but Sky stopped me.

"This isn't your room anymore. It's now an ancestor's room. A Shaman ancestor's room. The elders look after the needs of the ancestors. You will see her later. Right now you need some sleep."

"Sleep. Yes," I was starting to feel weak again.

Sky guided me down the hall a few more steps, and stopped at the door that had been Mother Wolf's room. The window to the room was open and Screech was perched on the window ledge. His yellow-green eyes followed me.

Wolf was lying on the floor beside the bed. On the bed was the brown envelope Wolf had taken out of Tom's hand.

Sky reached down and moved the envelope to the old relic of a dresser beside the window, and then seated me on the bed. Exhaustion was consuming me. I tried to lift my legs up onto the bed, but didn't have the strength. Sky lifted them for me, and then shifted me around and gently pressed me back into the pillows.

"Vision Quests awaken the spirit, but drain the body. You must rest. I'll wake you when it's time."

"When it's time for what?"

After that I don't remember anything. The relaxation of sleep was upon me so fast I didn't know whether Sky had answered me or not.

My sleep was dreamless.

Screech woke me, with his thoughts about eating, "*Hungry. Must hunt. Wolf protect.*"

His voice, sounding like escaping steam from a boiling tea kettle, woke me with a start. For a moment I didn't know where I was. The surroundings were foreign to me.

The pictures on the wall were different. The dream catcher beside the bed had turquoise stones and white shells woven into it, the one I was used to was threaded with multicolored stones and no shells. The bed was bigger. The room had the stagnant odor of old things, mixed with the fragrance of cinnamon, cloves, and lavender.

Then I remembered...this was Mother Wolf's room.

Screech, impatient with not getting an answer from me and succumbing to his hunger thought to me again, "*HUNGRY. HUNT NOW.*"

"*Stop that screeching. It hurts my head. Yes. Go. Eat.*"

"*Hurt Red,*" his voice was so quiet, I could barely hear him. He paused for a moment, I could feel his pain for hurting me, and then he added, "*Screech hurt Red. Yes.*"

"*I'm okay. You just surprised me.*"

"*Wolf protect. Screech hunt.*" His steam kettle voice was almost a whisper. Then he was gone from my mind.

He flew off the window ledge, and was soaring high in the sky within seconds.

Wolf stood and stretched as well. *How long had I been asleep?* I wondered.

I roused myself enough to sit up on the side of the bed.

There was a light tap on the bedroom door.

"Come in," I said.

The door opened. Sky entered the room carrying a large tray that held a plate of freshly baked bannock, a cup of coffee, a bowl of venison stew and a big bowl of kibble. Without saying a word, Sky put the tray on my lap. She took the bowl of kibble and placed it on the floor in front of Wolf. Her movements were graceful and her manner was one of quiet respect.

Wolf lowered his giant head and sniffed at the kibble. He raised his head, looked at Sky and then at me and finally laid back down beside the bed, uninterested in the food.

As for me, I was as hungry as Screech. I wasted no time and took the bowl of venison stew and greedily spooned it into my mouth. The stew tasted wonderful with the mixed flavours of meat and vegetables in a creamy savory gravy. In the distance I could feel Screech. He had caught a gopher and was eating it with the same enthusiasm, hunger, and enjoyment.

"Vision Quests take a lot of energy. They make you tired and hungry," Sky's voice was soft and light.

"Ravenously hungry. The stew is delicious. Thank you," I said between greedy mouthfuls.

Screech thought to me, "*Wolf want meat. Screech hunt. Feed Wolf.*"

"*Rabbit?*" I thought back.

"*Need Deer. Wolf Big.*" Screech thought to me a picture of himself trying to fly with a deer in his talons. I understood. "*Rabbit better,*" he thought to me.

I thought back to him with the image of a very fat rabbit, "*Wolf needs a big fat rabbit.*"

"*Screech hunt. Big Rabbit,*" he thought back to me and disappeared from my mind.

Sky sat down on the floor beside Wolf, asked his permission to touch him, he yawned and moved his head closer to her. She began to stroke his giant slivery-white muzzle.

"Mother Eagle, it will be dark soon and we are almost ready to send Mother Wolf on her journey to the ancestors. You will need to get dressed." She pointed to my dress on the chair and my moccasins carefully placed on the floor beside it.

I realized I hadn't removed my dress or moccasins before I had woke up in the bath tub. And I'd been so relaxed after my bath that I'd just put on the robe by the tub. And when I had woke this time, I had been so hungry that I had started to eat without noticing I was wearing one of Mother Wolf's nightgowns.

Sky watched me as I stopped eating and looked at the nightgown, "You were so tired. You fell asleep right away. I took off your bathrobe because it was damp, and I found the nightgown in the drawer, and put it on you," she said, continuing to stroke Wolf's muzzle, "I hope you don't mind."

I gave Sky a polite nod of understanding, and returned to spooning the stew into my mouth savouring every bite. It seemed to me that nothing had ever tasted so good.

Sky stopped patting Wolf and got up, "I'll leave you to enjoy your meal. There's a couple of things I need to do to help the elders with Mother Wolf's preparations. I'll come back later." She left the room as quietly as she had entered it.

A few minutes after Sky left, Screech returned and tried to land on the window ledge with a huge rabbit in his talons. In a clumsy motion, he dropped the rabbit inside and finally settled on the window sill.

Screech bobbed his head up and down and from side to side, clearly he was talking to Wolf. Wolf stood, walked over to the Rabbit, and picked it up in his giant jaws. I opened the bedroom door, and he left.

After I finished eating, I brushed and braided my hair, and put on my embroidered white rawhide dress and moccasins.

I took a few moments to run my hand over the eagle on my chest, admiring the beauty and detail of the embroidery. When I finally looked up, Sky was standing in the doorway. She greeted me.

"Mother Eagle, we are ready. It is time to send Mother Wolf on her journey," she announced. She walked down the hall to the front door of the cabin. I followed.

Screech was already outside and in the air circling the cabin. Wolf was quickly finishing off the rabbit. When he was done, he walked over to take his place beside the travois that held Mother Wolf's shrouded body. Jojo stood quietly while Constable Tom, who was dressed from head to toe in a beautifully beaded buckskin jacket, pants, and moccasins held the lead rope wrapped around Jojo's neck.

I looked at the small thin bundle wrapped in a rough woven turquoise colored blanket. It looked similar to the sun blanket she had wrapped me in the first night we met. But this was a solid color and was wrapped around her so tightly that she looked like a turquoise mummy.

"Turquoise is the color we use to represent spirit," Mother Wolf's young voice whispered in my head.

Other than the sound of one person chanting and a single drum beating, there was silence. No birds chirped. Not even a leaf rustled on the trees. It felt as though the world was silent. I could feel Screech in my mind as he circled effortlessly, high in the sky, but he was also quiet.

Men, women, and children had gathered around the old cabin-clinic. They waited in motionless reverence and silence.

Sky guided me to stand beside Constable Tom. He acknowledged my presence with a slight nod of his head. He gave a gentle tug on Jojo's bridle and began walking. We walked and led Jojo a half mile down the dusty gravel road that ran from the cabin-clinic to the resting place of the ancestors.

I remembered the place. Mother Wolf had brought me here to give me a complete history lesson about Our Mothers. I wish I'd paid more attention at the time.

As we entered the ancestors' final resting place, Mother Wolf appeared beside me dressed in her white rawhide dress, looking young and completely healthy.

And before I could say a word, she raised her hand and said, "Say nothing, child. Only you, Wolf, and your eagle have the eyes to see me."

"*Land now,*" Screech thought to me.

I automatically extended my left arm with the long sleeve, and prepared for the weight of his landing, but the sleeve of my dress seemed to harden helping me to hold my arm steady for Screech's landing. My arm lowered only slightly from the speed and force of him taking his perch.

Screech balanced himself. His sharp talons gripping my arm without penetrating the rawhide sleeve.

"*Screech loves Red.*" He looked forward, and was completely quiet. I could feel his love filling my body and mind like a warm soft blanket on a cold wintery evening. He comforted me. All seemed right in my world with my eagle.

Then I was caught by the thought of how strange it was to be having a funeral ceremony for Mother Wolf while she stood at my side. And then, as though she had heard my thoughts and question, she answered me.

"Those left behind need to mourn and honor those who have left. Those who have left, honour the living by not interfering with their mourning."

I turned to speak to her and she raised her hand. I remained silent. She placed her hand on my arm. The ceremony began.

The ceremony was elegant in its simplicity. All eleven of the Mothers who had preceded Mother Wolf were in attendance although Wolf, Screech, and I were the only ones to see them. The Mothers chanted and hummed in the background, as the chief and elders performed the ceremony. Mother Wolf translated the bits that I couldn't understand.

She coached me through the sweetgrass ceremony and then through the final prayers for her safe passage to the other side. When it was all done, they gave Mother Wolf the highest honour possible. They placed her on a funeral pyre and set it ablaze.

Mother Wolf was pleased and honoured.

She wanted me to thank Tom for getting all the clearances for the pyre.

She whispered in my head as she watched the flames, "Getting clearance for this must have been a paperwork nightmare. He is a good man and a good grandson." She gently squeezed my arm. "This is an honour only bestowed on the Shamans. And sometimes, the paperwork can't be completed in time. I owe him a debt of gratitude. We will take special care to watch over him. Please make sure you give him my message of thanks."

"I will."

For just an instant, I sensed that something was looking through the early evening darkness. And this something was close to me. I could almost feel it breathing on me. I shivered. The feeling left me as abruptly as it had started.

Then Mother Wolf's quiet young voice said, "The trials, trouble, and the Watcher will come soon, but not just yet. We will prepare you and watch over you. Don't worry, child."

I could feel Screech squeeze my arm with his talons, he looked at me with a piercing stare, and for a moment I could feel his fear. He understood what I was feeling. He knew fear. My great strong Bald Eagle and Totem Protector felt and knew fear. He said nothing.

I said nothing.

Wolf gave a long mournful soul shaking howl and the ceremony was over.

PART III

THE HUNT

Chapter Eight

Things settled into a routine at the cabin-clinic. At first I didn't feel qualified to help Mother Wolf's patients, but she was always at my side, guiding me through every step.

She was only seen by me, Wolf, and Screech. She was invisible to all those who came to the cabin-clinic. And the other Mothers were always close at hand. They all helped teach me everything from making complex poultices and delivering babies to suturing small wounds.

But this wasn't ever a smooth operation with twelve strong willed women arguing over the proper way of doing things, or deciding the best treatments for patients' ailments.

Each Mother had a special poultice recipe, or treatment they thought was better than the others. Sometimes the arguments became so heated Screech would take me in his mind and we would fly together over the peaceful forests, lakes, and streams, leaving them to fight it out without us. This practice of mentally disappearing with my beloved Screech annoyed the Mothers, which in turn, amused the hell out of Screech and me.

I adored my Screech. He was deliciously mischievous, a perfect soulmate for me.

But in the end, all the arguing between the Mothers would be resolved and we had a lot of all-is-forgiven-parties.

I liked those parties. We would all take a long walk on the forest trails, each Mother and each Totem through their Mother shared their knowledge with me about the ways of the great mother—Mother Earth. They taught me about her creatures and her plants.

It was on these walks that the Mothers expressed how pleased they were with my progress, especially Mother Spider and Mother Diamondback, along with their respective Totem Protectors.

Mother Spider was pleased with how well I could use her and her Totem's powers to see into the webs of illness and how well I used that vision to diagnose the ailments of my patients. And Mother Diamondback was impressed by my ability to use distillations to treat migraines, arthritis, and a myriad of other long term and painful illnesses. I had become so adept at using her and her snake's power that the city doctors sent patients to me the same way they had sent patients to Mother Wolf for treatment.

During the walks in the forest with the Mothers, Screech and Wolf kept me company as well. Wolf was vigilant on the ground, while Screech searched the skies. Ever since Mother Wolf's funeral, I had sensed a constant alertness in the two of them. They never left me alone. They never slept at the same time. One was always on guard.

When I asked the Mother's about this, they just responded with, "They are your protectors. That is what they do."

But I also sensed the Mothers weren't telling me everything. I felt they were intentionally keeping something from me. When I probed them for answers, I was given the hand in the air signal meaning they weren't going to tell me anything more.

The Mothers and I managed to make it through the fall and winter and into the spring with me as student and them as teachers without any casualties among us or our patients, even during the somewhat difficult delivery of Sky's baby. Although the Mothers argued, all of us and Sky successfully delivered her beautiful baby girl.

Sky decided to call her baby, Jessica. I was touched, but Screech thought *Red* would have been a better name.

When the cases and treatments were too complex for us, I always sent the patients into the city for care. The same way Mother Wolf had always done.

By late spring I was settled in and I had a comfortable routine. But at dusk everyday there was still a feeling that something was watching me. Following me. Patiently waiting.

Dusk was always the time when the Mothers, Wolf, and Screech gathered closest to me. When I asked what was following me, all the Mothers would hold up their hands and say in unison, "Their time and your time have not yet come. It is your time to learn. It is their time to wait."

It was the Mother's routine and constantly annoying response. Finally, I would give up and just appreciated the easy comfort of their company.

It was all routine until the morning when little seven-year-old Monica Whitefeather and her mother arrived at the cabin-clinic door.

Monica's mother, who was normally calm and reserved, was standing in my doorway shaking and wide-eyed holding her daughter in her arms. Monica's tiny leg was wrapped in a blood-soaked towel, and she was crying and sobbing uncontrollably. I lifted Monica from her mother's arms and tried to calm both of them.

"What happened?" I asked as I carried Monica and led her mother into the kitchen that doubled as a treatment room.

"Monica fell down the ravine," her mother said.

"And you hurt your leg," I said to Monica.

Between sobs, Monica nodded her agreement.

"It's okay. We'll get you fixed up in a jiffy," I reassured her, sounding like Mother Wolf.

As we entered the kitchen-treatment room, Mother Wolf, visible only to me and our Totems, materialized in her favourite chair beside the kitchen door. Wolf settled himself beside her. Screech sat on the open window ledge. A light morning breeze carrying the scent of impending rain blew in the window. The only sound was Monica's sobs.

I sat Monica on the kitchen table and began to remove the blood soaked towel from her leg. Monica sobbed more. Her mother cleared her throat uncomfortably, as I revealed her daughter's wound. A half inch thick twig was skewered through the soft tissue and muscle of her calf.

Mother Wolf guided me as she always did. Mother Spider also appeared and helped me to look inside the injury. I could see that no major blood vessels were involved. But the muscle of her leg had been badly injured.

"She'll need pain and bleeding control," Mother Wolf said.

I went to the cupboard and removed the bottle of pain mixture. I'd been creative in my labelling since I'd taken over the clinic and had labelled the bottle 'pain vomit'. The Mothers, in particular Mother Wolf, were unimpressed with my labels, but allowed me to put my mark on the concoctions they trained me to make. Next to the pain vomit remedy was the bottle labelled *'blood plug'*. From the corner of my eye I could see Mother Wolf shake her head.

"Child, those labels are embarrassing," she said, taking the opportunity to chastise me knowing I wouldn't argue with her while I had a patient in the room.

Ignoring Mother Wolf, I went back to the table, opened the little drawer under the table top, and removed a teaspoon.

I uncapped the pain vomit bottle and was instantly confronted with the aroma of rotten eggs. The fragrance was so potent Monica stopped sobbing and tried to hold her breath.

"Yeah, I know. It stinks. And it tastes even worse. But it works. It'll get rid of the pain." I poured out a small dollop of the brownish syrupy liquid into the tiny teaspoon.

I offered her the spoon of pain vomit, "You want the pain to go away?"

She gave me a nod.

"Then you have to swallow this. Maybe if your mom holds your nose while you swallow, it'll be easier."

Following my cue, Monica's mother pinched her daughter's nose.

Monica closed her eyes and opened her mouth. *Brave little girl,* I thought.

"Better than some little girls I know," Mother Wolf said, and smirked at me.

Screech shook his head and flutter on his window ledge, "***Pain is better. Medicine...stink.***"

I thought a smile to him. Sometimes I thought that he was developing a wry sense of humour.

After making a face at the taste of the pain vomit mixture, Monica stopped crying. I waited a few moments for the medicine to take affect.

"Less pain?" I aked.

In a small weak voice Monica said, "Yes, but tastes bad."

I opened the drawer under the table top once more and pulled out a fruit lozenge. I gave it to Monica, and she immediately busied herself with opening it, and popping it into her mouth.

"Okay Monica, I want you to lie down. Mrs. Whitefeather, maybe you can rest her head in your arms and talk to her while I have a closer look at her leg," I instructed as I opened the bottle of herbs labelled "blood plug" and put on a pair of sterile latex gloves.

The twig was poking out of both sides of her calf. One end was the piercing point of the branch, and the other end was splintered and broken.

Mother Wolf said, "We'll need to clean the wound, stop the bleeding, and put some antiseptic on it. And bandage it with the twig in place. This is something Dr. Ross should have a look at."

"Mother Eagle what kind of poultice would you recommend for this wound?" Mother Diamondback asked.

I thought to all the Mothers, "Witch hazel and winter green will be good antiseptics, and some willow to help with the pain."

"Well done," said Mother Spider in her best cheerleading style.

I was glad she thought I was doing well, and the Mothers weren't arguing about the treatment. I wanted to get little Monica on her way to the doctor as quickly as I could.

I cleaned the area with sterile water and sprinkled a liberal amount of blood plug on both the entry and exit point of the wound.

As I treated Monica's wound, I tried to distract her by asking her questions, "So what were you doing at the ravine?"

"I was going down to feed the fish in the creek," Monica said, her sobs were subsiding as the pain vomit took effect.

"Tell me about the fish." I started dressing the wound.

"They're really small, but there's one big one that's a bully. He takes all the food I give them."

"You know bullies don't always get their way. Mother Wolf used to tell me that when you tickle the belly of the dragon, you eventually get burned."

Monica seemed to be getting very groggy, and then I saw Mother Wolf standing beside Monica, stroking her head and humming. She was helping Monica to fall asleep.

I wrapped a poultice around her leg, leaving the twig exposed on both sides, and tightened it to reduce any further bleeding. Monica was asleep and felt nothing.

I wrote a note to Dr. Ross telling him what I had done and what meds I had given her. He was familiar with most of the medicines and poultices we used in the clinic. He supported our natural medicines and approach. I assured Mrs. Whitefeather that he would take good care of Monica.

I had just finished writing the note when someone knocked on the front door. I called out the usual greeting.

"Have a seat in the living room. I'll be with you in a minute."

It was normal for people to show up at my door. Appointments were usually not made.

Mother Wolf didn't have a phone and I had carried on that tradition. Wolf had been her messenger, taking notes and meds to people on the reserve. I'd followed in her footsteps, both Screech and Wolf delivered messages and meds for me. Everyone knew that was how it worked and the children especially liked it. Screech was rapidly becoming a celebrity. He was getting fat on the offerings left for him. He'd never tasted deer before he had become a messenger, and he was beginning to develop a fondness for venison.

If there was an immediate emergency, the Mothers and I usually saw it coming and were prepared. That all worked better than a phone.

Everyone always waited their turn when they came to the cabin-clinic, so I continued with my treatment of Monica. Mother Wolf seated herself on her chair beside the door, but I noticed both Wolf and Screech were restless.

"*What's up?*" I gave Screech a quick thought it was in slang but we'd been working on getting more in tune with each other's thoughts. Sometimes it worked and sometimes there were very messy misunderstandings. This time Screech surprised me with his cleverness.

"*Time...is...up,*" Screech's thought was filled with a feeling of worry and a slight hint of fear.

Mother Wolf was looking out the kitchen window and seemed to be talking to the Mothers. I couldn't hear what they were saying.

It was difficult, but I needed to focus on Monica and her mother, so I did. Monica was between waking and sleeping.

"Feel a little better, Monica?" I asked.

"Yes," she slurred. "Tell Mother Wolf I liked the dream she sent me about the boy who tickled the dragon's belly." She gave me a broad sleepy smile.

I understood what the Mothers had been up to with their humming. Dreams were the way the Mother's communicated with the living, except me, of course.

"She has heard your thanks Monica. Now Mom," I turned to Mrs. Whitefeather preparing more poultices for her daughter. "I've written a note for Dr. Ross, and he will understand what I've done. If it's okay with him, you can use these poultices when you change the dressings. Don't let her have anything to eat or drink before she sees the doctor."

"Hi, Monica. Mrs. Whitefeather. Mother Eagle," Tom said, as he walked through the kitchen doorway. "I'm sorry to intrude like this, but I couldn't wait, it's urgent."

Tom looked concerned and distracted at the same time.

Mother Wolf had disappeared, and Wolf was standing beside me at the table. Screech was fidgeting on the kitchen windowsill.

The air in the room seemed colder. I shivered. And there it was, that feeling of something watching and waiting.

I was also annoyed that Tom had walked in on my patient and me. I could feel some strong colorful expletives forming on my lips, but I said nothing. Even I didn't use that kind of language in front of children.

I ignored Tom and focused on Monica and her mother, "All right, we'd best get you off to the city to see the doc."

I put the poultices into a plastic bag and gave them to Monica's mother. I lifted Monica and cradled her in my arms.

"Mother Eagle, thank you. I left in such a hurry, I forgot to bring you tobacco," Mrs. Whitefeather said.

"It's okay. The best gift is making sure our little Monica gets better."

I nodded to Tom to move out of the doorway, and carried Monica out to the car. I placed her in the child seat.

"I'll wash the towel and return it to you later. I have a remedy that will remove blood. I'll send it back to you with Eagle or Wolf."

The prospect of having Wolf or Screech visit their home excited Monica and she said, in a groggy voice, "We have fresh venison."

Monica's mother buckled her daughter into the seat, went around to the driver's side, and opened the door.

"Then I'll send Eagle. Venison is his favourite treat." I closed Monica's car door, "Journey well."

Monica's mother slid into the driver's seat and nodded to me. "Thank you, Mother Eagle. Journey well." She closed her door and drove away.

Tom was waiting for me in the doorway when I came back to the cabin. He held the door open.

"I'm sorry for the interruption, but a Federal Investigator showed up this morning at the station looking for Jessica Seeker," Tom said as I entered the cabin.

"And what did you tell him?"

"Nothing. I left him with a cup of coffee, a newspaper, and a polite, 'I have an important errand to run. I'll be back.' And then I came out to see you."

"Do you know what he wants with Jessica Seeker?" I asked, walking toward the kitchen with Tom following me.

"He said a murderer was back in Wheaton, and he thinks you can help out on the case."

Wheaton and murderer were two words I had hoped I would never hear together in one sentence again. I didn't want to answer Tom. I ignored him. He remained quiet.

The air turned cold. I shivered and noticed that Wolf was no longer in the kitchen and the door was open. He had opened the kitchen door like he always did when he wanted to go outside, and as always, he hadn't closed it. But I knew the coldness in the room wasn't the cool morning air, it was something more.

As I cleaned the table, wrapped up Monica's bloody towel and put it in the sink for washing, I sensed someone watching. Waiting. It was a familiar feeling. It was the feeling that had been with me for more than a decade.

I took off my latex gloves, threw them in the garbage, and looked at the window ledge. Screech wasn't there.

As I closed the kitchen door, I looked out across the yard and saw that Screech was sitting on the top of the old shed that was Jojo's home. Wolf was sitting on the ground in front of it. Both of them were looking at the house. I could hear the Mothers humming.

I finally turned to Tom, "How did he know to look for me here?"

"He said the killer had made a demand to have you come back to Wheaton. So the Wheaton police tracked you down through your arrest records and your parole officer's final report. They found your last known whereabouts was in Silver Falls near Pinewood County and the town is in our jurisdiction. Seems they thought with your record, they should start with our police department to see if we'd had any run-ins with you."

"Tell them their records are wrong. I'm Mother Eagle. Jessica Seeker no longer exists. And even if she did, she couldn't help them before and she sure can't help them now."

"He's a very determined man, Mother Eagle. He's come a long way to look for you. I'm not sure he'll believe me. He's not the type to take '*no*' for an answer."

Then I could hear Mother Wolf's voice drifting to me across the yard, "Child. The time has come."

Screech was in my head, "**Screech protect Red.**"

"Tom, I'm sorry. But he'll have to take '*no*' as an answer. I'm not going back to Wheaton. And I'm sure as hell not going to help them out. That town hates me and the feeling is mutual."

"Seems this federal guy thought you'd feel that way, if you were here, of course. He gave this to me. It's for you." He handed me a folded piece of paper.

As I unfolded it, I saw it was a photocopy of an original document. There was a large black blotch on the corner.

I touched the blotch and looked at Tom, "Blood?"

"Yes. The Detective said this was a copy of a note that was attached to the last victim's body."

"A young girl? About twelve or thirteen?"

"Thirteen."

I read the note aloud, *"More will die unless Witchy-woman gets her ass back here."*

"The federal investigator said someone named Duggan figured the Witchy-woman was you. Seems that's the nickname the town gave you after you helped the police with a murder almost eleven years ago."

I felt my legs getting weak and sat down in Mother Wolf's chair by the kitchen door, "Witchy-woman and Constable Duggan are relics best left in the past."

"The Detective called him Commander Duggan."

"I guess he's been promoted since I was in Wheaton."

"Mother Eagle, I would never tell a Shaman what to do. But in this matter, I believe I can offer some advice."

I looked up at Tom, and noticed that although he seemed to be casual and relaxed leaning against the doorway between the kitchen and living room, there was nothing relaxed about the muscles in his face. His jaw was tight, and his brown eyes were searching me with his penetrating policeman's stare.

"Tom, I can't go back there. No matter what you have as advice," I said and felt Mother Wolf in my mind.

"Come. Talk with us," Mother Wolf's request rang in my head with the tone of a command.

Tom shifted his position and leaned against the doorway again. He measured his words as he spoke.

"These are children who are dying. It seems to me that a healer like yourself would want to stop it."

"Bring food for my wolf and your eagle. They are hungry and their feelings of hunger are distressing them and disturbing us. Quickly, child. We need to talk to you immediately," Mother Wolf's thoughts had an ominous urgency to them.

I got up and walked over to the fridge. I pulled out a tray of raw deer meat. Tom watched and said nothing more to me.

I took several slices of the meat and placed them on a plate, and put the plate in the new microwave one of my patients had given to me and quick-warmed it. Screech liked his meat warm, especially when he hadn't hunted it for himself.

"Excuse me Tom, I have to feed Eagle and Wolf," I said. I was always careful not to mention Screech's name to anyone, including the Mothers, since Sky had told me to keep his name to myself.

"Shaman's business," Tom said.

"What?" I looked at him, surprised by his observation.

"Every time they talk to you, you try to hide it. But I can see that same faraway look on your face my Grandmother used to get when the Mothers talked to her," he said and shrugged.

The microwave made a dinging sound. I opened it, gathered up the plate of meat, and walked to the kitchen door. In just a couple of strides, Tom was at the door before me and opened it. As I exited, I was close enough to him to smell the fragrance of leather mixed with the spicy aroma of sweetgrass and sage. I had never noticed it before. I liked it.

I walked across the yard to the old shed. Screech lowered his regal white head, and thought to me, "*Screech hungry,*" then he created a picture of a deer for me, and added, "*Deer. Deer good.*"

I held up the plate of raw meat, he glided down and picked up a slice of meat with effortless grace. I knew this was just a snack for both him and Wolf, but I would give them more later, after I talked with the Mothers.

Screech landed on one of the old buildings in the yard. He held the meat against the roof with his powerful talons, and then ripped at it with his beak. He tore a long strip loose, snapped his head backwards, and swallowed it whole. For a moment he allowed me to savour the meat with him. It was his way of thanking me for providing a meal when he couldn't hunt for himself, and then he left my mind. His hunger stayed with me, and my stomach protested with a hunger pang. I, too, hadn't eaten breakfast this morning and was as hungry as my eagle was.

I placed the plate with the rest of the meat on the ground in front of Wolf. He cocked his head and looked at me with his large blue-green eyes. I knew he was trying to talk to me, but only Mother Wolf could hear him, the same as I was the only Mother who could hear Screech. Mother Wolf had explained that all the Totem Protectors could hear and talk to each other, but they never talked directly to the other Mothers.

The Mothers were always gracious in translating their Totems' thoughts when required, and Mother Wolf translated for Wolf.

"Wolf thanks you for the food," Mother Wolf said, as she materialized in front of me. She was her young self, dressed in the white rawhide dress with all the Totems embroidered on it. I knew this was going to be a serious discussion, because she never wore the dress unless it was a ceremony or she wanted to have a serious discussion about my talents and me.

"Please tell Wolf he's very handsome and he is welcome. Eagle and I love him," I told her. Our Totems always wanted to be told they were handsome, brave, and loved. They liked the praise as much as they liked to eat.

Mother Wolf passed along my greetings to Wolf and then nodded toward the kitchen door where Tom was standing.

"I think we should go around the back. Out of sight," she said and disappeared.

I walked around to the back of the building. All the Mothers and their Totems appeared one at a time behind Mother Wolf. They materialized as shimmering white transparent silhouettes and then solidified into their forms as young women. All twelve of them dotted the landscape behind the shed.

There was the faint sound of drums and humming in the air. A slight fragrance of burning sweetgrass was carried on a light breeze. I knew the Mothers' tactics well, and I knew they were creating a feeling of calmness and tranquility. I could feel myself fighting but surrendering to the effect.

I didn't want to think about those young girls and their murders in Wheaton. Finally, I willingly gave into the calmness they were gifting to me.

"My child," Mother Wolf's voice was a soft whisper, "Your trials have begun. This is a test of your love, strength, and courage as a Shaman and Medicine Woman. You must decide with both your heart and your mind."

"Okay. I've decided, I'm not going back there."

"You choose to fail so easily," Mother Wolf said.

"There's nothing I can do for those children, or the people in that shithole of a town. Besides those people hate me."

"Mouth," Mother Wolf said and her face instantly turned into the giant wrinkled frown I was so used to seeing.

I turned to walk away, the calmness was leaving me, and I wanted to escape, but I couldn't move.

"You are frightened, my child," Mother Wolf said in her young voice. The giant frown was gone.

The drumming and humming was also gone, just the faint scent of sweetgrass lingered in the air.

"A family was ruined because of me. That town hates me and I don't blame them. I'm not going back."

Mother Spider and Mother Diamondback stepped forward, their Totems reached out to touch me. I put out my hand and Spider raced up my arm to my ear and stroked it with his hairy leg. I had long since lost the creepy feeling that act of affection used to give me. I put out my other arm. Diamondback slithered up my arm and wrapped himself around my shoulders gently caressing me.

"Mother Eagle," Mother Diamondback said, "This is your destiny. This is part of what you are meant to do."

"Mother Diamondback is right. You may want to run but you mustn't take that path," Mother Spider added.

Wolf walked around the side of the out building and joined us. He sat beside Mother Wolf and she stroked his huge white head.

Screech had finished eating. Now sated, he decided to offer his thoughts to me.

"**Screech protect Red. Screech strong. Red strong,**" Screech thought to me and followed it with a bird burp, "**Deer good.**"

"**Red knows Screech is strong. Red's not so sure about herself.**" Although Screech was quiet, I could still feel him in my mind.

"Wolf heard Eagle, and he wants you to know he won't leave your side either. This is what he has stayed behind to do," Mother Wolf said.

Spider crawled down my arm and hopped across to Mother Spider, and Diamondback slithered back to his Mother.

"None of us will leave you, Mother Eagle. You are loved by all of us. We are family." Mother Spider kissed her spider Totem on its furry black back.

Family. The thought struck me deep in my heart and ran into the marrow of my bones. It was true. They were my family. They were the only real family I'd ever had. I didn't want to disappoint them. But I didn't have the courage or strength to face the people of Wheaton. They hated me. And I didn't like them either. Even my desire to not disappoint the Mothers couldn't force me to return.

I hoped I sounded stronger then I felt, "Easy for you. You're on the other side. Nothing can hurt you. You weren't there. I was. I'm not going back."

"Not even to save a child's life?" Mother Wolf asked.

"Why can't you, all of you, do something? You seem to know all. See all. Why can't you help them?" I pleaded with them and tried to walk away again, but was still stuck, "Let me go. Please."

They released me, I was free to leave. I started to walk away.

"We can't be where you are not. If you are here, we are here. We can't intervene without you. And child, we can only see possibilities, not the final outcomes. Those outcomes depend on the choices of those who still live," Mother Wolf explained in her quiet young voice.

"Then those who are living in Wheaton will have to deal with the living and the dead in Wheaton," I said and took another step away.

"If that's your choice, Spider tells me the web shows many may die in Wheaton," Mother Spider warned. "And they will all be children."

My back was turned to the Mothers and their Totems, but I could feel all of them watching me. I stopped moving.

"You are a Medicine Woman, a Shaman, and kin to a whole line of Medicine Women Shamans. It's your path and choices that will continue the line or destroy it. Lessons you learn will add to our knowledge and abilities. Jessica Seeker no longer exists, only Mother Eagle survives and it's this one that we trust to continue the line. The past is dead—only the present lives," Mother Wolf said.

The fragrance of burning sweetgrass was gone and everything went silent. I turned. The Mothers were gone. Only Wolf and Screech were left. I could still feel Screech in my mind, but he, too, was silent. Then he left my mind.

I picked up the plate I had left on the ground for Wolf and walked back to the cabin-clinic. I had only one thought. Children were dying in Wheaton again, and I didn't have a foggy clue about how to stop it from happening. It wasn't my battle. I owed that town nothing.

Chapter Nine

Tom was sitting in Mother Wolf's chair by the kitchen door. I didn't look at him as I passed by, but I could almost feel the stare of his dark brown eyes searching me. He didn't say anything.

Screech landed on the kitchen windowsill, shook his huge magnificent head, and settled in. Wolf followed behind me and sat down beside Tom. Mother Wolf was not in the room, and that felt strange. She was always ready to give me a lecture on what I'd done right and what I'd done wrong with each patient I treated.

There was total and complete silence. No bird song. No wind blowing through the leaves of the trees. Nothing. The emptiness of the silence was beginning to hurt my ears.

"Okay," I said to Tom, and turned to look at him, "I'll need a few minutes to pack up some things," I immediately regretted what I had just committed myself to.

Tom nodded his understanding and said nothing.

I knew I was doing the right thing, but I wasn't happy about it. I was downright miserable. I could hear my own voice in my head telling me I was being stupid. Stupid. STUPID.

Screech fluttered on the ledge for a moment, began preening himself and entered my mind for only a brief moment, "*Screech like deer. Taste good.*" Then he left my mind.

I went to Mother Wolf's bedroom first. I had left it as her room, although she had told me several times that she no longer needed it and I should take it because it was a much bigger room. But, I felt comfortable in the smaller room at the back of the cabin. I rarely entered her room unless there were things I needed from it and this time I needed to get some items for my trip to Wheaton.

I looked for the small bundle of eagle feathers she kept in the top drawer of her dresser. I found them sitting next to the brown envelope that contained the papers to the cabin-clinic and her letter to me. I had put it away in the drawer the day of her furneral and had forgotten about it.

"It is time to look inside the envelope my child," Mother Wolf's young voice whispered in my mind.

I opened the envelope and pulled out its contents. The papers for the property were there, and attached to them with a paperclip was a note in Mother Wolf's shaky handwriting.

> *Dear Jessica,*
>
> *You will be tried in more ways than will be pleasant for you. You will face many of your fears and sometimes you will lose to those fears. But we, your Mothers, know your heart is good and it's strong. The decisions you make are your own. Make all of your decisions in accordance with your heart and what you believe and trust to be right. We will support and protect you in all that you do. No matter what your decisions may be. We love you.*
>
> *Journey well my child.*
>
> *Mother Wolf*

I thought to her, "You've known all along that this day would come, and yet you wouldn't tell me what the test would be."

Mother Wolf appeared in front of me. She was dressed in her blue-jeans, red plaid shirt, and quilted black vest...her "work clothes" as she always called them, but she was in her young form.

"I knew before I found you near death in the ditch that this was a possible outcome. But all things must happen in their own time and in accordance with free will. At any point you could have chosen to return to your old life. But you didn't, and you have arrived at this destiny...by your own choices. It could have been different. Predicting the future is not an easy task, as Mother Spider has told you many times. With every choice the possible outcomes change. We must always be cautious about how much we tell you. That kind of foreknowledge could interfere with your free will. But we have always trusted your heart. It's a good strong honest heart," Mother Wolf explained.

"Free will sucks," I said.

"Sometimes it does," Mother Wolf agreed, "But it does make life interesting, and most times...unpredictable."

She helped me find an old black duffle bag under her bed, and a small bright orange backpack in the closet. She helped me collect all the things she thought I would need, and I added some odds and ends of my own choosing and put them into the orange backpack. Before I left her room, I grabbed her old red plaid shirt and black vest from the closet. She smiled with approval.

"Work clothes, but I'm wearing my own blue jeans. Yours are really disgusting."

I went to my room and quickly packed a few of my clothes into the duffle bag. Mother Wolf told me to pack my white rawhide dress and moccasins. I carefully folded the dress and placed it with the moccasins between the other clothes I had packed.

I went to the washroom, changed into a clean pair of jeans and put on Mother Wolf's red plaid shirt and black quilted vest. They had been washed, but there was a faint hint of sweetgrass and sage smoke on both the shirt and vest.

I braided my hair with my favourite red rawhide strap and placed an eagle feather at the end of the braid. I looked through the cabinet under the sink and found a small brown zippered bag and put my toiletries in it.

I arrived in the kitchen with my full black duffle bag and bright orange backpack. I noticed Tom's left eyebrow rise and then fall quickly. He seemed to be amused.

"What?" I said.

"Your idea or Mother Wolf's?" he said and smiled.

"What?"

"The travelling attire."

I glanced at my shirt and vest, "My work clothes. I'm ready to go."

Suddenly the room was occupied by all the Mothers. They were all talking at once.

"Slow down. One at a time. I can't hear any of you when you all talk at once," I said out loud.

I started opening cupboard doors and packing the orange backpack with items the Mothers were telling me to take. I glanced at Tom and suddenly realized I had broken my rule of not talking to the Mothers out loud in front of other people. Tom nodded his understanding of Shaman's business.

"I'm just talking to myself. Can't a girl talk to herself?" I asked.

"You forget I'm a Shaman's grandson. I know the Mothers are talking to you. I can tell by the look on your face. Do they still argue?"

"All the time."

Tom chuckled. It was a deep easy chuckle. I liked the sound of it.

"Do you know of anyone who could look after Jojo while I'm gone? He's a bit grumpy and a lot of stubborn, but he'll do almost anything for an apple or pear."

"I'll see what I can do." Tom pulled out his cell phone to make the call. Within a few minutes he had found someone to look after Jojo.

I finished packing my orange backpack with all the items the Mothers told me to take.

I finally stood in the middle of the kitchen-treatment-room packed and ready to go. I felt Screech enter my mind.

"*Screech loves Red,*" he thought to me.

"*Red loves Screech,*" I thought back to him.

"*Screech go. Wolf go. Yes.*"

"*Yes,*" I said out loud, understanding that Screech and Wolf wanted to come with me.

I was suddenly aware that I'd have to transport Screech and Wolf somehow. Wheaton was more than twenty hours away by car, how would I make this work? I'd have to figure out something, but for now we needed to get to the city.

"*Screech fly to the city. Meet us—*" Screech stopped me mid-thought.

"*No. Screech protect Red. Screech follow Red.*" Screech was determined and forceful in his thoughts to me.

I had long since learned there was no point in arguing with Screech once he had made up his mind. I had never won a disagreement with him. I knew I wasn't going to win this one.

Mother Wolf materialized beside Wolf and stroked his huge white head, "Wolf says he'll ride in the back of Tom's patrol car," she said and vanished.

The rest of the Mothers also vanished saying, "We are all with you. Journey well, Mother Eagle."

In my mind, Screech showed me the red leather sleeve one of my patients had made for me to protect me from his talons. I left the kitchen and went to my room and retrieved it. On the way back I wrapped the thick red leather sleeve around my arm, noticing all the pock holes Screech's talons had made in it. The red sleeve wasn't as efficient as the sleeve of my white dress but it worked, and over time Screech had learned to adjust his hold on my arm when I wore the red sleeve.

I returned to the kitchen. Tom, Wolf, Screech, my black duffle bag, and bright orange backpack were gone. I could feel Screech in my mind, and he was giving me a picture of the cabin-clinic from his bird's eye view. He noted a rabbit heading for the edge of the forest, and for a moment I felt his desire to hunt, but it passed quickly. Through his eyes I could see Tom putting my bags in the trunk of the car, and Wolf standing beside him.

I closed all the windows and locked the kitchen door. I quickly wrote a note to place on the front door telling everyone I was away, and I didn't know when I would be returning. I wrote down the phone number for Dr. Ross in the city. I put the note on the front door and locked it. I slid the key under the scruffy outdoor mat. It was a rather silly thing to do because everyone on the reserve knew where the key was, but it was a city habit I'd kept.

As I approached the patrol car, Tom opened the back door for Wolf. Wolf sniffed the seat and was reluctant to enter, until Mother Wolf appeared on the back seat beside the window on the other side and beckoned him to enter. He still hesitated. Finally he slowly lowered his giant white head, and climbed into the car. He was a snug fit in the back seat. Mother Wolf stroked his head saying, "My Wolf is brave and strong."

The short ride to town was quiet. Even Mother Wolf was silent. Screech was in my mind and invited me to fly with him, so I did. It was pleasant flying with him. All the troubles of earth seemed far away. There was just the sound of wind rushing past and sights of the forest and river below. Occasionally, Screech would swoop down to get a closer look at a rabbit or gopher on the ground. I could feel his hunting instincts rush through me and the thrill it gave him.

When we arrived, it was still early in the morning and the town was just waking up. A few people were on the street and a couple of cars drove past.

Screech had kept up with us. His route had been straight, while we had to follow the bends in the road. As I stepped out of the car he thought to me.

"*Screech land.*"

Screech was never patient and he wasn't tired, but I sensed he didn't want me out of his sight.

I put out my arm and he glided down. I had become accustomed to his weight and I no longer lost my balance when he landed. His talons dug into the leather as he settled. I could feel the pressure as he squeezed my arm, but he was careful not to puncture the leather. I liked the feel of him sitting on my arm. He lowered his head as he always did when he landed, waiting for me to kiss his head. I brought him close to my face and kissed him.

"*Red likes flying with Screech,*" I thought to him.

Tom had let Wolf out of the car, and was busy pulling my bags out of the trunk when I joined him.

"Mother Eagle. This federal investigator is a royal pain in the butt," Tom warned me, handing me the bright orange backpack; he motioned he would carry the duffle bag.

"It's okay Tom, I've had my share of pain-in-the-ass lawmen in my time. Besides I have Our Mothers, Eagle, and Wolf to protect me." I slung the backpack over my shoulder and headed toward the police station.

I walked inside the station and was greeted by a startled receptionist at the front desk. Wolf gave her one of his deep looks. Screech ignored her looking around the area with his normal curiosity.

"Michelle. This is Mother Eagle," Tom said, greeting the receptionist in his smooth, deep voice. She nodded to me and Tom quickly ushered me around her desk and into the back area where we gathered a few more strange stares from constables working at their desks.

"Where's the federal investigator?" Tom asked one of the goggle-eyed constables.

"Conference room," one of the constables pointed to a wooden door with a glass window in it. The door was on the opposite side of the room.

Tom put my duffle bag on the floor beside a desk and crossed to the conference room. I followed him and stopped a few feet away from the door and waited. Tom knocked and opened the door.

Tom said, "Detective Dorset. Jessica Seeker is here. We all respectfully call her Mother Eagle."

Tom swung the door wider. Both Wolf and Screech looked at the doorway. I could feel Screech in my mind but he said nothing. Tom stepped aside to let Detective Dorset enter the constable's common area, but instead Dorset just stood in the doorway and stared at me.

Dorset was a man of medium height. He had light brown hair and eyes. He had a thick moustache over his thin upper lip. His skin was smooth and pale.

Wolf gave a low throaty growl, and Screech glared at him. Detective Dorset gave them a dismissive glance and looked back at me. He continued to stare at me. Unlike everyone else in the room, he paid no further attention to my entourage of animals.

This man made me feel uneasy. There was something about him that caused a strange unsettling feeling deep in my gut.

"Commander Duggan went to a lot of trouble to find you. Not that he really wants you back in his town," Dorset said.

"We have history."

"As I understand it, not a good history." Dorset formally introduced himself, "I'm a Federal Investigator, they respectfully call me, Detective Gary Dorset."

His sarcasm wasn't lost on me. But I remained polite.

"I'm Mother Eagle, Shaman and Medicine Woman, for the Pinewood Reserve," I replied in a formal and cool tone.

"Mother Eagle, Shaman, and Medicine Woman. Not Jessica Seeker, the psychic. Got yourself a new gig, 'eh?" Dorset said.

Dorset's upper lip disappear under his moustache as his mouth stretched into a smile that was neither warm nor friendly and faintly resembled a sneer.

"I'm here because you told Constable Tom you needed me in Wheaton for a murder case. I'm not here to debate credentials with you," and like Wolf and Screech, I took an instant deep dislike to the man.

A constable's phone rang. Suddenly a flash of light like a door opening from a dark room into a bright sunny day ripped through my mind and I saw a young boy doubled over in pain. I only had visions like this when something serious happened to one of the people on the reserve. Those visions took a lot of energy from me. I lost my balance for a moment. Screech squeezed my arm. And the vision disappeared. But I knew without a doubt the constable's son, was suffering from an appendicitis attack and it had ruptured.

"You'll need to get your son to the hospital right away. He has appendicitis and it's ruptured," I said, hearing my voice loud and clear before I could even think about what I was saying.

The phone rang once more. The constable answered it. There was a quick exchange of words about the constable's sick son. He told whoever he was talking to that he'd call an ambulance and he would meet them at the hospital. As soon as he was finished, he made a quick call for an ambulance, excused himself, and left.

I was dizzy and weak. I felt Screech squeeze my arm even harder and then he relaxed before his talons punctured the leather sleeve. Tom was at my side and helped me to sit down in a nearby chair.

"Are you okay Mother Eagle?" Tom said.

"*Red sick,*" Screech thought to me.

"I'm all right," I thought to Screech and said to Tom, "Just a bit dizzy. I don't do that often. It only happens when someone is in immediate danger."

Dorset came closer, and stood over me, "Nice little parlor trick. Was that for my benefit?"

"Mother Eagle is a Shaman and a Medicine Woman. You show her the respect she deserves, or you can leave," Tom warned Dorset.

"*Screech hunts Weasels. Screech eats Weasels,*" Screech thought to me, showing me a picture of him hunting the Detective.

Screech was bobbing up and down while he tightened and released his grip on my arm. I could feel his rage growing toward the man that he would call Weasel from now on. I knew that if I allowed it, Screech would attack Dorset without a moment's hesitation.

"*I don't like Weasel either. But I think he'd taste really bad,*" I thought back to Screech.

"*Bad taste. Not good,*" Screech thought and gave a loud shriek.

Everyone in the room was startled in to silence.

Dorset looked at Screech and then glared at me, "What's wrong with your bird?"

"My eagle doesn't like you. And for that matter, neither do I."

"This isn't a popularity contest, or a party of parlor tricks. You're here to help me stop a serial killer from killing anymore young girls. He wants you in Wheaton whether you and I like each other or not."

"Then I suggest that we quit farting around and get a damn move on," I said, and noticed that Tom didn't react to my cussing. His face was unreadable. A professional cop face.

Dorset continued to stare at me. His eyes were cold and piercing. Then he turned and walked into the conference room. I could see him pick up his briefcase, grab his suit jacket, and return to the doorway.

"Say goodbye to your zoo. We've got a plane to catch," Dorset commanded.

"I don't go anywhere without my Totem Protectors."

"Well, you'll have to because there's no way they're going on the plane."

"They don't go, I don't go."

"What? You've got to be kidding me."

"Mother Eagle is a Shaman. Eagle has chosen to be her protector. They are inseparable," Tom intervened with his deep powerful voice.

"We don't have time to screw around. Jessica gets on that plane willingly or under arrest. It's her choice." Dorset reached into the handcuff pouch on his belt, withdrew his cuffs, and stepped toward me.

Wolf was instantly between us, growling with his teeth bared. Screech opened one wing and swatted Dorset.

Dorset, surprised by my Totems' reactions, stepped back.

"I guess we'll have to drive," I said.

"Drive. It's a twenty hour road trip at the very least and just over an hour by air."

"I fly," Tom said.

He had our attention.

"I have access to a Twin Otter. I fly hunters into the back country for a friend during hunting season. I'll make a call and see if it's available," he said.

"Make it quick. A little girl's life is depending on us." Dorset moved away from me, and put his cuffs back in the pouch on his belt. He stared at me.

The air seemed to become thick and heavy. It was hard to breath. Darkness was growing around me.

The darkness seemed to move away from me slightly as Wolf sat down between Dorset and me. He never took his big blue-green eyes away from Dorset.

Mother Wolf, invisible to everyone around us, appeared beside Wolf and rubbed his muzzle. I knew she was talking to him.

"We don't like this Dorset fellow. He has no respect for anything or anyone. Child, stay alert. You and innocent children are in great danger," Mother Wolf warned.

I could hear the drums and the Mothers chanting. Normally the Mother's chanting gave me comfort. But for some reason, their chanting and drumming wasn't working. Goosebumps crept along my arms. The darkness felt as though it was sucking all the energy out of the space near me. This strange darkness seemed to be alive and evil. Sadness, anger, loneliness, pain, and sorrow surrounded me.

"*Screech protect Red,*" Screech thought to me.

I had heard Screech tell me that he would protect me many times, but this time he filled my mind and heart with his thoughts. I felt something I had never felt before—the power of his unconditional love. Screech's devotion and thoughts were giving me strength. I knew we could not be separated... ever. And I didn't want it any other way.

"*Red loves Screech. We are together forever,*" I thought back to him.

"*Yes. Screech protect and love Red,*" he said, and gripped my arm slightly tighter.

Screech, for the first time, had made a complex sentence. He surprised me, and I felt my pride for him welling up inside me. Yes. He and I were strong together.

Dorset stepped away and went back into the conference room. The darkness lifted and melted away. I could feel Screech relax on my arm.

"*Red and Screech are family. We are strong. Yes.*" I thought to Screech.

"*Yes. Screech eat Weasel. Now. Yes?*" Screech said and I could swear I heard him laugh in his Screech-like way.

Chapter Ten

Tom walked across the grass field toward the small two-engine plane he called a Twin Otter. I followed with my backpack over my right shoulder and Screech on my left arm. Wolf followed me. Detective Dorset followed at a distance behind all of us. Wolf had made it clear with his actions and growls, that Dorset was not allowed anywhere near me, and that decision on Wolf's part was about to become a serious problem.

Tom opened a hatch on the side of the aircraft and carefully placed my duffle bag in it. At the same time Screech took to the air, and Wolf sat on the ground between Dorset and me.

I gave my backpack to Tom and he placed it carefully in the hatch and then took Dorset's briefcase and stuffed it in alongside my bags.

It was time to get on board.

Tom looked up at Screech, then at Wolf, and finally at me "Okay. It's going to be tight quarters in there. I think Wolf should sit at the back. I've removed two rows of seats for him and I've put down a couple of blankets to make him comfortable. I thought Eagle could sit up front with me. You and Detective Dorset could sit in the middle seats."

Tom looked at Wolf again and then at me, I could tell he was thinking about the problem we had had with Wolf and the patrol car. In my mind I called to Mother Wolf for her help. She appeared next to Wolf. She touched Wolf's huge silvery-white muzzle and he shook his head. She climbed into the airplane, and beckoned to Wolf to follow her. He hesitated for a moment, then took a long stride, leaped, and was inside the plane. The plane bounced slightly with his weight as he entered.

Wolf settled down on the blankets at the back of the plane with Mother Wolf at his side.

"My Wolf wants you to know he loves you and he doesn't like airplanes," Mother Wolf said to me.

"Thank him for me, and tell him how brave and strong he is," I thought back to her.

"*Screech,*" I thought.

"*Screech fly. Follow Red,*" he thought back.

"*Plane flies faster than Screech. You'll have to ride inside with me.*"

Screech was quiet and said nothing. He circled overhead and watched. He gave me a vision of what he saw.

"What about that bird of yours?" Dorset asked.

"He's a Bald Eagle. And he wants to fly himself. We're discussing it. Give us a minute."

"This is crap, let's go," Dorset said, and climbed into the plane. Wolf rose up as high as the ceiling of the plane would allow and began to bare his teeth and growl at Dorset. "Wolf," Mother Wolf said, allowing me to hear her, "Let him be."

"Jessica," Dorset shouted out to me, "Call off your overgrown bulldog."

"Wolf, don't attack him. You might get some rude disease from him," I said and then I heard Mother Wolf laugh.

Through the doorway of the plane, I could see Wolf sit down, but he continued to growl deep in his throat. Dorset carefully and slowly took his seat, while taking quick glances over his shoulder at Wolf. Wolf leaned closer to Dorset's head, sniffed, and growled again.

"Well, let's get a move on. I don't want to spend any more time in this tin can with this zoo than I have to," Dorset called out to us.

"Mother Eagle, take all the time you need. I'm just going to run some checks before takeoff." Tom climbed into the plane and took the pilot's seat.

I called Screech to my arm and he landed with more than his usual force, indicating he wasn't happy about the situation.

"*Screech if you follow we will be separated. How will you protect me when you are far away?*" I thought to him.

"*Screech protect Red,*" he thought.

"*Then Screech must ride inside with me.*"

"*Screech inside. Screech eat Weasel. Yes?*" he thought, and gave me a clear picture of him biting Dorset's weasel nose off.

"*No. Screech will be a good eagle and sit in the front of the plane with Big Bear,*" I thought, using Screech's name for Tom.

"*Screech good Eagle. Eat Weasel. Yes?*"

"*No biting Weasel. No eating Weasel, even when you are hungry.*"

Screech let out one of his loud frustrated cries that nearly deafened me, and then fluttered over to the open door and entered the plane. His long sharp talons scraped the floor. He eyed Dorset as he passed, and took the opportunity to take a peck at him, deliberately missing him.

I visualized the front of the plane showing Screech where to sit.

I climbed in and Tom came back and closed the door.

He made sure we were all buckled up, "Some people don't like the engine noise. If you need them, there's earplugs in the seat pocket." He glanced at Dorset, turned to me, and gave a quick wink.

Tom went back to his pilot seat and started up the engines. I heard Wolf groan as the engines fired, and I felt Screech's mind in mine. He let me feel his talons puncture the seat cushion as he wrapped them around the metal frame.

"*Red loves Screech. Screech is a great protector. He is very brave,*" I thought to him.

He didn't answer. I felt him withdraw from my mind as we taxied for takeoff.

The roar was loud inside the plane as the engines accelerated and we lifted off the ground. Once we were airborne the noise subsided a small amount, and it was possible to talk over the noise, if one spoke loudly.

"So I've never worked a case with a psychic before. What's your little parlor game like? I mean what do you see, how do you see it?" Dorset said.

"What I do and how I do it, is not any of your business."

"Hey, I'm just trying to understand. We'll be working together over the next while and I'd like to know what to expect."

"I suggest you don't expect anything. I'm really not sure I'll be much help at all."

"Humble, too."

"Just honest."

"So how do you...see...know... whatever it is you do?"

"I get visions. Sometimes when I'm sleeping and sometimes when I'm awake, but mostly when I'm sleeping," I said, trying to be heard over the roar of the plane's engines.

"And these visions, what are they like?" he said.

"Sometimes they're like little movies. In 3D and surround sound. And sometimes they're just glimpses that are hard to interpret or understand," I said, trying to keep a friendly tone. Although, I wasn't enjoying discussing this with him and I was equally unhappy with having to shout over the engine noise.

"So how long have you been doing the Medicine-Woman-Shaman thing?" he asked. Even over the engine noise I could hear the sarcasm in his voice.

"Look Dorset, I didn't ask for this. You asked me. I really don't care what you think of me or what you think about what I do. But understand this. What I do isn't a parlor game or trick. It's real."

"Hey, don't go all PMS on me. I was just asking a few questions," he said.

"I've got a few questions of my own. For instance...tell me what happened to the girl whose blood was on the note Tom gave me."

"We found her in a shallow grave just outside of town. She was the third girl that has shown up dead in less than three weeks."

"How did they die?"

"They had all been...bled out. There were mild indications of a struggle. Some bruises. The killer had drugged the girls. He was smart though. Never left behind a stitch of evidence. Complete dead end, other than the letter. And it didn't have DNA or fingerprints. Nothing."

"Were they molested?"

"If you mean sexually assaulted, no."

"What were their ages?"

"Two were twelve and the last one was thirteen."

"Did they have anything in common, other than being young girls?"

"You know, if you weren't into this Medicine-Woman-Shaman thing, you might make a good detective," he said, and gave me his cold, thin, unfriendly sneer. His top lip was buried under his moustache. The sneer vanished, and he added, "The only other thing they had in common was their school."

I found myself drifting back to the time I lived in Wheaton when the two young girls disappeared. A cold shudder rippled through me. It felt as though someone had opened a window and a freezing wind was blowing in. I heard Mother Wolf's voice in my head.

"Child, this is not like the last time. You are not alone. We are with you. All of us and our Totem protectors," she whispered lightly in my mind. I could hear the drums and the humming.

Wolf moved forward with a groan, and placed himself in the aisle between my seat and Dorset's seat. I could feel the pressure of his body bending the armrest toward me.

At that moment, Screech entered my mind. He seemed a little calmer than he had been earlier, "*Big Bear flies...good. Red okay. Yes?*"

"*Yes. I'm okay. And no one flies as well as Screech,*" I thought to him, trying to show him what I saw and felt when I flew with him.

"*Fly forever,*" Screech withdrew from my mind.

"So what do I call you? Jessica or Shaman or Medicine Woman?" Dorset asked.

"Mother Eagle, will be fine."

"Mother Eagle." His mocking tone dripped off the words, like dew off a spider's web.

"If you don't mind, I'm feeling very tired." I reached into the seat pocket, pulled out the earplugs, and opened the sealed plastic bag, "I started out early this morning with a patient. I'd like to grab a little sleep before we get to Wheaton."

"Be my guest, but before you drift off to dreamland, would you get your bulldog to move to the back of the plane?"

"Wolf. Would you mind moving to the back of the plane? Mr. Dorset is uncomfortable with you lying here," I said.

I could hear Mother Wolf in my head, "I was never fond of your sarcastic wit, child. But I beginning to feel it does have its uses," she said and chuckled.

Wolf lifted his huge white head, rested it on Dorset's armrest, and glared at Dorset letting out a low rumbling growl.

"I guess he's comfortable where he is, so you'll just have to get used to it. It's a short flight." I turned away, put the earplugs in my ears, and closed my eyes.

I didn't sleep. I heard the Mothers humming and the rhythm of the drums beating. Then I felt that old familiar but unwelcome sense of someone or something watching me.

Chapter Eleven

I t was early afternoon in Wheaton when we landed. I felt Screech in my mind as the plane came to a stop. He was off his seat and coming down the aisle. I could hear his talons scratching on the metal of the floor. His pupils were large in his yellow-green eyes when he stopped and looked at me.

"*Screech hungry. Screech hunt,*" he thought to me and let me feel his hunger. I felt a pang in my own stomach and remembered I was hungry too. In the chaos of the morning, I'd forgotten to eat.

Wolf had maintained his position in the aisle between the seats for the whole trip, but after we landed he moved to the back of the plane. Tom stood behind Screech, slightly bent over with his head touching the top of the plane. He was like Wolf, a little large for the space. He gave me a questioning look, and glanced at Screech.

"Mother Eagle, I can't open the door," he said.

"*Screech, Big Bear can't open the door to let you out. Move closer to me. Yes,*" I thought to Screech.

Screech moved down the aisle closer to me and Tom opened the door, stepped back, and let Screech exit first.

"*Rain coming,*" Screech thought to me as he flew into the sky, showing me a gopher he had already spotted in the field beside the small private airport. Before I could caution him about watching out for airplanes landing and taking off, he was hunting the gopher and had captured it. I felt him as he enjoyed his first bite and my hunger started to ache in my belly. I needed food, too.

Dorset had unbuckled his seatbelt and was about to stand but Tom stopped him saying, "I think that Wolf and Mother Eagle should go first."

Dorset said nothing, but gave a long loud groan of contempt for the process.

Wolf, like Screech, wasted no time getting off the plane. Mother Wolf appeared at his side.

Fortunately, because Tom had landed at a small private airport outside of town, we didn't have to go through a terminal.

When everyone was out of the plane and we had gathered the luggage, we walked across the tarmac to a small parking lot. Screech had finished off his gopher, and flew above us.

Two patrol cars were waiting for us. The officers driving the cars stepped out to greet us. I called Screech to my arm. When he landed, I heard one of the officers say, "What the hell! Is that a Bald Eagle...and a wolf?"

I could hear Tom let out one of his deep throated chuckles as he walked beside me carrying my duffle bag, bright orange backpack, and another bag that looked like a oversized soft-sided briefcase.

"Mother Eagle,I think you just might shake up this place," Tom said.

"It won't be the first time."

Wolf and I went in one car. Tom and Dorset went in the other. Screech flew above us. I later found out that Tom had called ahead to make sure that two cars were sent for us.

The constable who drove us into Wheaton was quiet, and didn't say anything. I was thankful for that.

When we arrived at the police station, Dorset grabbed his briefcase and left us to sort ourselves out. Tom and the constable who had driven me, helped with my luggage. Screech perched himself on my arm. Wolf was by my side and Mother Wolf had disappeared.

Wheaton was a rural town. It was the kind of place where everybody knew everybody's business. Strangers were not happily welcomed and weren't invited to stay long. As I looked around, I could see it hadn't changed much in the years I'd been away.

Tom interrupted my thoughts about Wheaton, "I can take our bags over to the Wheaton Hotel. They've booked rooms for us there."

"You're staying?" I was surprised and happy. I knew he could hear the relief in my voice. It was truly a comfort knowing he was going to stay.

And this also explained the extra bag. The one that looked like a soft-sided oversized briefcase.

"You're our Mother Eagle. I wasn't going to leave you alone with a bunch of strangers, so I took a few days of special leave to help you out. So what kind of help would you like?"

At that moment my stomach cramped in pangs of hunger. Screech had been in my mind but hadn't spoken to me since the airport. Suddenly he squeezed my arm, thinking, "*Red hungry. Must eat. Yes?*"

I thought to Screech, "*Hungry. Yes.*" I said out loud to Tom, "Actually, I'm starving. I haven't had anything to eat today."

"Then Mother Eagle, food is the first thing to be taken care of. What would you like?" he said in an easy deep voice.

"Just a ham and cheese sandwich would be fine."

"Considerate it done. I'll drop our bags off at the hotel on the way. But, first, if you like, I can go in with you," he glanced at Screech and Wolf.

Again, I was happy Tom had stayed with me. His being here in a place I knew was full of enemies was a welcome solace.

"Thank you, but I've got Wolf and Eagle to look after me, and the Mothers. I should be fine," I said, although I didn't feel fine. I truly hated this town.

Then Screech squeezed my arm and thought to me, "*Wolf hungry.*"

"Ah Tom, if you wouldn't mind, could you get something for Wolf. Eagle got himself food at the airport but Wolf only had a small snack at home this morning."

"Not a problem. Two lunches coming up," he said and handed me my bright orange backpack. "You may want to keep this with you. And as Mother Wolf would say, I'll be back in a jiffy,"

He hefted my black duffle bag over his left shoulder and grabbed his soft-sided briefcase with his right hand, nodded to me, Screech, and Wolf. He turned and walked away with a smooth long stride.

Screech thought to me, "*Red like Big Bear. Yes? Screech like Big Bear.*"

"*Red hopes Big Bear will bring food quickly,*" I thought to Screech. I wasn't answering Screech's question because although Screech said '*like*' I had a feeling he meant a little more than '*like*'. Besides, I couldn't think about that sort of thing now. I had to focus on why I'd come to Wheaton. There were young girls in danger, and I had to figure out a way to help them.

I turned and faced the police station. Wolf stood close beside me. I could feel his body against my leg.

"Okay, everybody is on their best behaviour," I said out loud, and sent a quick thought to Screech, "***And Screech, no eating anyone, especially Weasel. Please pass that message along to Wolf as well.***"

Screech didn't answer me but I knew he was talking with Wolf, because Wolf let out a groan of disapproval.

We walked into the station. Dorset was waiting for us.

"You had to bring the zoo with you," he said.

Wolf answered with a growl.

"Like I told you. They go where I go."

"Keep them under control." He turned and led me through the common room where some of the Wheaton constables were working.

I heard some of the comments as we passed through.

"What the hell?"

"Never seen this before."

"Is this the woman everybody's been talking about?"

I stopped half way across the common area and said in my loudest and strongest voice, "I'm Mother Eagle, Shaman, and Medicine Woman of the Pinewood Reserve. These are my Totem Protectors, Eagle and Wolf. I have given them orders to not eat anyone. But it would be good to remain on your best behaviour because they sometimes don't follow orders when they think someone is threatening me in word or deed."

Screech held his head high and looked around the room. Wolf released a low rumbling growl in his throat. I felt pride surge in me. They would protect me with their lives, and I could sense that every one in the room knew it.

Dorset looked around the room at the surprised faces, "You know her as Jessica Seeker. She's here, as most of you know, at the request of the killer we're hunting." He looked at me, "The commander is in the squad room waiting for us," he said and walked toward a closed door just off to the side of the common area.

He opened the door and held it, allowing me to enter before him. It had been his only gesture of politeness since we had met.

I entered the room.

On the far wall was a corkboard and thumb tacked to it were pictures of the three dead young girls they had found. As I looked at the board, the darkness and coldness that had followed me from the time I had first left

Wheaton, began to settle in around me. At the same time, I had the familiar but unpleasant feeling that someone or something was watching me. Close by, but separate from the coldness and darkness. It was waiting.

Screech squeezed my arm tight enough to puncture the red leather arm protector. I reigned in my thoughts, suddenly aware that I was sending them to Screech.

Commander Duggan coughed and cleared his throat. I hadn't noticed him. My attention had been focused on the pictures of the girls. I turned in his direction and saw a man the years had not been kind to. He was once a muscular man with a full head of dark brown hair. Now his belly draped over his belt and his hairline had receded to the back of his head, leaving a fringe of grey streaked fuzz running from ear to ear. And like a flower in the hair of a young maiden, he wore a cigarette tucked behind his left ear.

"What in the hell are these animals doing in my station?" Duggan bellowed.

"They go where she goes," Dorset said.

"Then she and them, can go back outside where they belong."

Wolf growled, and Mother Wolf appeared beside me, seen only by me.

"Fine." I turned to leave.

"Just stay where you are," Dorset commanded, and turned to Duggan, "I'm not anymore impressed by this zoo than you are, but she will not work with us unless they are with her. We have no choice."

"Maybe you don't have a choice, but I do. She and those animals can leave my station house right bloody now," Duggan said.

I took a step toward the door to leave, as Screech thought to me, "**Screech eat Badger. Yes?**" He sent me a picture of himself landing on Duggan's belly, with his talons digging deep into Duggan's belly fat and then he started biting Duggan's lip.

I couldn't help myself, I laughed aloud.

"And what do you find so funny?" Duggan asked me.

"My Eagle doesn't like you and it seems he would like to make lunch out of your lip," I said. I tried to stop laughing at the pictures Screech kept sending me, but I wasn't being successful.

"Dorset, get her out of here." Duggan pulled a gold lighter out of his shirt pocket and began twirling it between his thumb and forefinger.

"This is the investigation of a serial killer, and need I remind you, that this is a federal case? This is my case. Do I need to call my bosses?" Dorset said.

I eased my way to the door as Dorset and Duggan started their dick measuring contest. Neither of them was paying attention to me. Wolf, Screech, and I slipped away without making a sound.

I quickly made my way to the closest constable. The man was busy typing on his computer, completely immersed in what he was doing and ignoring everything around him.

"Could you tell me where the girls' bodies are? I'd like to see them," I said in as calm a voice as I could muster over the yelling of Duggan and Dorset.

The constable looked at me with a start. Then he quickly looked at Screech who was staring at him.

"Ah, they'd be at the funeral home. Two of them are being buried tomorrow. Ah…the funeral home is a block and a half, straight up the road east of here," he said, not taking his eyes off of Screech, and pointing in the direction of the funeral home.

"Thank you," I said and left.

When we stepped outside, it was clear Screech had been right about the rain. It had started to drizzle.

I adjusted my backpack over my shoulder, and thought to Screech, "*Screech. Do you want to fly?*"

"*Yes. Yes,*" he thought to me and immediately leapt off my arm and headed up into the rain, circling overhead while I walked. "*Screech fly Red?*"

"*Red loves to fly with Screech, but I need to think,*" I said. Screech didn't answer but I could feel him in my mind.

Wolf walked along side me and from time to time he stopped to stretch relaxing his muscles. Mother Wolf appeared beside me.

"Wolf is happy to be out in the open. It's been a little cramped for him," she said.

"Mother Wolf, I'm not sure that I should even be here."

"You are where you need to be, child," she said. I could feel her presence and an unsual sensation. It felt as though she had put her arm around my waist and gave me a squeeze, "We are here with you. And we will help. You will know what to do when the proper time comes. Follow your heart. Trust your instincts."

And as quickly as she appeared, she disappeared.

I wished the Mothers were more direct and helpful, because I really had no idea of why I needed to see the girls' bodies…I just knew that I had to.

I didn't even know what I would do when I saw them. What would I find? What would I do with what I found, assuming that I found anything at all.

It was a short walk to the funeral home, and lost in my thoughts, I almost walked past it. Wolf nudged my leg and I looked around and saw we had reached our destination.

A large black awning with scripted white print displaying the name *Peace Valley Funeral Home* protected the front entrance.

I looked up and saw Screech circling around overhead. He was magnificent with his wings spread wide, effortlessly gliding above us. I patted Wolf on his huge white head, and thought to Screech, "***Land now, my beloved Screech. Yes?,***" and I put my arm out for him.

He landed. Shook himself. A few tiny droplets of water sprinkled on me.

We all entered the funeral home together.

Chapter Twelve

As we entered the funeral home, I noticed the lobby was a wide and open area decorated in light blues and creams. Overstuffed ivory-white chairs and sofas were arranged in small intimate groupings. Heavy ivory drapes hung from thick golden rods and were tied back on either side of tall windows. I felt like this was a place for whispering and weeping.

The aroma of fresh cut flowers drifted through the air. It all seemed upscale and expensive for a small town like Wheaton.

A middle-aged portly woman with short blonde hair and dressed in a grey business suit greeted me from behind a mahogany desk on the left side of the entrance. She seemed to be politely proper and reserved, but the look in her eyes indicated she was startled by Wolf and Screech.

"May I help you?" she asked.

"Yes. I'm ah...I'm working with the police, in regard to the young girls who have...ah...recently passed away," I said a smidge above a whisper, attempting to sound official but sensitive, "I was hoping it might be possible to see them."

"May I ask your name, please?"

"I'm Mother Eagle, but I'm also known as Jessica Seeker."

"Oh." Her demeanor changed from polite and reserved to cold and suspicious, "I'll have to talk to the funeral director. Please wait here."

"Thank you," I said as she turned her back and went through the door behind her desk.

Screech shifted his weight from one foot to the other, and bobbed his head.

"*Between close.*" He squeezed my arm and showed me a vision of flying in the sky as the sun was setting. "*Between. Life. Death. Sad. Scared.*"

I felt a cool breeze on my face as I flew with him in his vision. But I couldn't hear the wind as I did when we had flown before. We seemed to glide. No earth below and no sky above. It was darkness below and above was the pale glow of a fading sunset.

"*Ghost Walkers,*" Screech thought to me. "*Between. Bad place.*"

Before I could think back to him for an explanation, the woman was back followed by a short slim man dressed in a charcoal grey suit.

"Ms. Seeker, this is Mr. Barrette, the funeral director," she announced, and sat down behind her desk.

Mr. Barrette crossed the floor, and stood in front of me. He looked at Screech and Wolf, but unlike any of the others he didn't seem to be affected by their presence.

"I'm told you're called Mother Eagle," he said in a soft low voice that any baritone would be envious of.

"Yes. Shaman to the Pinewood Reserve peoples."

"Your Totems?" he nodded respectfully to Wolf and Screech.

"Ah...yes."

He looked at them and then nodded to each of them, "You are all welcome here at Peace Valley Funeral Home," he said.

For the first time since I had left the reserve I felt welcomed.

"Mr. Barrette, this is the first time in Wheaton that a... any one...has greeted me and my Totems with such respect. Thank you."

"My father was French, but my mother was full blood Mi'Kmaq. I have great respect for tradition. Respect as befits a woman of your standing. How may I help you?"

"I'm working with the police, and I'd like to see the girls that were...ah...murdered."

"I see...all right. Your eagle is especially welcome here. He knows the ways of the dead better than any of us do. Please, follow me," he said, leading us down the hallway to the back of the funeral home. "Two of the girls have already been prepared for the funeral services tomorrow and the third is in the process of being prepared."

He led us into a room with two caskets.

I walked up to one of the caskets and lifted the lid. The embalmers had done a fine job. The young girl looked as though she had simply fallen asleep.

"*Red talk…Ghost Walkers. Go Between. Screech help. Screech protect,*" Screech fluttered from my arm and onto the head of the casket so lightly and gently the satin batting barely moved.

Mother Wolf, invisible to Mr. Barrette, appeared beside me and said, "Child, you will have to go…Between. We can help with the ceremony. You have everything you need in the backpack. You'll need to put all the girls together in a circle on the floor."

"And just how do I ask to do that?" I thought to her.

"Just ask, child," she said in her matter-of-fact tone, like I should ask for a drink of water.

"Mr. Barrette, I need to perform a ceremony with the girls. I'll need a private space. One large enough to place the three girls in a circle on the floor," I tried to sound as matter-of-fact as Mother Wolf had sounded.

Mr. Barrette was finally shaken. The muscles in his jaw twitched, he sighed, and finally said, "Well…I'm not sure we can do that without the parents' consent."

"*Girls. Ghost Walkers. Lost. Screech. Red. Help,*" Screech thought to me. I could feel him struggling to explain himself. There was a feeling of urgency in his thoughts to me.

"Mr. Barrette, I appreciate the respect you have shown us. And I'm relying on your understanding of the old ways. Have you heard of Ghost Walkers?" I aked.

"Lost souls caught between life and death. Yes, I heard stories about them. They suffer terribly." He looked at Screech, "As I understand it, only strong medicine and the assistance of Totems who can go Between can help these lost and tortured spirits."

He knew more about Ghost Walkers than I did. Sky had been reluctant to speak about them, Screech was vague, and now this stranger was talking about them like he understood the situation. And I didn't have a foggy clue about Ghost Walkers. A person could fill the International Space Station with what I didn't know. I wasn't prepared for any of this.

Then inside my head I heard Mother Wolf, "I know my child. There was just so little time to teach you. But we can guide you through whatever you need."

"We have to help the girls. My eagle is very distressed about their condition," I thought back to Mother Wolf.

Then I spoke to Mr. Barrette, "My eagle tells me the girls are Ghost Walkers," I waited a moment to see how he would react but he revealed nothing of what he was thinking, so I continued, "My eagle says that...he and I can help them."

Mr. Barrette was quiet for a long moment and then said, "You must be a very strong Shaman, Mother Eagle. There are few who would dare to venture Between because, as I understand it, it's extremely difficult to return once you have entered."

"My eagle assures me that we can do this together."

"Your eagle. He is your personal Totem?"

"Yes."

Mr. Barrette stared at Screech for a long time, and said nothing. I broke the silence.

"These girls have suffered so much, how can we deny them rest? Please let me and my eagle do this."

Mr. Barrette slowly shifted his gaze from Screech to me. "I've seen this ceremony done once before. The Shaman died. Have you done this before?"

"No, I haven't but I have an Eagle for a Protector. Did she have an Eagle as her personal Totem?" I asked.

"Not a she, a he. And I don't think he did."

"I was chosen by the eagle, and in his choosing of me, he knew he had a Shaman that was strong enough to cross and return." I tried to sound more confident than I was.

"*Screech protect Red,*" Screech thought to me and for the first time when I looked into his eyes his gaze held me firm. I couldn't look away. His pupils grew large and small and large again, he struggled to make his thoughts clear to me, "*Screech go...Between...come back. Screech and Red help.*"

"We're fortunate that everyone is done for the day and there are no funerals. We're pretty much alone. Oh dear me...Mother Eagle...I know you mean well. But...if I were to allow you to do this and people found out." He rubbed his chin in deep thought, finally speaking as though he was thinking aloud, "The idea of those poor girls suffering is horrifying. But there isn't time to get their parents' permission. You've put me in a terrible position."

"I can help them. Please. No one needs to know. We can keep it a secret," I pleaded with him.

He thought longer, rubbed his chin harder, and finally said, "The only place we have that will be private enough for you is the cold room. Help me move these girls down the hall," he instructed as he reached up to close the lid of the casket holding the young girl I had been looking at.

At the same time, I put out my red leather clad arm and Screech hopped onto it. His grip was firm but it felt lighter than it had ever felt before. I could feel him in my mind but he didn't speak to me.

I could hear drumming and humming.

The Mothers were also with me as I followed Mr. Barrette pushing the second casket. The caskets were on stretcher-like dollies and moved easily. We moved quickly down the hall.

Mr. Barrette led us to a large embalming room. The floor and walls were lined with pale green and grey ceramic tiles. Two aluminum embalming beds sat side by side in the centre of the room. At the back of the room was a long wall with a large aluminum refrigerator door in the middle.

Mr. Barrette went to the door and pulled on the handle. The door opened with a slight hiss as the suction was broken. I felt the cool air rush out. It wasn't freezing but it was very cold.

"You won't be able to stay in here long. But you'll be private," he said as he opened the lid on the casket he had been pushing. He carefully lifted the young girl out and went into the refrigerator with her, I followed him.

The refrigerator was a large brushed aluminum room. There were two stretchers along the wall. On one stretcher was a body covered in a green sheet. Mr. Barrette saw me looking at the stretcher with the body.

"She's the other girl. Where would you like me to place this one?" he said.

"Right there," I pointed to a spot in the middle of the metal floor.

I went back out and opened the lid on the second casket. The girl inside was small and had a purple braid extension in her golden hair. She was like the other girl. She looked as though she was sleeping.

Mr. Barrette returned and stood beside me for a moment, then he lifted the young girl out of the casket, took her into the refrigerated room, and placed her gently on the floor.

Screech hopped from my arm and onto the floor. He tugged at my backpack. I slid it off and he pulled it into the refrigerator. Wolf made himself comfortable in a corner of the embalming room, yawned, laid down, and settled his giant white head on his paws and closed his eyes.

"He knows he can't go Between. I've asked him to rest here. He trusts Eagle, me, and our Mothers to protect you," Mother Wolf said as she appeared next to me.

I went into the refrigerated room.

As I entered, I saw that Mr. Barrette had gathered the green sheet carefully around the third girl who was on the stretcher and laid her down like the others.

"Do they need to be arranged in a circle?" he asked as he placed her gently on the refrigerator floor.

"Yes, with their heads toward the middle. Just the way you have placed them," I said, not even knowing how I knew.

At that moment there was a commotion in the hallway. I could hear the once calm voice of the receptionist from the front desk calling loudly in a distinctly angry voice, "Sir, you can't go in there without the expressed permission of Mr. Barrette, our funeral director."

From the doorway of the refrigerator I could see Dorset running into the embalming room, red-faced with anger, and breathing hard. He stopped suddenly and the receptionist banged into him making him unbalanced on his legs for a split second. Mr. Barrette left the refrigerator and entered the embalming room.

"What is going on here?" Mr. Barrette demanded.

Dorset straightened himself and tried to regain composer.

"I tried to tell him he's not allowed back here without your permission," the receptionist said, not giving Dorset a chance to answer.

"Yes, I heard you telling him that all the way down the hall," Mr. Barrette said.

"That woman is not allowed to be here," Dorset said in an over commanding tone, while pointing at the refrigerator door and me.

"Mr..." Mr. Barrette said.

"Detective Gary Dorset. Federal Investigator assigned to the case of the kidnapping and murder of the three girls here in Wheaton. And that woman..." he wagged his finger at me, "Has not been given clearance to be here."

"Detective Dorset, last time I looked this was a free country and citizens are allowed to go where they please. And in my funeral home, which is private property, people are allowed to go where I let them go. Ms. Roberts, would you see Detective Dorset out, please." Mr. Barrette started to return to the refrigerator.

"Then I'll join her," Dorset said, following Barrette.

From down the hallway, "Hello, anybody home?" It was Tom's deep smooth voice, "Hello?"

"Tom, we're down here," I shouted.

Screech decided to join in with a high pitched shriek that bounced off the walls of the refrigerator, the embalming room, and down the hallway, temporarily deafening everyone. Wolf was on his feet and instantly barring the refrigerator doorway, blocking Dorset from entering. He lowered his head and released a slow rumbling growl. He stared at Dorset, raising his lips high to show his large white sharp teeth. The fur along his spine stood on end.

Tom strode into the embalming room carrying a fat white bag with a red maple leaf logo on it. Even with all the commotion I could smell the sweet aroma of fresh baked bread, my stomach twisted with hunger.

"Mother Eagle you ordered lunch. They told me at the station that you were here. I picked up a big thick ham and cheese on freshly baked rye bread and a double side order of ham for Wolf. Mother Eagle will that suit you?" he said, in a calm smooth voice as he carefully surveyed the situation.

I could tell he'd figured out the problem quickly, but was remaining calm and had an air of control about him.

"Suits me just fine. But I'm afraid it'll have to wait a bit longer. I'm busy right now," I said.

I walked over closer to the doorway of the refrigerator where Dorset was trying to push past Mr. Barrette and Wolf to gain entry. I had to admire the man's determination or insanity. No one I knew would ever challenge Wolf.

"Detective Dorset, Wolf has been very patient with you. I commend him for that, but if you give me one more ounce of trouble I will give him permission to make dinner out of you and he's very hungry. Is that crystal clear?" My voice echoed off the aluminum walls of the refrigerator.

"I've seen him rip the hind leg off a deer with one bite. Not a pretty sight." Tom gave me a quick smile and wink, "I assume you are fond of both your legs. Why don't you just let Mother Eagle do her work? After all that's what she's here to do, isn't it?"

Wolf added emphasis with another growl and started to creep forward in Dorset's direction.

Dorset backed off and moved away from the door. He said nothing more. Mr. Barrette stepped back into the refrigerator with me. I could see Tom put the bag of food on a nearby counter, and then he stepped closer to the door, and motioned for me to come closer to him.

"I know what you're going to do. Most Shamans won't even try it. You can be trapped by the Between," he said, his brown eyes were soft but were searching mine, and his brow was furrowed with worry lines.

"I have my Eagle and the Mothers to guide me. I'll be okay. Those girls are Ghost Walkers. Eagle tells me they are suffering and they need us," I said, trying to sound as matter-of-fact as Mother Wolf had always sounded.

Tom reached in his pocket and pulled out two braided strands of hair and forced one into my hand, "This is Coyote. He's my Protector and I will ask him to watch out for you. He's a bit of a trickster but as a Totem Protector he can help you see the tricks that are played on the mind. Be wary in there because there are many Ghost Walkers, not all are innocents like these young girls. Stay frosty and alert."

"Hey, frosty is my middle name," I said.

"With due respect, this is no time to be a smart ass, Mother Eagle," Tom said.

"Mouth, Constable. But thank you, I'll be careful," I said and tenderly tucked the braid of coyote hair into my vest pocket.

I entered the refrigerator. Mr. Barrette had carefully laid the girls so their heads were facing toward the middle of an imaginary circle. Their bodies arranged in these positions resembled petals on a grotesque flower.

"It will get very cold in here," Mr. Barrette said, taking off his suit jacket and wrapping it around my shoulders, "If you're not done in ten minutes, I'm coming in. If you're done before, there's a handle on this side of the door that opens it. May the ancestors protect and guide you Mother Eagle," he said, as he walked to the refrigerator door. "Journey well."

He closed the door behind him as he left.

Journey well was a good wish, and also a goodbye. I hoped it would turn out to be the first and not the latter.

I began to work quickly as Mother Wolf guided me through the steps. I rummaged through the bright orange backpack and took out all the items Screech and Mother Wolf instructed me to remove. A bag of tobacco. A bundle of eagle feathers. A large quartz crystal. A turquoise stone. A small length of twine.

I walked to the centre of where the girls' heads were situated. I connected the circle by running a thin arched line of tobacco between the girls' heads. Screech instructed me to place one eagle feather on each girl's mouth. He explained that this would help us to communicate with the girls. Then he told me to place the quartz crystal on one girl's forehead, the turquoise stone on the next girl's forehead, and to place the small length of twine on the last girl's forehead.

Mother Wolf explained the crystals and twine, "The quartz crystal is like a scrubber and battery. It attracts good energy and repels the bad. The turquoise stone is the color of spirit and allows us to connect with spirit. The twine binds us all together in the past, present, and future. The tobacco, as always, is a gift to the ancestors and to show reverence for all the gifts that are bestowed upon us by the creator. It is a gift to show great respect. These are all energy gifts Eagle will need for the Between. Journey well, Mother Eagle."

I held out my red leather clad arm and called Screech. He flew onto my arm without disturbing the air in the room.

"*Red sit. Yes?*" he thought to me.

"*Yes. Red sit,*" I thought to him as I settled down in the middle of the circle surrounded by the girls. I crossed my legs in front of me.

"*Screech sit,*" Screech thought as he hopped down and nestled himself into my crossed legs, "*Screech protect Red,*" he thought as he nuzzled his head into my chin. I kissed the top of his head.

Mother Wolf dressed in the white rawhide dress, appeared first on the outside of the circle. For a moment, I wished I had been wearing my white rawhide dress. But I was still wearing the clothes I had travelled in. I started to feel I needed the extra protection the dress could offer to me.

Mother Wolf began to chant in words I didn't understand. She was soon joined in a circle around the girls by the rest of the Mothers and their Totems. The room filled with the sound of drumming and chants.

I felt Mother Wolf join Screech inside my head, she whispered, "Child, getting into the Between is easy. Getting out is the tricky part. Before you enter, you must concentrate on something that holds you here in life. Something that is important to you."

"I'll hold on to my Eagle," I said, being careful not to say Screech's name.

"That goes without saying, but you need something that is not in the Between. Eagle will be with you."

I thought of the Coyote braid Tom had given me, "I will hold onto Tom and his Coyote Totem."

"Good choice, child. The Mothers all approve," Mother Wolf said.

Suddenly the chanting became louder and the drums were almost deafening.

"*Screech fly Red*," Screech thought to me. His words were like thunder in my head. The room began spinning round and round. I felt like I was being drawn out of my skin and into the air.

This flight was nothing like I had experienced with Screech before.

"*Hurt a little*," Screech thought to me, and I remembered when Mother Wolf had said something would hurt a little, and it always hurt a lot.

And this was no different. It hurt like hell.

It felt as though shards of ice were ripping through my body. My stomach, all my insides, and muscles seemed to be twisting. For a split second, I wondered if my white rawhide dress would have protected me from the pain, but the thought was quickly replaced with nausea and I'm not sure whether I vomited or not. And just as suddenly as it had started it was over. The pain was gone and I wasn't flying, I was hovering in total blackness.

"*Between*," Screech thought to me, he sounded sad, "*Red hurt. Yes?*"

"*It did hurt a little*," I thought back to him, putting an emphasis on the '*little*'.

"*Going...Between...alive...hurts. No hurt...when...dying*," Screech thought to me.

"*Did Screech hurt?*"

"*A little*," he thought back to me. I could feel him shiver. But he quickly blocked his feelings from me.

The darkness melted away in patches and images started to form and then the images evaporated into a mist before I could make out what they were. As I looked down at myself, I saw I was wearing my white rawhide dress. It was settling in around me as though it were giving me a reassuring hug. All the embroidered animals on it seemed to be alive and moving.

"Red think dress. Red get dress. Between...think. Happens," Screech struggled to make his thoughts clear to me.

Screech was on my arm but he had no weight. I could barely feel his grip.

"Mothers. No go Between," Screech thought to me.

I could hear the Mothers chanting, but I couldn't see them. For a split second I thought about how this was an amazing trip. Like no high I'd ever been on.

Then a man materialized in front of me. He was a drug pusher who had pimped for me when I first ran away and was living on the street. He was also my drug supplier. He had been killed by a rival gang a couple of years ago.

He had a bottle of cheap whiskey in one hand and an assortment of drugs in the other.

"Hey, Jess girl. Damn, you're looking fine! Wanna join me? Got some of your favourites... TNT, black pearl, green dragons, kit kat, and even some good old skunk. Let's party babe!" He teased me with his offerings.

I had an overwhelming craving for a hit. I wanted to get high. It was like he was offering me water after I'd been lost in the desert and was dying of thirst. I wanted it. Just one last hit. I was raising my hand to take the drugs, as Screech intervened.

"No. Ghost Walker. Kill Red. Screech die. Stop," Screech shrieked in my mind.

I could feel Screech filling my mind with thoughts of flying. Sunsets and sunrises. All the things he knew I loved. But I wanted the hit more. Just one last time. I didn't want to fight the aching urge to get high. I knew I needed to focus. Concentrate on Screech's thoughts. But I couldn't.

"Hey, Jess. Just one last hit. You want it. Why not sweet cheeks?" the pusher urged.

"Red. Screech. Between forever. Fight. No think," Screech forced his mind to fill my thoughts, *"Screech love Red."*

Finally, with great effort, I lowered my hand and stepped backward. I knew from Screech's thoughts that taking the drugs from this man would trap my beloved Screech and me in the Between. No matter how much I wanted the hit, I loved Screech more. I couldn't let us become trapped in this place. And I had to help the girls.

I concentrated on the thoughts Screech was giving to me. I fought the cravings. The man slowly dissolved into a mist. As the man vanished, I began to hear shouts, groans, moans, and crying all around me.

"*Are people making those sounds?*" I thought to Screech after the dealer disappeared.

"*Ghost Walkers. Yes. Lost. Afraid. Angry. Pain. Many here,*" Screech's thought was a whisper and sounded like he was struggling to think.

"*What do I do now?*" I thought to Screech.

"*Think girls. See girls,*" Screech said and gave me a faint aerial picture of the girls in the circle on the floor of the refrigerator. They looked even more like petals in a grotesque flower. As I looked at them from above, I heard girls crying.

The darkness around me turned into shades of magenta and gold. Mist gathered around me.

Chapter Thirteen

ppearing in the swirling mist of color, one of the girls materialized. She was the blonde girl, with the purple braided hair extension. Her eyes were closed and she was shaking. Two more girls appeared beside her, one with light brown curly hair, and the other had dark hair. Their eyes were closed. They were the same size as their bodies in the morgue. They were all wearing different outfits, but their clothes were grey, dirty, and drab.

"***Talk to girls,***" Screech thought to me.

For a moment I didn't know what to say to them.

"***Screech. Red. Help girls cross.***" Screech encouraged me.

"I am Mother Eagle and this is my Totem Protector Eagle. He and I can help you to leave this place and cross over to where you are supposed to be. You can trust us." My voice sounded hollow, like an echo across a canyon.

The girls all inhaled at the same time, opening their pale frightened eyes, and spoke together as a chorus, "We trust you, but you came to us from the living. You are in danger here."

"My Eagle protects me," I said.

"You are in danger from yellow-eyes," they said as a chorus.

"I don't understand," I said, frustrated with more riddles. Even the dead couldn't give me a straight answer.

The girls raised their hands and opened them. In each palm there was a tiny droplet of blood. On each of their arms were long deep slashes from their palms running halfway to their elbows. There was no blood in the wound. I had seen the same slashes in the pictures of the dead girls' bodies in Duggan's office.

The tiny droplets of blood they had on their hands, dripped off and hung in the air.

"Women's blood," they said as a chorus.

As they lowered their arms down to their sides, the gashes on their arms began to bleed.

"I still don't understand," I said.

"We're lost. We can't cross. He took away the bridge. We are alone in this place. Help us," they said in unison, and they began to weep. Their pain, suffering, and fear were as palpable as the beating of my heart.

"Red help," Screech thought to me.

"How?"

"Spider. Diamondback. Medicine. Think."

As I thought about the spider and the Diamondback snake, the spider and snake on my dress began to move and then climbed off my dress. Spider climbed down and rapidly built a huge web shield around each girl, and Diamondback used his body to create a circle of protection around them. The girls became motionless and quiet. Their eyes closed.

"How did that happen?" I thought to Screech.

"Red think. Spider. Diamondback. Dress help Red. Dress loves Red," he thought back to me.

"So thoughts here become real." I thought to Screech, finally understanding what he had been trying to tell me.

"Yes."

"Okay, now what?"

"Girls remember. Lost love. Help them," Screech thought back to me. He seemed to be getting weaker.

"What the hell do I know about love? Let alone lost love."

"Screech help Red."

Screech gave me a picture in my mind of the Vision Quest Mount, and I could see Mother Wolf lying on the ground. The sadness of that loss filled me I could feel the tears running down my cheeks. There was pain like no other pain I had ever felt. Then he showed me a picture of her when she appeared to me after she had died, and how happy I felt. The joy of her return was a joy like no other.

"Lost love. Love. Eternal. Connects all," Screech thought to me.

"Girls," I said, "Have you lost someone you love?"

Two of the girls answered 'yes'. The third girl with blonde hair and purple braid was silent, but they all continued to weep.

"Think about the person you've lost. Think really hard about that person. Think until you see them," I said, and waited. Nothing happened.

"Screech, this isn't working," I thought to him.

"Screech help. Red remember."

Remember what? I wasn't all that familiar with love. I knew hate, anger, revenge, distrust, but love that was such a new thing to me.

"Red love Screech?" Screech thought to me, there was sadness in his thought.

"Yes. But that's different."

"No."

My thoughts swirled and whirled in my head, I truly didn't know how to help these girls find love again.

"Flying lesson now," Screech thought to me, and then a picture of fledglings being pushed out of the nest appeared in my mind. A hand materialized in my mind, like the hand the Mothers always showed me when the discussion was over. Suddenly Screech's thoughts were blocked and he disappeared from my arm.

"What the frigging hell is going on here. What flying lesson?" I shouted at the black void around me.

Suddenly, I was filled with pain. My throat tightened and burned. My eyes stung with tears. The sorrow was so painful I thought I might explode from it. The loneliness was unbearable without my Screech. It was too painful to think about losing Screech.

Loneliness. Sadness. Pain.

"Screech. Where are you? Come back," I thought to him and then screamed out to him. There was nothingness. Emptiness.

Then I remembered what the girls had said about the loneliness, and I understood how much pain they were suffering. *Those poor children,* I thought and looked at them spun in webs and surrounded by Diamondback. Silent statues forever trapped in pain and loneliness. How could I help them remember love? How could I remember lost love and bring back Screech? I knew that was the flying lesson he was teaching me.

Then thoughts of Screech filled my mind. I remembered flying with him and how wonderful that felt. I thought about how he liked to tease Wolf when he was in a mood for mischief. I remembered how much he loved to hunt and eat. I thought about how good it felt when he told me he loved me and how fiercely he protected me. I suddenly got it.

"Flying lesson learned," I thought to Screech, *"I love you. I miss you and you can come back now."*

A screech broke the silence as Screech appeared on my arm.

"Lesson...learned. Yes. Help girls," he thought to me.

"Remember all the good things you can about the people who have gone away. Remember how good they made you feel. How you loved being with them, seeing them, talking to them. Remember how much they loved you. You must remember!" I pleaded with them.

Suddenly, an old grey-haired woman appeared beside the girl with brown curly hair. The old woman bent forward and kissed the girl on the forehead. A quartz crystal fell to the ground. The web around the girl dissolved. She opened her eyes.

"Grandma," she cried and threw her arms around the old woman. "I missed you so much."

The old woman gave the girl a hug, "I heard you crying, but you had forgotten me. I couldn't reach you."

The old woman began to lead the girl away, and then the girl turned to me, "Yellow-eyes takes the bridge away and leaves us here. He looks for you. He uses woman's blood. Stop him," she said and evaporated into the darkness with the old woman.

I heard a distant giggle and the happy chatter of a young girl catching up with her grandmother. The talking faded away.

A mist appeared by the next girl who had said "yes" to losing someone she loved. The mist materialised into a young man who appeared to be in his late thirties and dressed in a military uniform. The girl with dark hair opened her eyes, the web melted, and the girl shouted with excitement, "Uncle Teddy! You're here!"

"Yes. I'm so glad you didn't forget me. You had me a little scared for a while. I heard you crying, but I couldn't find you." He took her hands and twirled around with her. She laughed with delight.

"Thank you. Your ability to love is deep and serves you well. Be safe." Uncle Teddy said to me just before he and the young girl evaporated into the darkness.

That left the girl with the blonde hair and purple braid, still frozen in the spider's web.

"What about this one?" I thought to Screech.

"Lost...no one."

"She hasn't lost anyone to death?"

"*No,*" he thought to me, *"Red. Screech. Help."*

"Help? How?"

Screech shivered slightly, *"Hurt a little."*

"Hurt a little," I thought to Screech. I remembered the last pain we had gone through. I didn't want to do it again.

"Think Mother Wolf. Remember...Vision Quest," he said and blocked his thoughts from me, but I could feel him tremble as his talons dug deep into the sleeve of my dress, *"Red think...all Protectors. Dress help."*

As I thought about the Totems on my dress, they came to life, moved from my dress, and wrapped themselves around the girl just as they had been wrapped around my dress. Then a tiny thread of twine reached out from the girl's forehead and seemed to beckon to me drawing me closer. I touched the tiny tendril of twine and suddenly it was like a rope made of steel drawing me to the girl and binding me to her.

I began remembering the night of the Vision Quest, following Screech's guidance. I remembered the wonderful creatures, flowers, and aromas.

I heard Screech in my head, *"Hurt a little. Now."*

And it hurt a lot. It felt like shards of ice were ripping through me. My body felt like it was being stretched in every direction at the same time. My mind swirled and I could see light passing by me in every color imaginable and a few colors I'd never imagined. It felt as though my whole body was on fire. So many fragrances and aromas filled my nostrils, although I wasn't sure I still had a nose. I tried to hold the thought of Mother Wolf and the meadow, but the thoughts swirled, evaporated, and reappeared. It was almost impossible to stay focused.

Suddenly, it all stopped.

I was standing in the beautiful meadow I had been in with Mother Wolf the night she had died. It was all there as it had been that night, the wonderful flowers, the music, and the amazing and beautiful creatures. I could feel the joy and love of the place. It was warm and bright here. Screech was on my arm, the Totems were back on my dress, and the girl was holding my hand and standing beside me. She smiled up at me. I could tell from the look on her face that she loved this place as much as I did.

"It didn't hurt when Mother Wolf brought me here," I thought to Screech.

"Red drink medicine," Screech paused, I could tell he was thinking of a way to explain his thoughts to me, and then he added, *"Medicine. Red dying. No pain...when dying."*

The young girl squeezed my hand, looked up at me, and said, "I was here before, but the man stopped me from crossing the bridge. I got lost. He's very evil."

We walked hand in hand through the field and I remembered walking with Mother Wolf. The flowers moved away and created a path to a bridge. The bridge was covered in arches of colors that glowed and shimmered. It was pulling us toward it. I had never seen anything so beautiful. I felt joy. Freedom. I could barely wait to cross it.

When we arrived at the bridge, Screech whispered in my mind, *"Girl cross. Now."*

"Okay. We'll take her," I thought to him.

"Alone," his voice was a faint whisper, I could feel him trembling on my arm, but he kept his mind blocked to me.

"Will she be okay?" I thought to him.

"Yes. Hurry," he said in a thought so faint I almost couldn't hear him. But the urgency of his request was loud and clear.

I could hear the Mothers humming and drumming, but I couldn't see them.

I could feel the pull of the bridge and the desire to cross it. I wanted to go to the other side where I could feel joy and happiness beckoning to me. Suddenly, I felt faint, and the images started blurring around me. I could feel darkness starting to engulf my thoughts.

"NOW," Screech shrieked in my head and then left my mind completely.

I looked at the girl smiling up at me, and said, "You must cross the bridge before it disappears again. Go."

I fought the desire to cross with her. I wanted to go to the other side of the bridge with her. But in a faint whisper I heard Screech say, *"Must stay. Destiny. Not finished."*

I reluctantly let go of the girl's hand, and said to her, "Time to go."

"He had yellow eyes," she said, and walked up and over the bridge.

I was still fighting with every fibre in my being to keep from crossing the bridge with her, but I could feel Screech filling my mind and holding me. His voice was weak. He was trembling on my arm. I looked at him and the pupils in his eyes were so large I could barely see the yellow-green ring of his irises around them.

"Must go. Think Big Bear," He thought to me so weakly I feared for my beloved eagle's life. He showed me a picture of Tom handing me the braid of coyote hair.

I held on to the vision he sent me. I remembered how I liked watching Tom walk, how I liked the scent of leather and sweetgrass that was always around him. I even thought of him holding the big bag of lunch he had brought for me and Wolf. I clung to every thought I could remember of him. I clung to them with every ounce of strength I could summon. I clung to my beloved Screech.

The daggers of ice ripped through me. I felt my body being twisted from my insides to the outside. It hurt so bad I could hear myself screaming. The nausea, the turmoil of thoughts, the flashing of passing lights, and the aromas were beating against my senses. It felt like the torture would never stop.

Suddenly, it was over.

I was back in the refrigerator with the girl's bodies and Screech. I was dizzy and everything seemed to be out of focus for a moment.

My beloved Screech lay limp on my lap, then he raised his head, and fluttered his wings slightly. I raised his head, kissed him, and thought, "*Screech. My beautiful strong brave eagle. Red loves you.*"

"*Love Red. Screech hungry. Must hunt,*" he thought to me, his mind left mine and his body went limp.

I could hear the Mother's chanting and drumming. I felt Mother Wolf, Mother Diamondback, Mother Spirit Bear, and Mother Spider beside me.

I shouted out loud to them, "My beloved Eagle. What happened to him?"

I heard myself screeching his name, but the sound of the screech reverberated off the walls of the refrigerator. I heard Wolf howl outside the door.

Chapter Fourteen

The refrigerator door burst open. Wolf and Tom filled the doorway.

"Wolf, keep everyone back," Tom said as he entered the refrigerator. He crossed the room in two strides, and knelt beside me.

As though he clearly understood Tom's direction, Wolf blocked the door and growled. Mother Wolf appeared beside him. I could hear her in my head.

"Child, in your medicine bag is a small vial of white crystals. It's Golden Foxglove. Put a few grains of it in your eagle's mouth," Mother Wolf thought to me.

I tried to pull at the braided necklace that held the medicine bag around my neck, but my fingers felt frozen and numb from the cold. My hand was shaking and didn't seem to cooperate with my will. Then I felt Tom's warm hand cover mine.

"The medicine bag," he said. His deep voice was soft and almost a whisper.

I nodded to him, and he pulled the medicine bag from out of my shirt.

"White vial. Golden Foxglove," I said, trying to clear my mind and battling the urge to pass out.

Tom found the tiny vial of white crystals, removed the stopper, and gave it to me.

"Place a few of the crystals in Eagle's beak. He has used a lot of energy, and needs a little boost until he can get food," Mother Wolf said to me.

I still couldn't control my hands. I felt as though I were freezing. I trembled from the cold and fumbled with the vial.

"Tell me what to do," Tom said, and gently removed the vial from my hand.

"Put a couple of crystals in Eagle's beak," I said to him.

He shook the vial and a few of the crystals fell into his hand. He quickly put the crystals as far into Screech's beak as he could. He made sure Screech's beak was closed and the crystals couldn't fall out. I could see Screech's throat moving as he swallowed the crystals.

Tom placed the stopper back in the vial, and put it back into the medicine bag. He returned the bag to its place under my shirt.

I'm sure it was only seconds, but it felt like hours. I stroked Screech's head and throat, "Please come back to me, my beautiful beloved eagle," I said aloud and thought to Screech.

The Mother's were chanting louder, I felt them surrounding me. Screech shivered slightly, and tried to lift his head.

Then in the tiniest of whispers I heard him say, *"Red, okay? Yes?"*

"Red is fine. Is Screech okay?" I thought back to him as I cradled his head next to my chest. My hands were still trembling.

"Screech okay. Red brave. Red strong. Screech hunt. Now," Screech said, and his mind left mine.

"Is your eagle all right?" Tom said.

"He's going to be okay. He needs some food."

"I think you need the same," Tom said in his soft, deep voice, as he wrapped me tightly in the suit jacket the funeral director had given me.

"I need to gather the feathers, stones, string, and stuff."

"There are no feathers or stones, just you, Eagle, and the girls," Tom said.

I struggled to focus and looked around. The eagle feathers, the crystal, the turquoise stone, and the twine were all gone. Even the circle of tobacco was gone. Only the girls remained.

"Energy gifts, my child. Your eagle used them to help you and the girls," Mother Wolf thought to me.

Tom tucked one big arm under my legs, wrapped the other around my waist, and lifted both Screech and me up together. His arms were warm and strong. I felt protected and secure in his arms.

He carried us out of the refrigerator and into the embalming room. Wolf let us pass but made sure he stood between us, Dorset, the funeral director, and the receptionist. Tom sat me on one of the embalming tables, carefully lifted Screech from my lap, and placed him on the table beside me. He unfolded my legs from their crossed position and let them dangle over the edge of the table. Wolf guarded me while Tom returned to the refrigerator and collected my orange backpack.

Everyone remained silent. Even the Mothers. Tom returned from the refrigerator.

Screech was beginning to move and he shivered several times. Wolf raised his huge silvery white head and sniffed Screech, then he walked over to the counter where Tom had placed the bag with our lunches. The bag was easily within his reach. He grabbed the bag and brought it back to the embalming table, giving the others a quick glance. He let out a low, short growl as a warning for everyone to stay where they were.

I could feel Screech in my mind, and I could feel his hunger. He was ravenous. And so was I.

Tom took out the ham sandwich and placed one half of it in my trembling hand, "By the looks of things, Wolf seems to think you're in need of this."

I didn't need any advisement about eating. I devoured the half sandwich without tasting it, while Tom removed the meat he had bought for Wolf. He offered the meat to Wolf, but Wolf refused to take it. He rested his head next to Screech and gave a whimper. Tom understood, and tore off a small piece of the ham and held it near Screech's beak.

Screech lifted his head, grabbed the meat, and gulped it down. After eating almost half of the ham, Screech gained strength, stood up, stretched and looked around the room.

"Meat good," Screech thought to me and burped.

"It's ham. You feel better?" I thought back to him.

"Ham good. Screech okay. Wolf need ham," Screech thought to me, as he pushed away the next piece of ham Tom offered to him.

"Tom, Eagle wants Wolf to have the rest of the ham. Wolf can have the other half of my sandwich. He's hungry too," I said, and handed the last of my ham sandwich to Wolf.

Dorset, who had been remarkably quiet decided to end the peace, "So what was all that shit about?" he said.

Tom turned around, "You're talking to Mother Eagle, and you'll do so with respect." His deep, rich voice was filled with the tone of command and annoyance.

"Listen cowboy, I'll talk to her anyway I like. She's here to solve murders and find a missing girl, and she had damn well get her ass in gear, pronto. No more screwing around. Is that clear?" Dorset said as he stepped forward. Tom stepped forward to meet him.

Wolf stepped between the two men, showing his teeth, and growling at Dorset.

"Enough. I need some rest. Tom, would you take us to the hotel?" I said, feeling as tired and as drained as I sounded. I had no desire to deal with Dorset.

"Screech hungry. Weasel nose good. Ham better. Deer better. Weasel nose okay. Yes," Screech thought to me. Screech ruffled his feathers, partially stretched his wings, and raked his talons on the stainless steel table.

Screech was back to being himself and that felt good. I could feel some of my strength returning and I chuckled at Screech's request, *"No you can't eat Weasel, yet,"* I thought back to Screech.

I put out my red leather protected arm and Screech bobbed his head and stepped up and onto my arm. Unfortunately, for all of us, he didn't do it quietly. He let out a loud hunting screech that hurt everyone's ears, including mine.

"What's with that bird of yours?" Dorset said.

"Oh he's angry because he's still hungry, and I won't let him eat you." I took Tom's out-stretched arm to balance myself as I slid off the table.

Tom grabbed my backpack.

"This is all crap. Do you or don't you know where the missing girl is?" Dorset demanded.

"At the moment I don't know. I wish I did but I don't," I said as Tom and I proceeded toward the exit door of the embalming room.

Mr. Barrette stepped toward me, "Mother Eagle, I'll need my jacket," he said, and I slipped his jacket off my shoulders and handed it to him, "Are the girls okay?"

"They're fine. They are safely across."

"Then you are a powerful Shaman," he said, taking his jacket, "It has been an honor to meet you."

"Thank you. And thank you for helping us. But my eagle deserves all the credit. He's a powerful Totem Protector."

"And brave. Your Wolf is a fine companion as well. Please tell them that for me," Mr. Barrette said.

I passed along his compliments to Screech, and I knew he would share them with Wolf. Screech bobbed his head to Mr. Barrette and Wolf rubbed his muzzle on Mr. Barrette's hand, something Wolf seldom did to a stranger.

Dorset was following us as we left the embalming room, "And what do you plan to do now?"

"Rest," I said.

"Rest. Dammit woman there's a little girl missing. The clock's ticking," he said.

"Believe me I understand that. But I need to rest and think. I'm no good to anyone in this condition," I put up my hand the way Mother Wolf and all the Mothers did to me.

"That's enough Dorset. She'll get back to you as soon as she knows anything," Tom said, then added, "I wouldn't annoy her right now, because she has a wolf and an eagle that are still hungry and irritable. They would happily turn you into a snack."

Dorset dropped back and we left the funeral home. As soon as we exited Screech gave me a quick thought about getting more food and reminded me that Wolf was still hungry. He launched himself into the air and began looking for food. I told him he couldn't have cats or dogs because they were people's pets. Pets didn't translate well, so I just said, "*Protectors.*"

"Would you like me to call a taxi?" Tom asked, as he reached for his phone.

It felt good to be outside again, the rain had stopped and the sun was shining. My strength was returning and I wanted to walk.

"My eagle is hunting and I'd like to walk," I said.

"Okay."

Tom stepped around me and placed himself between me and the street. Wolf placed himself on the other side. I was sandwiched between them. I had the feeling they were both trying to be subtle about protecting me. It wasn't working. I knew what they were doing. The three of us filled the width of the sidewalk.

"How did you and Eagle help the girls? Did they tell you anything?" Tom's voice was soft, deep, and rich.

"My wonderful eagle was amazing. We helped them to cross to the otherside. They're no longer in the Between. They were so frightened. They told me about woman's blood and about a man with yellow eyes, who wouldn't let them cross the bridge. But they didn't say anything about the missing girl," I said and I couldn't stop the shiver that passed through my body, "The Between was so horrible. I hope I never have to go there again."

I wished I had thought of asking the girls about the missing girl. But it had been difficult to focus and think in the Between. A brutal place. I was just glad Screech and I had survived and made it back to this side.

"It's good you could help them. What you did was dangerous and courageous."

I was sure I could hear admiration in Tom's voice.

"I'm not sure I would have done it if I'd know how painful the trip would be and how terrible the place was. Tom, I'm really not a courageous person."

"Mother Eagle, an eagle wouldn't have chosen you if you weren't brave or courageous. Trust your eagle. He is the strongest Totem there is. But then again, for him to pair with you, he'd have to be brave and courageous himself," Tom made a deep-throated chuckling sound. I liked the sound of his voice and his chuckle. He was easy to be with. We walked along in a comfortable silence, until Mother Wolf broke in.

"Child, I'm sorry to interrupt your thoughts, but Wolf is painfully hungry," Mother Wolf thought to me, "He enjoyed the snacks, but he needs to have more."

"Tom, Wolf is still hungry. He's had so little to eat today."

"There's a grocery store beside the restaurant in the next block. We could stop in and get Wolf a whole roast of beef. What the heck. He's on an expense account. We'll get him a whole prime rib roast. He's earned it." Tom leaned around me, and patted Wolf on his muzzle.

Other than Mother Wolf and me of course, Tom and children were the only people Wolf would allow such offerings of spontaneous affection. From time to time, under special circumstances, Wolf would allow touching from others but it was rare.

We stopped at the grocery store and bought Wolf the biggest prime rib roast we could find. Then we went to the restaurant and ordered takeout. I bought another ham and cheese sandwich, a salad, and a coffee. Tom bought a hamburger, chips, and a pop for himself. We stopped at a park on the way back to the hotel, and had a makeshift picnic. Wolf ate his roast with a greedy enjoyment and passed along his thanks to us through Mother Wolf, while Tom and I ate our lunch.

Screech caught up to us at the park; he settled on the end of the picnic table, and was excited about finding a couple of gophers and a squirrel. He commented on how fat the animals were compared to home, but now he was sleepy from his feast.

Tom and I didn't talk much, and I was deep in thought about the girls and what had happened in the Between. I knew there was a clue in what the girls had told me about the man with yellow eyes and the woman's blood, but it was as clear as mud to me. My mind kept wandering back to the Sheffield house and the night the police had taken away Mr. Sheffield.

I remembered the young boy, about thirteen years old, with the pale hazel eyes who had watched from just inside the entrance of the house. His eyes were so pale they appeared to be yellow. Could he be the one? I felt the same as I had so many years ago. I felt the Sheffield family had something to do with all of this, I just didn't know what.

I was suddenly sidetracked from my thoughts. Wolf and Screech were becoming restless and strangely alert, as an old man with a white cane came through the park and approached our picnic table. Then Wolf and Screech seemed to yawn at the same time and relaxed quickly. They fell asleep as the old man stopped, sniffed the air, and looked at me. He removed his sunglasses revealing eyes that were glazed over with a white film, and he moved his cane back and forth in front of him stepping forward with each swing until he was close to me. His cane gently tapped my foot and he stopped. He sniffed the air again.

"Hmm. Fresh baked bread. Sweetgrass, herbs, leather, a bird, a dog, a woman, and a man. Am I close?" the man asked.

"Right on the money, sir," Tom answered.

The old blind man sniffed again, cocked his head and listened, then reached forward with his hand offering it as though he wanted to shake hands with me, "And this is where the lady is sitting I presume," he nodded in my direction.

I shook his hand, "I'm Mother Eagle."

"I'm Mr. Arnie Jackson," he said and continued to hold my hand, "I suspect the bird is large. As is the dog."

"An eagle and a wolf," I answered.

"Hmm," he murmured thoughtfully but he seemed unaffected by the strangeness of my animal companions, "And you son. Who are you?"

"Constable Tom Diamondback, Pinewood Reserve and County," Tom sounded like he had recited this many times.

"Both of you are far from home." The old man released my hand from our handshake, and tapped the picnic table with his white cane. He sat down beside me.

"We are," Tom's tone was cool but not unfriendly.

"You must be the lady all the folks around here are talking about. Quite the stir you're causing. Here to find a killer are ya? Cause ya didn't do such a good job the first time."

"Some might say that," I said.

"And some do say that. You, my dear, have the hand of a healer. Very powerful healer, I'd say," the old man settled himself. Wolf woke up and stretched, and then came close to the man and sniffed him. "The wolf is curious about me. And he should be."

"Why?" I asked.

"He knows I'm...different from most people. And he'd be right. But, I do know things. I listen. Folks think that because I'm blind, I don't hear too well either. A human foible, I suspect. Folks talk when I'm around, like I'm not there. I listen."

"What do they talk about?" Tom's mood appeared to have migrated from mild curiosity to professional interest.

"Mostly gossip. Lots of bad blood in this town. Lots of secrets. Take the old Widow Sheffield. Lots of talk about her," the old man mused.

"Mrs. Sheffield still lives here?" I was surprised that she had stayed.

"Yup. She sold the old house and moved in across from the school on Fiftieth. Sits on the front porch every day and watches the kids in the school-yard. Folks say it's because she misses her son. He left to go to school in the big city."

Mr. Jackson held out his hand in the air. Wolf slowly approached him, sniffed the old man's hand and then placed his muzzle under the man's hand. Mr. Jackson smiled showing his dark stained teeth. He appeared to be enraptured by the touch of Wolf's muzzle.

"Beautiful animal. He's big all right." The old man stroked Wolf's head and neck.

"Yes, he is," I said.

"Ya'all might want to talk to Widow Sheffield. Worth a visit to her I'd say. She's a lonely old soul. The townsfolk pretty much ignore her. They wouldn't do her any harm, mind ya, but they keep their distance. They say she's an odd old duck. I suspect she never got over all that trouble with her husband years ago." Mr. Jackson stood up.

"Is there anything else you think we need to know?" Tom asked.

"Maybe. Probably. But young lady, you should go pay your respects to the Widow. Might do both of ya some good," the old man gave me a wink with his left blind eye, put on his sunglasses, and prepared to leave.

"What's the widow's address?" Tom asked.

"Don't know, but folks around here say the place is haunted. Superstitious nonsense," the old man said, and walked away tapping his white cane on the ground as he walked.

As I watched Mr. Jackson walk away, I suddenly had a strange feeling about the Mothers. I felt as though there was something terribly wrong. They had all been quiet during our walk and our picnic. Suspiciously quiet. And none of them had said a word during the exchange with the old man.

"Mother Wolf, are you there? Did you have anything to do with Mr. Jackson talking to us?" I thought to her.

There was a long silence before she thought to me.

"We have nothing to do with that...man. He's a creature of his own design and talents," Mother Wolf thought to me, and mentally gave me a picture of a raised hand. She clearly didn't want to talk about Mr. Jackson or anything else.

The other Mothers were silent. There was a distinct chill in the air. I felt as though there was someone or something watching me.

"Is there something wrong?" I thought to Mother Wolf.

"There is so much danger around you, my child." She paused, and in the background of her mind I thought I could hear animal sounds. A raspy growl and a hiss. Then she continued, "Since you went Between, all the threads of possibilities around your strand in the web...have knotted together. Mother Spider can't unravel the knots...she can't see future events."

I could sense, by the way she concentrated on her thoughts, she was worried and hadn't really wanted to tell me about the knots in the web. I had always thought the Mothers were invincible. Strong. In charge. But they weren't. They had weakness, too. In a strange way they were more like me than I'd imagined. They weren't perfect super-women, and that thought made me feel closer to them than I'd ever felt before.

But I was still worried.

I didn't want Mother Wolf to know how worried I was about the knots in the web. I tried to be as calm as possible when I thought to her.

"So we have a few knots in our future. No problem. We'll work around it. But, I'm guessing Mother Spider can't help us find the missing girl? Or the killer?"

Mother Wolf seemed to hesitated before thinking to me. Again, there were animal sounds in the back of her mind.

"No. Mother Spider can't help us at the moment but I'm sure she'll have it sorted out soon," Mother Wolf said, and again I heard animal sounds.

"Mother Wolf, I keep hearing animal noises in the back of your thoughts."

"We have a...small issue...it'll be fixed in a jiffy," she gave me a mental image of a hand in the air and left my mind.

It appeared I would have to find the killer and the missing girl without help from the Mothers. I didn't have a foggy clue about where to start looking for either of them, other than Mr. Jackson's remarks suggesting I should visit Mrs. Sheffield. I had a gut feeling the old man was right about visiting her and, because I lacked a better idea, I decided to follow his suggestion.

Tom had cleared up the remnants of our picnic and was stuffing them into the paper bag that had held our lunch. He walked over to the garbage bin and dropped the bag in.

"Tom, can you call...the station, and get Mrs. Sheffield's address?" I called to him.

"Sure."

He pulled out his phone, thumbed through the display, tapped a phone number, and was talking to someone at the police station as he walked back to the table.

Within a couple of minutes he had the address and directions. She was only a few blocks away. Tom, Wolf, and I walked. Screech flew overhead. He was as silent as the Mothers.

I had the feeling that someone was still watching me. I looked around but saw no one.

Tom was quiet. When I spoke to him, his responses were short and indicated he wasn't interested in talking. It felt as though he was distracted.

He fidgeted and pulled out the braid of coyote hair from his rawhide jacket pocket and held it between his fingers. He whispered words I didn't understand and then tucked the braid away. I figured he was calling his Totem Protector to his side.

"Something bothering you?" I asked.

"The old man. He put me on edge. Something about him wasn't...right." He patted the pocket that held the braid of coyote hair, "I asked Coyote for his assistance. He sometimes helps me see through deception."

"Mr. Jackson was a bit strange."

"He was more than strange."

"It's been a weird day. I think we're all on edge."

"I suppose," he said as our eyes met, and he seemed to soften, "It certainly has been a rough day for you. Are you sure you're ready to visit Mrs. Sheffield? It could be...difficult." Tom looked away and patted Wolf.

"I don't want to talk to her. But I have to. Maybe she can tell me something that will help us. I just have a feeling about that family. I've had it for a long time. And...we have nothing. Not one friggin' thing we can actually follow-up. And Dorset isn't any help."

Tom looked at me again. His eyes searching mine, "Mother Eagle, I'll always take a Shaman's gut feeling over anything else. And Dorset. He's a piece of work. You're right. He isn't any help. Unless being a pain in the ass is considered helpful. Because he's a lot of that."

"Mouth." I cocked my head and playfully smiled at him.

Tom's left eyebrow rose and he smiled back at me. His eyes were soft and warm. There was a tenderness in the way he looked at me.

"Hmm," was all he said.

We both settled into silence.

I thought to Mother Wolf and the other Mothers, but they remained silent. I was beginning to miss their arguing and talking with me. I felt a chill pass through me again. My skin went into goosebumps and I could feel the tiny hairs on my arms rise. Wolf pushed his great large silvery white head under my hand and gave a low sigh.

Screech finally broke the silence, ***"Screech protect Red. Wolf protect Red."***

"Red and Screech fly," I thought back to Screech, and we were instantly flying. I was with him looking at the roof tops, streets, and cars below. The air didn't taste as fresh as it did over the forest but it was still a wonderful escape. On the ground I was aware of where I was walking but I didn't really pay a lot of attention. It was like I was walking in a daze...there, but not there.

"Why is everyone so quiet?" I thought to Screech. I wondered if he might know what the "little issue" was the Mothers were dealing with. Maybe there was some Protector gossip he could share with me.

"Mothers...thinking. See cat. Cat like squirrels. Cat good hunter. Screech no eat cats. Cats Protectors. Yes," Screech thought to me, and then made me focus on a cat in a back alley. The cat was hunting a squirrel.

Sometimes talking with Screech could be as frustrating as talking with the Mothers. I wished Screech could express himself better and stay focused.

"Screech shouldn't eat cats. Yes. Cats in the city are peoples' Protectors," I said, and then thought to Mother Wolf, "Hello, anybody home out there?"

The Mothers were still quiet. I had wished many times that they would be silent, but now that they remained silent, I felt alone. Forsaken. It was a feeling I hadn't felt in a long time. The feeling triggered the desire to have a drink or just to hide in a high of some kind. I remembered the craving I had in the Between. I pushed the craving away.

As we approached Mrs. Sheffield's house, Screech left my mind and we were no longer flying together. I suddenly felt a darkness around me. It felt vaguely similar to the darkness I had felt in the Between.

Chapter Fifteen

We stopped across the street from the house and I thought to Screech, *"Stay with Big Bear and Wolf. I'll go alone to the house. Tell Wolf."*

"Wolf knows. Red go alone." Screech landed on the school fence near Wolf.

"Tom," I said aloud, "I've asked Eagle and Wolf to stay here. I want to talk to Mrs. Sheffield...alone."

Tom nodded his understanding.

I noticed young boys and girls hanging around and talking in the schoolyard. I watched them for a moment and noticed a young girl was staring at me. She was off to one side of the yard and didn't seem to be interacting with any of the other kids. She appeared to be about twelve years old. Her hair was short, curly, and red, very much like my color. She moved closer to the schoolyard fence and me.

"Are you the lady everyone is talking about?" she called to me as she approached the fence.

"I don't know. Who have they been talking about?" I asked.

"They say you have an eagle and a wolf and you can see the future," the young girl said.

"Then, yes. I am the lady everyone is talking about," I said and thought to myself that news always travels fast in a small town.

I walked closer to the fence, and as I approached her, I felt like I was being watched. There was a slight chill in the air.

I quickly looked around and saw Tom was watching me. His expression was one of amused interest. He smiled. I smiled at him. But I still felt like there were eyes watching me and they weren't Tom's eyes.

I turned back to speak to the young girl.

"And what's your name?" I asked.

"Christy Abigail Turner."

"Nice to meet you, Christy Abigail Turner. I'm Mother Eagle."

"Hello, Mother Eagle."

She spun around and ran off toward the gate on the other side of the schoolyard. As she left, so did the feeling of being watched. The chill was gone and I could feel the warmth of the late afternoon sun again.

I crossed the street and went up to the veranda of Mrs. Sheffield's house. Mrs. Sheffield was sitting on the porch rocking back and forth in an old rocker. She looked much older than I remembered her. Her hair was almost all white. Her eyes were sunk into her head and circled by black shadows and deep wrinkles. She was watching the children in the schoolyard. She didn't look at me.

"Mrs. Sheffield," I said to her, "I'm Jessica Seeker and I'd like to talk to you." I thought it was better to use my old name. Judging from her distant stare at the schoolyard and her slumped frail body in the rocker, I thought I should be as careful and as gentle as possible with her.

"Jessie Seeker...back to cause more trouble." She continued to watch the children in the schoolyard.

"I'm truly sorry for the pain I caused you and your family."

"More girls are missing. That's why you're back, ain't it?"

"Yes."

"Kids are done. They'll be heading home. Getting close to dinner time." She stood up and beckoned to me, "Come inside."

I looked at the schoolyard one last time and noticed the boys and girls were leaving. I turned and followed Mrs. Sheffield into the house.

The inside of the house was stale. Old cooking odors and dust filled the air. It appeared as though the house had been locked up for decades. The bookshelves were coated with dust and the carpets were stained and in dire need of a good vacuuming.

Mrs. Sheffield seated herself on an old threadbare high backed cushioned chair and pointed to the sofa, indicating that I should sit down.

I resisted the urge to wipe off the seat cushion and sat down as close to the edge as possible. She looked out the front window, and I did the same. I could see my beloved Screech preening himself as he perched on the school fence.

Finally the old woman turned her gaze to me and our eyes locked on one another. Her gaze was piercing. It was uncomfortable looking at her. Her expression was one of anger and pain. I knew she hated me.

"Again, Mrs. Sheffield, I'm truly sorry—"

"What do you want?" she asked.

I realized I wasn't sure about what I wanted. I hadn't thought it through. I was following the advice of Mr. Jackson and some gut feelings I had. I was lost. I thought to the Mothers for some guidance. They were still silent. I felt a strong urge for a good strong shot of whiskey or something even stronger.

"I've become a Shaman and Medicine Woman. I'm called Mother Eagle by the people of the Pinewood Reserve. The police have...ah...invited me to help out on the case," I said, feeling I had to justify myself somehow.

"Medicine Woman...I don't put much stock in the supernatural, but I do see my husband, Robert, from time to time. Not as a ghost or anything. He comes to visit me in my dreams. He looks sad most of the time but he never talks to me," she looked at the dusty bookshelf.

There were only two pictures on the shelf that didn't have dust. One picture was a wedding photo of her and her husband smiling together with his arm around her. The other picture was of a young boy. A handsome young boy dressed in a T-shirt and ball cap.

I noticed his eyes were a pale shade of hazel. His eyes appeared to be yellow. I remembered the girls talking about the man with yellow eyes. I remembered my visions and the name I kept hearing the day I talked to the police over eleven years ago. Robert Sheffield's name rang in my head the same as it had so many years ago. I remember seeing the boy's pale hazel eyes staring out at me from the doorway of the house.

"The picture of the boy—who is he?" I asked.

"My son, Robert Junior, but we called him Robbie," she said as a smile slowly began to form on her lips. "His father would be proud of him. He's done well for himself."

"Where is...Robbie?" I asked in a soft and gentle voice, being careful not to break the warmth of her present mood.

"He went up to Hull to get his training as a Licensed Practical Nurse. Then he went to work in a palliative care facility. Mostly older people. They were all in a bad way. Most of 'em were dying. He loves looking after people. He's such a deep and sensitive young man."

"He sounds very special," I said, still trying to keep her in the pleasant mood. She seemed to be enjoying the nostalgia of the moment.

Still staring at the picture, "He was always a smart boy. Quiet but smart. He didn't speak until he was five. Doctors thought he had a speech problem. But I knew he was fine. A mother knows these things."

"Yes, a mother knows her child better than anyone," I said, knowing that was bullshit talk because I never knew my parents or my mother's love. My mother didn't know a thing about me.

Mrs. Sheffield turned her gaze back to me. There was genuine tenderness in her eyes as she spoke, "He always watched the people and traffic go by the front window. One day a car hit a dog right in front of our house while Robbie was watching. Poor child. I hated that he had to see that."

"It would be difficult for a child," I said.

"It was. His father went out immediately to check on the animal, but it was terribly mangled. Dead. The car kept on driving. I don't think the driver ever knew he had hit the dog. It was so small." She stopped for a moment, and looked off in the distance as though she were reliving the event. "My husband found an old blanket and wrapped the dog in it. Robbie wouldn't leave the window, even though I kept trying to pull him away."

Mrs. Sheffield shifted in her seat, and then refocused on Robbie's picture.

"Robbie spoke his first words that day. He said, 'Is it dead?'" She paused fidgeting with the top button on her blouse, and finally added, "I tried my best to comfort him, telling him the dog had gone to a wonderful place called Heaven."

I gently coaxed her, "Did he talk after that?"

"Yes. But he was always very quiet. Not a chatty child at all," she said turning her gaze to me, the anger and hatred was back, "I think he was very sensitive, especially after his father's death. I think that's why he wanted to help people. That's why he became a nurse and started working in that long-term care-home."

"What is the name of the home?" I asked.

"The Elysian Fields Care Center in Hull." Her eyes narrowed as though she was becoming suspicious of me and my questions.

Trying to keep my tone friendly, I said, "Does he talk with you much. Text...call...email?"

"He used to call sometimes, but I haven't heard from him in almost a year. He was staying with my sister and her husband up in Hull until her husband passed, and then...he just disappeared. He's probably trying to deal with his grief. He was very close to my sister's husband."

"I'm sorry to hear that. It must have been difficult for Robbie. Being a sensitive young man." I waited for a moment, and then quietly asked, "How did your sister's husband die?"

"He was a diabetic. It seems he died of insulin shock. But he wasn't alone, Robbie was with him. My sister said Robbie tried to help, but there wasn't anything he could do," she said as her eyes narrowed further. Then, she stood up and looked out the front window.

I followed her gaze and looked out the window. I saw a van, marked with the town of Wheaton's blue and yellow police logo, pull up and park across from the house. I knew without seeing them—Duggan and Dorset were in the van. I guessed that when Tom called to get the address for Mrs. Sheffield's house, it alerted Duggan and Dorset to our activities and location.

"I think we're done here," Mrs. Sheffield said and pointed to the door, "I don't want or need your apologies. What is done is done. Understand that you're not welcome here. We don't need any more of your trouble."

"Thank you for your time," I said.

Mrs. Sheffield said nothing more, and waited for me to leave.

As I walked from the house to the van, Dorset and Commander Duggan stepped out to greet me. Tom and Wolf, in just a couple of strides, were between me and the men. Tom crossed his arms over his chest. Wolf growled, and the fur on his spine instantly rose to attention as the men tried to approach me. Screech released a loud glass-shattering shriek, and landed on the top of van, scraping his talons along the roof.

Duggan seemed to ignore Tom and my Totem Protectors' protests, and continued to approach. Then he stopped. He twirled his gold lighter between his two fingers, and adjusted the cigarette tucked behind his ear. Dorset stopped a few steps behind him.

"I understand you created quite the hubbub at the funeral home. In the future, before you go off to play detective, you clear it with me," Duggan said, then pocketed his gold lighter and adjusted his belt around his more than ample belly.

"You clear it with both of us," Dorset added and steped up to stand at Duggan's side.

"Whatever," I said, knowing rules were invented for me to break—especially rules made by these two clowns.

Duggan looked at Tom, "Are you the Constable, that Detective Dorset has been telling me about?"

"I don't know what Dorset has told you. But, I'm Constable Diamondback." Tom's answer was crisp and cold.

"What are you still doing here?" Duggan asked.

"I'm on special leave to be Mother Eagle's...ah, assistant and security detail," Tom said.

"You have no authority here, understand," Duggan said.

"Understood." Tom's deep voice carried a hint of contempt.

"Seems our killer has left another note for you." Duggan reached into his pocket, pulled out a note, and handed it to me. The note was encased in a plastic folder.

I read it aloud, *"Hello Witchy-woman. I'll take another one soon. Tag. You're it."*

There were splotches of red on the note. The splotches were blood.

"They found the girl's body over by the river. The note was attached to her clothes. They figure she's been dead for about twenty-four hours. That makes four," Dorset said. His voice was cold. His brown eyes were emotionless.

"Then she was dead before I came here. Before you came to get me. I didn't have a chance to save her." I felt a knot forming in my stomach. A sense of helplessness filled me.

"Why didn't I see her Between?" I thought to Screech.

"Thought three. Not four. Between...thinking," Screech thought to me.

I wanted to scream. To pound on something. I filled with rage and sorrow at the same time. This girl was dead and there would be another.

I knew I had to find Robbie Sheffield. My heart and my gut told me it was him. His yellow eyes. The girls telling me he had yellow eyes. I had no doubt. He was the Robert Sheffield my child-self had been looking for eleven years ago.

I said to Duggan and Dorset, "We have to find Robbie Sheffield immediately. He's the killer."

Duggan protested, "What? Are you out of your mind, woman? You've caused this family enough grief. I'm not allowing you to cause them anymore trouble."

"I think Robbie is the killer."

"And what makes you think that?" Dorset demanded.

"He has yellow eyes." I immediately regretted saying it.

"Dorset—remember, you wanted this wing-nut here," Duggan said.

"The killer wanted her here and it appears he still wants her here." Dorset snatched the note from my hand.

"There's nothing more we can do now. I think Mother Eagle needs a rest," Tom intervened.

"Red rest. Yes," Screech thought to me.

"I'm very tired. I need some time to think, if I'm going to be of any help to you," I said, as I thought back to Screech, *"Red needs to fly with Screech."*

Screech raked his talons along the roof of the van, *"Red fly. Yes."*

"Yes," I thought to Screech. I felt his mind in mine as he lifted off the van and flew away. I felt Tom helping me into a seat. Then from Screech's aerial view point. I saw Tom help Wolf into the back of the van. After that, I was high in the air flying with Screech.

"Where are the Mothers?" I thought to Screech.

"Here," he thought back.

"But I don't hear them or see them."

"Between...change...Red. Mothers thinking. Red rest. Screech protect." Screech seemed to be struggling to explain the strangeness of the Mother's new behaviour, then he gave up and filled my mind with sights and sounds of our flight together.

He didn't let me think of anything else until we arrived at the front of the hotel.

Mother Wolf suddenly appeared beside me as I was getting out of the van, "Child, we are here. You need a sweat," was all she said and disappeared.

"What?" I said out loud, as Tom took my arm and helped me negotiate the steps.

"Mother Eagle, please tell Eagle that we'll open the window of your room before he goes berserk," Tom said.

It took me a moment to figure out what was going on, I heard Screech screeching and Wolf was howling back to him. I heard other sounds as well. Some sounded like chirps, others like squeaks; still others were like hisses and roars. It was a cacophony of animal sounds. My head was so full of noise, that I couldn't think the words to Screech, so I just showed him a picture of me opening a window and suddenly the noise stopped. All was calm.

"Tom," was all I could say just before everything went black.

Chapter Sixteen

When I felt the darkness leaving me, Tom was laying me on my bed in the hotel room. He had my backpack slung over his arm.

"Red okay. Yes? Screech land now," Screech thought to me.

"Red okay. Yes." I thought to him, but I didn't feel okay. I felt dizzy and confused. I called out to Tom, "Screech needs to have the window opened."

Tom opened the window. Screech landed and Tom turned his attention back to me, "And you, Mother Eagle, need some rest."

"Mother Wolf says I need a sweat."

"I think she's probably right but all we can do here is get you a nice hot bath. You rest here and I'll get it ready for you," Tom said and disappeared into the bathroom carrying my bright orange backpack.

I was happy he was with me. He understood more than I understood about the ways of the Shamans. He was right, I needed a good long soak in a hot tub, which in my way of thinking, was a great substitute for a real sweat when a sweat lodge wasn't available.

There was so much racing through my mind. Thinking about the fate of the young girl the police had found, and how she was probably lost in the horrors of the Between. Knowing that I had to find Robbie Sheffield before he found another victim. Thinking about another girl in danger, knowing I couldn't reach the Mothers, and Mother Spider's web was in knots, was making my mind swirl. I wanted it all to stop.

My body was hurting. My brain was hurting.

My frustration and fear collided, exploding into a rush of tears. Screech began to get agitated on the windowsill. Wolf was instantly at my side. In the distance I could hear the cacophony of animals again. As I started to focus on the distant noises, the noises got louder. I reached out to Mother Wolf, "Please help me."

I heard Mother Wolf in my mind for only a brief moment, "Sleep, child," she said.

I felt my body relax to her command. The Mothers sent me a dream. Instantly I was in that wonderful paradise of exotic strange flowers, wonderful music, aromas, and vibrant colorful sky. Mother Wolf helped me lie down on a soft mound of grass and in my dream, I fell asleep instantly.

I don't know how long I slept but when I woke, I was back in the hotel room and Tom was sitting on a chair beside the bed.

"When I looked in here you were sound asleep so I turned off the water for your bath. I'll go run it now."

I closed my eyes and heard Tom running water into the bathtub.

"Child you'll need your dress and moccasins," Mother Wolf whispered in my mind.

I felt weak and had to gather strength to get my duffle bag, put it on the bed, and remove my white dress and moccasins from it.

Tom came out of the bathroom carrying the orange backpack, as I was placing my dress on the bed.

"Wolf and I will wait for you to finish," Tom said as he opened the bathroom door for me.

"Screech. I'm just taking a warm bath. Stay with Tom and Wolf," I thought to Screech. He settled on his window perch.

I walked into the bathroom. The steam engulfed me. I could hear the water filling the tub. After I entered, Tom closed the door.

Tom hadn't turned on the bathroom's exhaust fan. The steam from the bath filled the room and fogged the mirror. The air was lightly scented with mint, pine, and lavender. There was also the lingering aroma of burnt sweetgrass and sage. He had also put tobacco in the four corners of the room.

I turned off the water, stepped out of my clothes, and lowered myself into the hot steamy water. It felt wonderful and I felt some of the tension in my body slip away. As I lay soaking in the hot fragrant water I heard soft drumming.

The Mother's all appeared around me. Their Totem Protectors were not with them. They were all humming and chanting words I didn't understand. They were more intense than they usually were.

Mother Wolf spoke in thoughts to my mind. Her voice was almost a whisper, "This was needed, enjoy for a little while...but you can't linger here. You'll need to put on your dress, when you are done. You need its powers. We can't hold this back much longer."

She vanished. The Mothers vanished. I groaned.

I could have stayed in this bath for the rest of the day but Mother Wolf seemed unusually anxious. I enjoyed the luxury for a few more minutes, then I got out of the tub, wrapped myself in a towel, and opened the door a crack.

Tom turned quickly, "I'll step out while you change,"

"You don't have to leave, just turn your back. I'm a little shaky right now. I'm not sure I should be alone," I said, ashamed I felt so weak and admitting it. I wasn't comfortable allowing anyone to see me weak.

The room was filled with the scents of sage and sweetgrass. Tom had been busy again while I was in the bath.

Tom turned his back to me and I changed. It was comforting to feel the silky leather dress flow over my body and mold itself to me. I slipped on the moccasins, and they felt reassuring on my feet. The fear, confusion, and whirling in my mind subsided. I could feel my dress giving me strength. I walked to the window and put out my arm for Screech and he climbed onto it.

"Screech protect Red. Screech loves Red," He thought to me as he embraced my mind.

"Red loves Screech," I thought back to him. I kissed his head as he leaned forward. I began to feel stronger as my mind cleared.

"Tom, you can turn around."

Tom turned and as he turned all the Mothers appeared again, with Mother Wolf in front.

"Child, no questions. Take Screech with you into the bathroom. You need privacy right now. No need to stress Tom out. No questions, just do as I ask. Please," Mother Wolf instructed as the other Mothers chanted and drummed.

"The Mothers want to talk with me," I explained to Tom.

He nodded his understanding as I turned and entered the bathroom again, closing the door behind me.

In the distance there were sounds of many animals squeaking, chirping, hissing, and growling, but Mother Wolf kept talking, "You must focus on my voice. Do you understand? This is vital."

"I understand," I said.

"Good. This is new for all of us. We are learning to cope with it, and we need you to cooperate. Do you understand?"

"Yes," I wanted to say more but it felt like I wasn't being allowed to talk. My dress would tighten after I spoke and threatened to squeeze the breath out of me if I spoke more.

"When you and your Eagle crossed into the Between, our Totem Protectors tell us you called for their help. You and your Eagle brought the Totem Protectors on the dress to life. You made a connection with our Totems that has never been made before. Your pairing with the Eagle has made you both very powerful. You two are the strongest pairing there has ever been with the Mothers," Mother Wolf paused as though she was looking for the right words to say next.

"I understand. My Eagle is strong, brave, and magnificent," I said to Mother Wolf and thought to Screech. I could feel Screech embrace my mind like an affectionate hug.

"You are so young to have such strong powers and responsibilities. You'll need to use all the wisdom and good judgement you can muster. You must understand what I'm saying to you." Mother Wolf's voice was firm and commanding as she materialized in front of me. She was her thirty-something self, dressed in the white rawhide dress.

"I understand," I said.

"I don't think you do understand. But my warning will have to do at the moment," she said as the humming stopped and the cacophony of animal noises filled the room.

The noise subsided slightly, as Mother Wolf spoke, "Each Totem Protector wishes to speak to you. We've barely been able to hold them back. That's why we've been silent, but we cannot restrain them any longer."

Then Mother Wolf spoke to the Mothers with words that were unfamiliar to me and then translated her message, "I've told the Mothers in the ancient language to keep their Totem Protectors polite and orderly. The Mothers are busy deciding which Totem will speak first," Mother Wolf said to me and then spoke with the Mothers again. Finally she turned her attention back to me, "Mother Eagle, Spirit Bear will be first."

I could hear a deep rumbling groan that relaxed into a name. Screech helped by explaining that Spirit Bear was telling me his true name in bear speak. I was surprised by this because only each Mother knew the actual name of her Protector. It was the Mother's power with her Protector and by telling me his name he was giving me a direct connection to him and his powers. He explained that his name was a special gift and I wasn't allowed to share it with anyone, other than Screech. He didn't tell me his name for his Mother. Her name was a sacred secret he couldn't and wouldn't tell.

His facility for language and sentence structure was more sophisticated than Screech's, but then again he had had many years of practice. His deep mellow tone was similar to Tom's deep voice. I understood why Screech had called Tom, Big Bear.

Spirit Bear explained that he could help souls cross to the bridge and beyond, but he couldn't go Between to help lost souls. He sounded sad when he spoke about the Ghost Walkers he couldn't help, but he was excited when he talked about Screech, his pairing with me and our combined abilities. He was hopeful that the three of us could free more of the Ghost Walkers and help them cross. Screech and Spirit Bear lavished each other with great praises and words of affection for me and Mother Spirit Bear.

All the others took their turns speaking with me, sharing their true names. It also appeared that most of them had liked the name Toadstool and used it frequently when talking to me. They all had pet names for their Mothers and like Spirit Bear, they didn't share those names with me. I noticed that Screech had never shared his pet name for me with them either.

I began to feel comfortable with strange squeaks, hisses, and, for a lack of a better term, accents all the Totem Protectors used when they spoke. As each of them talked with me, the animal that represented them on my dress moved and seemed to cuddle into me. They all explained how powerful my Screech was among them and offered up great praises to him and me. Of course they all praised their own Mothers in the most affectionate terms.

The Mothers were astonishingly quiet during all of the exchanges.

When all the Totem Protectors were finished talking I asked, "So now everyone including the Mothers can hear my thoughts?"

"No, child. We can only hear or know what you allow us to know," Mother Wolf paused for a moment and seemed to be thinking about how she would explain this, and then continued, "It's like you don't always know what your eagle is thinking. He...ah...leaves your mind and does not allow you to enter his thoughts. It's the same between you and us."

"So you don't always know what I'm thinking?" I asked.

Mother Wolf and a few of the other Mothers laughed.

"Child, you have the most closed mind of us all. We rarely, know what you're thinking. Our Totems tell us your eagle is a perfect match for you because he rarely lets them know what he's thinking," Mother Wolf clarified the situation.

"Good." I was happy they couldn't always read my thoughts. I would have to talk with Screech and see how I could refine my ability to keep my thoughts to myself.

All the Mothers and their Totems went silent again. I could feel a sense of uneasiness within the group. I could also feel that every Mother had called their respective Totem Protectors closer to them. Finally, Mother Spirit Bear broke the silence.

"Mother Eagle, there are some Mothers who are uncomfortable sharing their Totem Protectors with you. They are also concerned about what your eagle and you have done," Mother Spirit Bear said.

Her statement was followed by a murmuring among the Mothers. They spoke with words I didn't understand.

"They feel you are young and a bit...impulsive. They worry that you may not have the maturity, wisdom, discipline, and training to handle the great powers you've...acquired," Mother Wolf said.

"Do they trust my eagle?" I asked.

"Of course they trust your eagle." Mother Wolf sounded surprised that I would ask such a question.

"Then they should trust his choice of me. I understand their concern. I'm concerned as well. But I have all of you to teach and train me. We'll figure this out and work on it together. We are, after all, family," I said.

Mother Wolf was silent for a long moment. There were still some whispers in the ancient language that I didn't understand.

"Toadstool, the Mothers are very impressed with the wisdom of your answer. Some even think you have great promise." There was a hint of pride in Mother Wolf's voice.

"And what do you think?" I asked.

"Mother Eagle. I've always known you've had great promise, right from the day I pulled you out of the ditch. It's only you that hasn't believed it," Mother Wolf said and touched my face with gentle affection the same way I'd seen mothers lovingly touch the faces of their children.

Then the Mothers started whispering again and the Totem Protectors began chirping, squeaking, hissing, and groaning as they talked with one another. There were too many conversations going on and it made my ears hurt. But in all of it I could make out one word that was constantly being repeated—"Watchers".

Finally, I couldn't take the noise any longer.

"Please, stop. I can hear everyone talking and it's making my ears and head hurt. Please, stop. And who are the Watchers?" I called out over the noise and commotion.

Suddenly there was quiet.

"We are truly sorry, Mother Eagle." Mother Badger's gravelly voice was similar to the sound of her own Totem Protector, "We forgot that you can hear all the Totems and us. It will take time to adjust."

"Mother Eagle, there's much you and all of us need to learn and know. Unfortunately we don't have time to sort everything out at the moment. But the Mothers collectively agree and feel that you need to visit the young one called Christy Abigail Turner. It's the only thread of possibilities Mother Spider can see relatively clearly in the web. She seems to be an important thread," Mother Wolf said and vanished.

All the Mothers and their Totem Protectors vanished with her. Frustration boiled up in me. I needed more help. More information. Not more unanswered questions and riddles.

"I asked you a question. Who are the Watchers? We are not frigging finished here. You can't lay all this crap on me, and just bugger off without answering my question. Get back here. Right bloody NOW," I shouted at the empty bathroom.

There was no answer, not even the word "mouth".

"Girl...in danger. Mothers...worried," Screech thought to me.

I knew Screech was right, but I was still frustrated and angry. I knew he could feel the anger in my thoughts, and I was about to turn my anger on him for siding with the Mothers.

I was interrupted by Tom knocking on the bathroom door.

"Are you okay in there?" Tom called through the door.

"No. I'm not okay, and I'm in the mood to kick some surly Mothers' butts," I said, and yanked the bathroom door open.

Screech wasted no time flying in a flutter from my arm to the open window. He paused on the ledge for only a moment. He gave me a quick look and then launched himself into the air.

"Red angry. Screech fly...alone," he thought to me. He shut his mind so hard it felt like he was slamming a door shut in my face.

I tried to reach out to him, but he didn't respond.

"Okay, fly alone. Everyone can be a royal pain in the ass, for all I care. Piss off world," I said out loud.

"I see the conversation with the Mothers went well," Tom said.

"You can piss off too."

"I will if you're finished with the bathroom," he said, and gave a deep throated chuckle.

"And what's so friggin' funny?"

"You are."

"Me?"

"You're just funny to watch when you're angry. I suspect you'll owe your eagle an apology when you finally cool off. Don't let the Mothers get to you," Tom continued to chuckle as he entered the bathroom and shut the door.

Funny when you're mad. Ha. Ha. Ha. I thought. I went to the window and looked outside. I saw Screech flying high in the sky. The day was getting late and the sky was beginning to turn a light purple. A soft cool breeze blew past me.

I remembered there were young girls in danger. I reluctantly admitted to myself that Screech and the Mothers were right. I could sort out what the Watchers were later. I had to find Robbie Sheffield and the Mothers wanted me to talk with Christy. Then it hit me. *Oh, shit. Could Christy be Robbie's next victim?*

"Red, okay. Yes?" Screech finally thought to me. His voice was soft and almost a whisper.

"Red is confused," I thought to him. *"I'm sorry I was so angry. I didn't mean to hurt you my beloved and beautiful Screech."*

"Screech love Red. Yes," Screech thought back to me.

"Red loves Screech. Yes," I sent him images of me scratching the feathers on the top of his head, and then thought to him, *"We've got to find Robbie. I need to talk to Christy."*

"Find Yellow-eyes. Find Rabbit," he thought to me, and created a picture in my mind of Christy.

"Why do you call her Rabbit?" I thought back to him.

"Rabbits fear. Rabbits run. Hunters hunt Rabbits. Yellow-eyes hunter. Hunt Rabbit," Screech thought to me in the matter-of-fact way he always thought about his prey.

Tom walked out of the bathroom, "Feeling better?" he asked.

"Yes and no," I mumbled. In all of this, I couldn't shake off the question about the Watchers. I really wanted to know who or what they were, so I decided to ask Tom, "Can you tell me who the Watchers are?"

"Shape-shifters and according to the legends, they are usually no end of trouble. Coyote, my totem, is protection against them. Your eagle and the Spirit Bear are also good protection against them. Why do you ask?"

"The Mothers and their Totem Protectors were talking about them. But they wouldn't tell me who or what they were."

The color seemed to drain out of Tom's tawny face. He turned his back to me and stepped away.

"Watchers scare Big Bear. Coyote. Screech. Protect him." Screech thought to me.

"Eagle says he and your coyote will protect you," I said to Tom, as I sent Screech a thoughtful hug and praised him for his generosity.

Tom spoke quietly in his deep, soft voice, "The two of you must have used some powerful medicine when you were Between. The Watchers rarely take much interest in the affairs of mere mortals. And that kind of attention almost always gets our Shamans into serious trouble. I'd rather not talk about them."

"You're as infuriating as the Mothers. The whole lot of you are really pissing me off. Shit-damn-fuck." I stomped my foot and fully expected to hear Mother Wolf's 'mouth' warning. But there was only silence.

Tom turned and glared at me. His brown eyes were piercing and his jaw muscles tightened straining his mouth as he spoke, "Another girl is likely in danger. What would you like to do...Mother Eagle?"

His tone and the curt way he said my name was unsettling. He was clearly a formidable man when angry. And he was angry at me. I felt my cheeks blushing in response, but chose to hide how much his anger affected me. And he was right—another girl was in terrible danger.

"I think... Robbie Sheffield... is the killer, and the Mothers want me to speak with Christy Abigail Turner. The girl I met in the schoolyard. I expect she's part of this," I said, and very quietly added, "I have a feeling...she might be his next victim."

"I'll call Duggan and get a car for us and I'll get the girl's address. Christy Abigial Turner. Right." Tom's voice had lost its friendly mellow quality and had a professional cop's brisk attitude.

"Thank you." My response came out somewhat more abrupt than I had intended. In a more cooperative tone I added, "I'll see what I can find out about Robbie."

I used the phone on the nightstand beside the bed, and with a few instructions managed to find the number for the Elysian Fields Care Center in Hull.

It took several minutes of waiting on hold with elevator music, but I finally got through to a lady named Eleanor McKay. She was the personnel manager of the home, and I was lucky to get her this late in the day. She had stayed late to finish up some paperwork.

I asked her about Robbie. She spoke highly of him and indicated that he was wonderful with all of the patients. He would spend hours with the residents who didn't have family to sit with them and hold their hands when "their time was at hand." Mrs. McKay seemed reluctant to say dying, and I suspected it was an old habit she had developed from years of talking with family members about their loved ones.

She said Robbie would always hold the patients' hands and talk quietly to them as they "passed." He seemed to be a comfort to them, giving them permission to "shed their mortal coils," "truly an angel of mercy."

She told me that about a week after Robbie's uncle passed away, Robbie had not come into work, and they hadn't seen him since. He hadn't picked up his paycheck or collected any of his things from his work locker. She had personally reported him missing to the police and had talked with his aunt, but he had just simply disappeared.

I thanked her for her help and hung up the phone. I took a bathroom room break and freshened up, but I didn't change out of my dress and moccasins. I felt I needed the support and physical strength they offered me.

A few minutes later, there was a knock at the door. It was Duggan and Dorset. Neither of them were happy about more zoo duty with me.

It was a short and quiet ride to Christy's house. Tom sat as far away from me as possible, and he had a detached coolness in his attitude. He was still annoyed with me.

Wolf was in the back of the van. Duggan and Dorset were in the front. Duggan drove. Screech flew above us and circled around from time to time waiting as we stopped for traffic signals and other cars. I flew with Screech in his mind.

When we arrived at Christy's home, everyone got out of the van. Tom opened the rear hatch door and let Wolf out. Screech landed on my arm and Wolf came over to stand beside me. Mother Wolf also appeared beside her beloved Wolf. During my talk with the Mothers and their Totems, Wolf was the only Totem Protector who hadn't spoken to me. I didn't know why and hadn't really thought about it until now. Maybe it was because he was still on this side of the Between and hadn't been there with us.

My thoughts were interrupted by Mother Wolf.

"Mother Eagle, I think that only we should go in to see the girl. All of these fellows may make her feel anxious." Mother Wolf glanced at the men.

"Agreed," I thought to her, and then spoke out loud to the others, "Gentlemen, I think it's best for me to go in alone to speak with Christy."

"Are you planning to take your zoo with you?" Dorset asked.

"Yes. I've found in my practice as a Medicine Woman that children, for the most part, like animals better than they like people. I tend to agree with them on that point." I turned on my heel, and headed toward the front door of the house before anyone could argue with me.

Mother Wolf thought to me, "Children know that animals don't lie. People do."

A rather barrel-chested man, dressed in a well-worn blue sweat suit answered the door. His eyebrows and hair were black, but his temples were streaked with grey.

"Good evening," he said to me, then looked at Screech and Wolf. His jaw dropped slightly as he surveyed us.

I remembered I hadn't changed out of my dress. What a sight we must have been to him—a woman in ceremonial dress with an eagle perched on her arm and a wolf at her side.

"Good evening," I said, mimicking Mother Wolf's casual tone, "I'm Mother Eagle, Shaman and Medicine Woman to the Pinewood Reserve, and I'm here to speak with Christy."

"Ah...yes. Christy said she had spoken with you earlier today." He stared at Wolf.

A woman joined him at the door, "Harold...who...what the heck," the woman said.

"She's the woman who talked with Christy today. She's here to talk to her again," the man said to the woman.

"Well then, let her in." The woman pushed past the man and made room for me to enter the house.

The woman was thin and fidgety like a ferret, but seemed to be the ruler of the household. I soon learned she was Anna Blockhold and the man she called Harold was her husband.

"I'm glad you're here. Christy was so taken by you. And from what I see, I can certainly understand why," Anna said, while keeping her distance from me and my Totems.

"I just have a few questions for her," I said.

"You're the woman everyone's talking about. The one they brought here to find the pervert that's killing all these little girls. What a monster!" The corner of Harold's lip seemed to twitch with disgust.

"Yes," I agreed.

"This whole thing has been giving Christy awful dreams and visions. She's such a gifted child, but she has a lot of... emotional...matters. Seems we're the only foster home that wants her," Anna said.

"She's a good kid. But can try a person's patience at times," Harold added.

"Stop that Harold," Anna gave him a solid but friendly slap on his shoulder, "Mother Eagle, you probably remember how it was when a girl is making the difficult transition to womanhood. Christy started her menstrual cycle a couple of months ago. Harold doesn't handle it well, having two females in the house with irritability problems." She winked at me.

"I just retreat to the man-cave and find a good game to watch and thank God I only have two women in the house," he said and gave Anna a quick kiss on the cheek.

"Christy is in her room. She didn't want to have dinner. She said she didn't feel well. I checked her temperature, but it was normal. I just figured she was having one of her spells. She gets those sometimes," Anna shrugged.

"It's really urgent that I speak with her," I said.

"Yes, yes. I understand. Follow me." Anna poked Harold and motioned for him to move.

Harold moved out of our way, and let us pass. Wolf paused for a moment in front of Harold, raised his huge silvery white muzzle to Harold's chin, and sniffed. Harold seemed to suck in his barrelled chest and stepped back.

"Wolf smells fear," Screech thought to me.

"Who is the man afraid of?"

"Man loves Rabbit. Hunter hunt Rabbit. Man worried."

"Well, he doesn't have to worry about Rabbit. We're all going to protect her. Yes."

"Protect Rabbit. Yes."

I followed Anna down the hall.

"Why does Wolf not talk to me like the other Totem Protectors?" I thought to Screech.

"Wolf not dead," Screech thought.

"There's so much I don't know."

"Need...more...flying lessons. Yes," Screech thought to me showing me the picture of the fledgling being pushed out of the nest.

"Unfortunately. Yes."

We arrived at Christy's door. There was a little wreath on it made out of homemade paper flowers with Christy's name on a ribbon across the centre.

"She's very artistic," Anna said, pointing at the wreath, "She made this all by herself. Made one for our door as well," Anna pointed down the hall to another door adorned with a wreath, but it had no name on it.

"They're truly works of art," I said, "I think it might be better if I go in alone."

Anna reached out to touch Wolf's huge head. I stopped her.

"It's likely best for you to ask his permission to pat him. He's not always friendly to strangers," I said and moved her hand away.

"It's okay. Wolf understands. He will allow her," Mother Wolf thought to me, startling me because she had been so quiet, I'd forgotten she was still with me.

"May I pat you," Anna said in the baby-talk way some people speak when they talk to animals and small children.

Wolf allowed the pat on his head and I knocked on Christy's door, "It's Mother Eagle, Christy. May I come in?"

I could hear her footsteps cross the floor. She turned the handle on the door.

"Mother Eagle, I was hoping you would come," she said as she opened the door, grabbed my hand, and pulled me into the room. "You brought your wolf and eagle. They are so wonderful. I'd like a pet, but I can't have one because none of the foster homes would allow it," she chatted on as Wolf and I entered the room.

Christy turned to her foster mother as she started closing the door. "Mrs. Blockhold would it be okay to talk to Mother Eagle alone, please?"

Christy closed the door, and we could hear Anna's voice through the door, "That would be fine, dear."

Christy's room was painted a pale grey with white trim. There was a bookshelf with lots of books. Some of the books seemed too old for a girl her age. In the corner was a small desk with a laptop computer. There was only one doll and it rested on a pillow in the center of her bed.

Although the room was neat and tidy, it appeared impersonal...other than a few drawings that were framed and hanging on the walls. Her name was written on the bottoms of the drawings.

"I see the man with yellow eyes, he's mad at you, and he's looking for you. I think he wants to hurt you. You must leave before he finds you," she said, her eyes were wide and her forehead was furrowed with worry. She came close to me, grabbed me and hugged me so tightly I could feel my dress pushing out against her.

I had begun to suspect that my dress was more mystical than I'd ever expected. It was clear it had one sole intent, and that was to protect me.

"Christy, you're squeezing too tight," I said, "And I'm safe, my eagle and the wolf are protecting me. Nothing will happen to me."

"I'm sorry," Christy said, "But, he's an evil man. Your wolf is big and your eagle is big, but he's...very very bad."

"Christy, how do you know about the man with yellow eyes?"

"I see him. I see him when he takes the girls. I see him in my dreams," she said and suddenly she was hugging me again. "You have to leave. I've seen him taking you...he'll kill you. You have to listen. No one else listens to me, but you have to."

My dress was expanding ever so slightly to keep her from squeezing me too tightly.

"Christy, I'm listening to you. But I can't go until we've captured him. That's the only way—" I stopped before I said that it would be the only way to keep other girls safe. I didn't want to scare her anymore than she already was.

In the distance, I could hear the Mothers humming and chanting. Although Christy couldn't see Mother Wolf, I could see her as she rested her hand on Christy's head. I knew from experience she was connecting with Christy. The humming and chanting grew nearer. I could feel Christy relax her death grip on me.

"I like the music," Christy said.

"You can hear that?"

"Yes. Can't you?"

"I hear it a lot," I said, and looked at Mother Wolf, "It makes me feel happy."

"This girl is special. Normally children and most people can't hear us until they are asleep or almost asleep and we enter their dreamtime," Mother Wolf said, as she stroked Christy's head.

"The music is nice to listen to. But I've never heard it before," Christy said and yawned.

"It's all my...Mother ancestors...singing for you, and they are happy you like it," I said, hoping I didn't have to explain it any further.

"He's really close. I can feel him. He's going to take someone soon. Maybe you." Christy shivered and yawned again.

She looked up at me, her eyes wide, and her lips were trembling. Then she released me. She went over to her bed and lay down on it. She gathered her pillow and her doll into her arms, curled up with them, and gave a little giggle as though she were listening to a voice I couldn't hear.

Quietly, off in the distance I heard Mother Wolf's voice, not the wheezing ancient voice, but her silky thirty-something voice talking to Christy.

"When you tickle the belly of the dragon, you will get burned. This bad man has tickled the dragon's belly. Mother Eagle is one dragon he shouldn't tickle. She has a flame that will burn bright and hot. Don't worry child, there are many who protect her and you. Sleep now, young one. We are listening to you," Mother Wolf whispered in Christy's ear.

Mother Wolf showed me the pictures she was showing to Christy. There was a beautiful dragon with scales of red, gold, and green. It dipped its huge head down and rested it gently on the pillow beside Christy and her doll. Christy was sound asleep.

As soon as Christy was asleep, Mother Wolf turned her attention to me, "And she's right. You're in great danger. We can all feel the danger is close. Too close."

"I can feel it too. What is it?" I asked, not sure I had thought it or said it out loud, because I was distracted by the same feeling of danger. I could feel someone watching me. "Is it the killer that's in the shadows?"

"We can't see who or what it is. Mother Spider is blind to the events that are coming. She hasn't been able to untangle the knots in the web," Mother Wolf said, and I could see the muscles in her thirty something face were drawn tight.

Screech began to squeeze my arm tighter, and the sleeve of my dress pushed back. Screech slowly released his grip.

"*Screech protect Red,*" he said, but he was looking around the room, his eyes were so wide the whites were showing.

Then Wolf released a low rumbling growl, he was looking out Christy's window. I went and looked out and saw Duggan and Dorset arguing with each other. I couldn't hear what they were saying, but I could tell by the way Duggan ground his cigarette butt into the ground under his heel that he was angry.

I quietly let myself, Screech, and Wolf out of Christy's room. Screech was still looking around with the whites of his eyes showing. The way Screech looked startled Anna and Harold who were waiting in the hallway outside the door.

"*Screech are you okay? You're scaring these people,*" I thought to him.

Screech looked at me and I could feel him relax, but he wouldn't let me into his mind and he wouldn't say anything. His eyes closed down until the whites were hidden under his lids. He looked less fierce, but he was still more alert than usual.

"Christy is sleeping. Thank you for letting me talk with her. I hope you have a good evening," I said, and hurried out of the house followed by Wolf. I didn't hear what they said to me as I left.

When we arrived at the van, Duggan and Dorset stopped talking. They were both glaring at me.

"So did she have anything to say?" Dorset asked.

"She says she has visions of the yellow-eyed man taking the girls. She says he's close by and he's going to do it again," I said as I opened the back of the van and let Wolf climb inside. Screch left his perch on my arm and flew into the air.

"Visions of a yellow-eyed man. Fucking repeat of a bad movie I went to eleven years ago. I'm not fallin' for that crap again," Duggan said.

"Did you know Robbie Sheffield has light hazel eyes? They are so light they look yellow," I said and walked around Duggan to the side of the van and opened the door.

"I'm taking you back to the hotel. You and your animals can get on your plane and go home. And you can take your deputy-dog Constable with you," Duggan said, cocking his head in Tom's direction.

"Duggan, have you forgotten? This is a federal case. I'm in charge and she stays," Dorset reminded Duggan.

"And this is my town and my police department. So screw you," Duggan said.

We all got into the van. All of us slammed our respective doors.

"Fine, I'll call my bosses and they'll have twenty guys down here. We'll take over your hick-town police department. You want that? I can do it for you," Dorset said, his voice was slow, calm, and menacing.

Tom leaned over and whispered to me, "It's been a proverbial...excuse the language...pissing contest between these two guys ever since you went into the house."

"I'm glad you came with me," I whispered back meaning every word of it, "I'm sorry I was angry earlier."

He looked at me. His eyes soften as he spoke, "Apology welcomed and accepted. I'm glad I came, too. We need to find this Robbie Sheffield guy."

"I have a feeling he's going to find me and soon," I said.

Duggan and Dorset continued to argue over whether or not I was going to stay. It didn't matter what their decision ended up being. I had decided I was going to stay. Robbie wasn't going to get one more girl. I decided I was the dragon and I was tired of being tickled. He was going to get burned and burned well, like hamburger on an open flame.

Screech was flying above the van, and I felt his mind enter mine as he thought to me, *"Screech hungry."*

"Screech hunt. Yes?" I thought to him.

"Danger. Screech not hunt. Protect Red. Wolf hungry," he thought back.

"Big Bear and Red will get food for Screech and Wolf," I thought back to him, and realized I was hungry as well and I could feel a weariness settling into my mind and body.

It was late. The sun had set and it had been a long day. I thought about how peaceful little Christy looked as she fell asleep, and I felt thankful that the Mothers could give her some peace.

"Would you like us to sing for you too?" Mother Wolf thought to me.

"Thank you. I would very much enjoy it, but not right now. I need to think," I thought back to her, as my mind settled into solving the murders of the young girls.

I needed to find Robbie before he took another child. But how could I find him? Where should I look for him? Was he the one I'd felt watching me through all these years? If so, how had he done that?

My life and my reality had changed so much since meeting Mother Wolf. I had never been part of the mainstream all of my life, but now I was even further away. I was wearing a dress that was mystical or contained strong medicine as the Mothers called it. I was talking with animals and my best friend was an eagle. I was mixing up concoctions from weeds, flowers, and insects and using them as medicine. Hell, I was helping to deliver babies. And everywhere I turned I was discovering reality was not at all what I thought it was. The Between. The Ghost Walkers. And something called the Watchers. If I was tweeting this it would be *OMG, WTF,* definitely not *LOL #IM SO SCREWED.*

I finally decided to fly with Screech and tried to clear my mind. It was always a relief to fly with him. His mind was so clear and easy to be with. He enjoyed seeing his surroundings. Life was a simple matter of survival. I loved my Screech.

"Screech loves Red," he thought back to me as he watched a squirrel scurry up a tree and I could feel his hunger.

"Screech did you hear what I was thinking," I thought to him.

"Red scared. Protecting...Rabbit. Yes," he thought to me.

"Can you hear my thoughts all the time?"

"No." He focused on a pigeon flying in the distance, *"Pigeons good. Screech not hunt. Protect Red. Protect Rabbit."*

I relaxed into Screech's mind and flight, enjoying the wind passing over his wings and watching the sights pass by below.

By the time we reached the hotel, Duggan and Dorset had finally agreed I could stay in Wheaton, but I was not allowed to talk to anyone or actively participate in the case unless they asked for my input. They dropped us off at the hotel entrance reinforcing that they didn't want me doing anything without their permission.

Tom, Wolf, and I had barely exited the van and closed the doors, when Duggan stepped on the gas and drove away leaving some of the van's tires behind in two black stripes on the pavement.

Tom decided to go to the restaurant and grocery store to get food for all of us. I told him to surprise me with his choice for dinner. Some comfort food was all I wanted.

"Do you think Duggan or Dorset could have someone watch Christy's house tonight and keep an eye on her until we catch Robbie?" I asked Tom before he left to get food.

"I'll give them a couple of minutes to cool off, then I'll call and arrange protection for her."

Tom headed up the street toward the restaurant. Screech landed on my arm and Wolf followed me as we entered the hotel. I was thankful the small hotel lobby was empty, and the desk clerk was not at his post. No one was staring at us. We were unseen all the way to my room.

As I approached the door to my room, I felt a cold chill run through my body. I could feel someone watching me. Wolf suddenly became tense and alert. He growled at the door. Mother Wolf appeared beside us.

"Be careful. Watcher," she said and then vanished.

Screech's eyes were wide again showing the whites around the edges of his beautiful yellow-green eyes. His pupils were dilated. The white feathers on the top of his head were pointed straight up revealing the pink skin underneath. His talons dug deeply into my sleeve. I could feel the rawhide sleeve of my dress pushing against him grip.

"What is wrong?" I thought to Screech.

"Screech protect," was the narrow thought Screech sent to me and then he closed his mind.

Chapter Seventeen

I slipped the card into the lock pad of the door, click—the lock released. I opened the door.

The sun had set a while ago and the room was dark. I could feel the cool breeze coming through the window I had left open for Screech. I felt for the light switch beside the door until I found it and flipped it. I released the hotel door and it swung shut.

The light above the small hallway entrance to the room lit the tiny area, but the room was filled with shadows. As I focused my eyes, I could make out a silhouette of a person sitting in one of the two chairs in the far corner of the room.

"Hello, Mother Eagle," the silhouette said and switched on the light that was sitting on the table between the chairs.

It was Mr. Jackson, the old blind man from the park. Screech started crouching and prepared to leap from my arm to attack. Wolf prepared to lunge. Then they suddenly stopped and relaxed, seemingly calmed by something the same way they had behaved in the park. Screech did a leap, and then a clumsy wing flutter in the confined space of the room and managed to land on the back of the chair next to Mr. Jackson. He fluffed his feathers, gave a little shake, closed his eyes, and went to sleep. Wolf strolled over to a spot on the floor at the foot of the bed, curled up, and also went to sleep.

"There. A little calming trick I use sometimes. And yes, I used it in the park. But when we were in the park, I couldn't resist your wolf, I did rouse him just enough to pat him. He has such wonderful fur and he's not as high strung as the eagle. But these two are dedicated in their protection of you. Unfortunately and for that reason, I have to...ah...settle them down. I've also blocked the Mothers from communicating with you or joining us. We can talk alone and uninterrupted. I thought it was time we finally met for real," Mr. Jackson said.

"You're a Watcher or whatever the hell that is?" I said hoping my voice sounded stronger than I felt.

"Alas, you're right. Mr. Jackson has been one of my favourite personas. But I'll have to change soon. I'll miss him. And yes, I'm the one that has been watching you all these years."

"I thought it was—" I stopped.

"The killer," he finished my thought, "Nope, it has always been little old me. You're killer is human and hides in darkness and anger. And is far more dangerous than I. I'm something...a little different." He paused and rubbed his chin as though he was thinking of a way to explain himself, "We've known for a long time, that you might turn up in this line of possibilities, so I've kept an eye on you until we knew for sure. When you and your Eagle went into the...Between, as you call it, we knew this line of possibilities was going to happen. So, I had to step up and introduce myself."

"So who are you or what are you? And what have you really done to my Totem Protectors?" I asked as I folded my arms across my chest hoping I could conceal the fact I was beginning to tremble.

"I would never harm such magnificent and innocent creatures such as the ones who have chosen to be your companions. They're merely asleep," he said, looked at each of them, and then back at me. "Oh, dear. The years have made me somewhat sloppy with my manners, after all this is your room." His tone of voice was a mixture of amusement and false sincerity.

He made a grand hand gesture like that of a head waiter in a posh restaurant ushering a prestigious patron to her seat. I felt an irresistible urge to sit on the edge of the bed facing him.

"You clearly have many questions. I'm not surprised, of course. Your meteoric rise to Medicine Woman, Shaman, and now psychic detective has been a rather large leap from the drug infested, death wishing, cheap prostitute who relished nothing about herself, humankind, or the like," he said as he removed his sunglasses revealing eyes that were a milky white devoid of irises or pupils.

"Who the hell are you, asshole, and what do you want?" I said feeling anger rapidly replacing my fear. He was about to meet the angry and pissed

JESSICA SEEKER AND THE GHOST WALKERS

off Jessica Seeker, not the Medicine Woman I had become. Plus, I hated his demeaning attitude.

"Ah, now that's better," he said, and gave a quick thin-lipped smile, "I've been told I'm becoming insensitive and boorish. It comes with the territory and my age, I suppose. Hazards of the job, as they say. Please forgive me," he said and rose from his chair, "Maybe this will make you more comfortable."

His eyes turned from milky white to clear white with bright translucent blue irises and black pupils, immediately mesmerizing in their intensity. He crossed over to me and put his hand out in front of him and held it above my head.

I wanted to jump up and push his hand away. I felt an overwhelming urge to just belt him. I wanted to hurl a long string of colorful expletives at him. But I couldn't move or speak. I was frozen where I sat.

"Ah, ha," he said as he held his hand over my head. "Definitely feisty. You and your eagle have the ability and power to cross into other dimensions, or realms if you will, and you have some other talents you don't know about, yet. Yes, you are by far more powerful than your predecessors. So the question is, are you a child with a box of matches and a can of gasoline? Or are you a boon to this poor lots' existence? I think it will be worth watching, if only for the entertainment of it all," he said as he lowered his hand to his side and returned to his chair.

"Who are you?" I said as my ability to speak returned.

"Some of your lot call me a Watcher, but I and my kind have been called many things over the centuries. We've been called Magi, Anunnaki, Ant People, Fish People, Gods, and Demons. The ancient Greeks and Egyptians had a pantheon of names for us. So if you wish, you can pick any name you would like. You could even make up a new name. The human vocal system at its present development wouldn't be able to pronounce my real name," he said and settled back in his chair like an old familiar friend who had just dropped by to have a coffee chat.

"I've been told you're good and bad...and trouble. According to the legends you can't be trusted and you interfere in Shaman business," I said, still frozen in place and unable to move.

"We try to observe and not interfere in the affairs of your species, but from time to time it is required for us to get involved. As fascinating as you all are, you have this uncanny ability to be horrifically self-destructive. That tendency is somewhat counterproductive to your hopeful evolution as a species. You lot just need time. We help to keep you developing, by making sure you get the time. But, I must admit, all of you are interesting to us," he said.

"That tells me fuck-all, you arrogant bastard."

He laughed out loud, it was a genuine full bodied laugh, then he leaned forward and stared at me with his intense translucent blue eyes, "I do so like you. You are by far one of the most interesting and powerful Mothers we've monitored. Some of us say you're trouble. Some of us think you have potential. But simply put, I've decided that we will just watch you...for now," he said and stood, "It's been a pleasure talking with you, Mother Eagle and Jessica Seeker."

"Now wait a damn minute. You've told me nothing. I deserve an explanation for your intrusion and a real explanation of who you are," I shouted at him.

"My dear, if that's the way you feel you haven't been listening, but what exactly would you like to know because our time together is growing rapidly shorter," he said.

"Are you good or are you evil? Do you mean to do us harm?" I asked, wishing that I'd had something better to ask but these seemed to be the most important questions I had.

"Good or evil. Do we mean your species some sort of harm? Such narrow and pedestrian concepts. Therefore, it is difficult to answer," he paused, scratched the side of his temple, closed his eyes as though he was in deep thought and added, "Say there is a battle between two groups. Each side has their feelings, thoughts, and perspectives. Each side believes that it is the right side. The just side. The good side. But, because the members of each side believes the other side is wrong, does that make it so. Good or bad. Right or wrong. It is all merely thoughts and ideas. There are more shades of grey than you could possibly ever imagine. Time is...and always has been the ultimate judge, jury, and historian...for us all."

"So, do you have a side?" I asked.

There was knocking on my door.

"Sorry, our time together...has run out. I believe your dinner has arrived. I will see you again. And you should try to slip in a little nap soon. You have a long night of choices ahead. I believe I should say 'Journey well,' Mother

Eagle," he said, and stepped sideways through the wall as though it were a door. He was gone.

"Dinner is served," Tom said through the hotel room door.

Screech opened his eyes and gave his wings a small stretch. Wolf woke up, shook his head, and yawned. I was unfrozen and able to move.

I opened the door and let Tom in. The aroma of the food was delicious and began to fill the room immediately.

"Hot hamburger sandwiches with mashed potatoes, peas, and carrots, with a side order of homemade gravy. A juicy roast for Wolf and Eagle to share. Comfort food for the whole crew," Tom said as he placed the bags of food on the table near the chair where the Watcher had been sitting.

I decided I was not going to tell Tom about my conversation with the Watcher. After all, it was Shamanic business. It was better to keep it that way.

Tom began unpacking the bags. He gave me a plate covered in aluminum foil and handed me a plastic knife and fork. My stomach announced its anticipation with a loud growl. He unpacked a plate of food for himself, and then filled two plates with slices of raw roast beef for Screech and Wolf. We all settled in and began to eat.

"This is a wonderful feast. Thank you," I complimented him.

"Being single and a terrible cook, I've become the master of take-out. I had the grocery store slice the meat for Wolf and Screech. I asked the restaurant to heat it. I hope it's warm enough. I didn't want them accidently cooking it," Tom paused and settled into a chair with his plate on his lap, then added, "I got hold of Duggan. He sent me a text. He is going to have someone park outside of the Blockholds and keep an eye on things for the night. He said they'll make arrangements for further surveillance tomorrow."

"Thank you. I appreciate that, but what about the other girls living in Wheaton? We've got to find Robbie."

"Agreed."

"I'm not sure where to start. The manager at the care facility didn't know where he was. Neither did his mother."

"Maybe we should ask the Mothers to see if they can help."

"I have."

"And what did they say?"

"They didn't know anything, but I'll ask again." I wasn't willing to tell him about all the problems the Mothers were having. I didn't think I needed to worry him with it.

I carefully reached out to Mother Wolf and thought to her. "Mother Wolf, I just wanted to apologize for getting angry earlier."

"Toadstool, you are always angry. We are used to it. We forget all of this is new to you. We forget you have so much to learn. We forget you didn't grow up in our culture or learn our ways. Sometimes, our forgetfulness makes us poor teachers. We are sorry, too," Mother Wolf thought back to me.

"I appreciate your understanding. How are things going with the web?" I asked.

"The web is still knotted. We've all been trying to use our powers to locate Robbie ever since you saw the picture of him in the Sheffield's house. We have managed to find his strand of possibilities, but it ends in the knots around your strand in the web. He's in Wheaton, but we don't know where."

"No surprises there," I thought to her.

I turned to Tom, "The Mothers say he's in Wheaton, but they don't know where...yet." I hoped I had sounded more optimistic than I felt.

Tom shrugged. "We'll find him. Just have to convince Duggan and Dorset to help out with some good old fashioned detective work. He can't be that hard to find. Wheaton isn't a big town."

Wolf had finished his portion of the roast. He walked over to me and laid his giant head in my lap. I had to raise my plate so he didn't knock it out of my hand. This surprised me because Wolf was not a spontaneously affectionate fellow.

"Mother Wolf do you think the Watchers are interfering? Do you think they could tie the web into knots somehow?" I thought to her.

There was a long silence before she answered.

"Yes, child. It's possible the Watchers are interfering."

"Mother Wolf, the Watcher was here and he talked to me."

Again Mother Wolf waited a few long moments before she thought back to me, "We know. He stopped us from communicating with you while he was here. He's the lead Watcher. He's in charge of all the Watchers." Mother Wolf paused, then sighed, and continued, "You are the strongest Mother there has ever been. And since you crossed into the Between, we have sensed the lead Watcher has been very close to you. There have been other times the lead Watcher has taken a personal interest in one of us. That's always caused us trouble. And, make no mistake, he has taken a personal interest in you."

He certainly has. I thought to myself.

Then Mother Spirit Bear said, "When my beautiful brave bear and I helped a young dying man cross the bridge, we entered the other side and returned. The lead Watcher visited me right after we returned. During my time in the world, he interfered with me and the Mothers several times. It was as though he was...testing me...us."

"Why?"

There was another long pause before Mother Spirit Bear thought to me again, "We...I don't know. But like you, I had visions. Visions that came in my dreams. He didn't stop those. Maybe if you can sleep and dream, you will get some answers. Our...spirit form doesn't allow us to sleep or dream."

"But, I can't sleep either. I just keep thinking about all those girls and the pain I felt in the Between with them. I have to find a way to stop the killer." I didn't hide the desperation I felt.

"We can help you sleep, if you would like," Mother Wolf thought to me.

"Okay," I thought to Mother Wolf and then looked at Tom. He had his distant stare, the one he always had when he knew I was talking with the Mothers.

"Tom."

"What did they say?" he asked, refocusing his attention on me.

"They can't see anything. They suggested I sleep and maybe I would have one of my visions and that might help us find Robbie," I said.

"It might work. Worth a try. I'll spend a little time on the computer and make a couple of calls...see what I can dig up. Might turn up a few leads while you're...getting some rest or some visions."

Tom gathered all the empty plates and stuffed them into the garbage. He closed and locked the window. Said his good nights to all of us, but he seemed reluctant to leave. I was a little reluctant to let him go. I found his company enjoyable and reassuring. But I needed to sleep. And I needed to be alone to sleep and have visions. Having him stay with me would have been too...distracting.

Tom waited outside my door and listened to me put the chain in place and lock the deadbolt.

"If you need me, I'm in room eight at the end of the hall. Dial zero-eight on the phone. Journey well, Mother Eagle," he said through the door.

"Journey well, Tom."

I could hear his footsteps as he walked away. Then there was quiet.

Screech settled onto his perch on the back of the chair. I noticed that his talons had scored a few holes, large and small, in the old upholstered chair back. Wolf settled on the floor at the foot of the bed.

I thought about changing out of my white rawhide dress but decided to just lie down for a short while on the bed before changing and showering.

Within moments, I heard the Mothers chanting and drumming. I was instantly asleep. I felt myself flying in the fresh morning air with Screech. I was listening to the soothing humming and chanting of the Mothers. It felt so good. So free. I was enjoying the escape. I didn't have any visions but the flight with Screech in my dream was refreshing and relaxing, until I heard Mother Wolf's voice break into my dream.

"Child, wake up. WAKE UP," she shouted.

Her voice and the interruption of my sleep, was as startling as a high-pitched whistle of a train breaking the quiet of a cold winter morning. I awoke sitting bolt upright.

"I'm sorry, Mother Eagle," Mother Wolf said as she materialized beside my bed, "You and Christy are in danger. We felt trouble for you both. But we can't see what it is."

At that moment there was banging on my door.

"We need you," Dorset said outside my door.

"Just a minute," I said and stumbled out of bed. I went to the door, unlocked it, and opened it.

Dorset quickly stepped in and closed the door behind him, "You've got to come with me to the Blockhold's home. We need you. I'll explain on the way."

"Did you tell Tom?" I asked.

"Duggan's looking after Tom. You're riding with me. They'll catch up with us. Let's go. Let's go," he said.

"Careful, Mother Eagle," Mother Spider was suddenly in the room.

I heard a small raspy voice in my head. I instantly knew it was her spider talking directly to me, *"I cannot see the weaves of the web. But I can feel vibrations on the web. I can sense danger for you and your Eagle. Stay alert. Journey well, Mother Eagle."*

Spider and the other Totems spoke well and had a better understanding of language than my eagle. But they had had years to develop their skills with their Mothers.

Screech and Wolf were ready to act and wide awake. I put out my arm and Screech took his perch on it. Wolf stepped in beside us as we hurried out the door and down the hall.

Wolf reluctantly climbed into the back of the van. Screech flew overhead. I sat in the front seat with Dorset

Once we were in the van, Dorset looked at my feet and said, "Do you sleep with your moccasins on?"

"Of course I sleep with my moccasins on. You never know when some asshole is gonna knock on your door and drag you out in the middle of the night."

I had forgotten I had gone to sleep wearing my dress and moccasins. I was glad I had. My dress made me feel safer somehow and I knew it was extra protection. But then I remembered I'd left my orange backpack behind. Something deep inside me regretted not taking it.

I could feel the Mothers were with me, and I could feel Screech in my mind, but everyone was quiet.

Dorset rambled on about the midnight shift change between him and the next watch at the house.

Midnight. Had I slept that long? I thought.

"I was just settling down in my room, when the officer on duty called me. He said he saw some strange activity outside...around the house and wanted to know what he should do. These backwoods cops are useless," Dorset said.

"What did you tell him?"

"I told him I'd call Duggan, and he should call in back-up, and wait till he had help. I told him I'd get you," Dorset said.

Just as he finished his sentence, we were pulling up in front of the Blockhold's house. I looked at the house. It was dark. There were no other police cars.

I turned back to Dorset and saw him pointing a gun at me.

"Keep your zoo under control or I will kill them," he said.

Wolf was snarling in the back of the van and was ripping at the seats with his claws and teeth trying to get at Dorset. I could hear Screech above us, and his screech was frantic and wild.

"Screech kill Weasel," Screech thought to me.

"No. Screech land. Now," I thought to him and sent Mother Wolf the thought, "Stop Wolf. Dorset will kill him." To make sure Dorset knew I was commanding Wolf, and I had control, I said aloud, "Wolf stop."

I was concerned that if Dorset thought I couldn't control Wolf, he would kill him.

Wolf stopped, but he had successfully destroyed the back seat closest to him and was making his way forward. He was only one seat away from Dorset and he had partially demolished it. Wolf continued to growl.

"Mother Wolf, he has to be careful. Please," I thought to her.

"Good," Dorset said as he threw a pair of handcuffs to me, "Put these on. I figure with your background you know how they work."

I did as I was told and put the cuffs on. But, I took my time and fumbled with them, thinking about what I could do and trying to understand what was happening. Dorset got impatient and tightened them on my wrists. I heard Screech land on the roof of the van. He scraped his talons along the roof.

"Screech, be good. Weasel will kill Wolf and me if you try to hurt him," I thought to Screech.

Screech immediately closed his mind to me. I couldn't hear his thoughts and I wasn't sure he could hear mine, but he stopped scraping his talons on the roof.

Chapter Eighteen

"Get out of the car. Don't give me any reasons to shoot you or your zoo, because I'll gladly do it," Dorset said as he opened his door and slid out of the van, still pointing his gun at me.

I found myself wishing I was as clever as those cops in the television shows. Have some smart move up my sleeve to get out of my predicament, but nothing was coming to mind. I did as I was told.

"Good. Well done Witchy-woman. Let the dog out. He's going in with us. The bird stays here," Dorset said.

I thought between Mother Wolf and Screech to keep everyone calm. I told Screech to stay on the roof. Screech didn't open his mind to me, but it was clear he heard what I was saying to him, and he stayed on the roof of the van. His eyes were wide open and circled by whites. He locked his focus on Dorset, his head and eyes following every move Dorset made.

I had the feeling he would ignore my warning if he could spot an opportunity to attack. I hoped he would stay calm.

Wolf, Dorset, and I crossed the lawn. Mother Wolf walked beside Wolf. She was invisible to Dorset. We all entered the house through the unlocked front door. As we stepped into the house I could see Anna and Harold sitting slumped over on their couch. An open box of pizza was sitting on the coffee table.

"About two hours ago, I brought them a pizza with my special blend of *spices*. They enjoyed it and crashed about half an hour ago. Perfect timing for the shift change. I sent the officer home, and took over." There was pride in his voice.

"Are they dead?" My heart was pounding so hard I could hear the pulse in my ears.

"No. Just drugged and asleep. They'll be out for hours. I don't waste death if I don't have to. Down the hall. Christy's room. I assume you know where it is. You first," he said and motioned me and Wolf forward with his gun.

I walked down the hall and opened the door to Christy's room. She appeared to be asleep. She was wrapped in a blanket like a baby snuggly fitted for an outing on a cold night.

"You're going to put her on your dog's back, or you can carry her. Your choice," he said.

"What have you done?"

"Just a little concoction I gave her in her juice…she didn't want pizza," he said, "She'll be fine for now. Get a move on. I suggest you put her on your dog's back."

"Like that's possible," I held up my hands with the cuffs on my wrists.

"Hey. You're the Witch. I'm just the guy with the gun. You figure it out and do it fast."

"How?" I thought to Mother Wolf.

"Wish we had Jojo. But Wolf is big enough and strong," she thought back.

"Maybe if he would crouch down beside the bed I could slide her across and onto his back," I thought to Mother Wolf.

As I sent my thoughts to Mother Wolf, Wolf laid down beside the bed. His back was level with the top. I knew Mother Wolf was directing him.

Christy was small and slim for her age, but moving her would be difficult with my hands in cuffs.

I slipped between Wolf and the bed. I slid my arms over Christy's head and down to her back, and lifted her up as best I could until she was across Wolf's back. I slid my arms out, and in an awkward maneuver I managed to roll Christy onto her stomach. She looked like a large bundle draped over Wolf's back. Wolf stood up and gently stepped forward. Then he growled and his eyes locked on Dorset and his gun.

I followed Wolf's gaze, and saw Dorset was staring at me with light hazel eyes—yellow eyes. He held out his hand and showed me the brown contacts sitting in his palm. He smiled and his top lip disappeared under his moustache.

I had been so busy with Christy, I hadn't noticed him removing his lens.

"Holy crap. You're Robbie," I said. I was hit by a wave of anger I couldn't suppress. Every ounce of my being wanted to attack him. Years of hate, fear, and anger ran through me like an electrical shock.

Wolf moved forward, threatening Robbie. He snapped his jaws several times. He started to salivate. Spittle flew from his mouth each time he snapped his jaw shut. This was not a warning of an attack. Wolf had every intention of killing Robbie.

Robbie stepped back and cocked his gun. He aimed it at Wolf's head.

Screech was instantly in my mind, **"Screech kill Weasel. Protect Red."** I could hear his hunting screech.

"Get them under control. Or you'll all die," Robbie shouted.

I had to fight back my own urge to attack. I also had to calm down Wolf and Screech. We weren't a match for a madman's gun.

"Calm Wolf," I thought to Mother Wolf. And to keep Robbie thinking I was in control of Wolf, I said aloud, "Wolf. Stop."

My mind was racing through thoughts. I gathered my will and focused my thinking. I calmed myself as best I could. Everything seemed to slow down. Suddenly, I was an observer watching a movie in slow motion.

"Screech stay where you are. Weasel will kill Wolf and me with his gun. Please be calm. We're safe for now," I thought to Screech, and did my best to hide my own fear and anger. I could feel Screech in my mind. He didn't answer me. But he didn't shriek again.

I knew Mother Wolf was calming Wolf. He stopped snapping his jaw, but there was drool hanging from his lips. He didn't step back and his muscles were tense. He was poised for a killing lunge. I had seen Wolf hunt. I knew Robbie would be dead in a split second. But, I didn't think Wolf could out maneuver a bullet.

As the situation calmed down, Robbie relaxed slightly. But he kept the gun cocked and ready to fire. His upper lip twitched and he smiled again. It was clear he thought he had regained control.

"Hiding in plain sight," he said, as he tucked the contact lens into his suit coat pocket. "Some hair dye, a moustache, and brown contact lenses."

"How did you fool Duggan?" I asked, stalling for time to think my way out of the situation.

"A little hacking and a trapdoor entry with the Wheaton Police computer's data and security systems. They found Detective Dorset and what I wanted them to know. Easy stuff in a backward town like this. I wanted to toy with you a little longer. But once you visited my mother, and the cops found that girl's body sooner than I had planned on, I figured I'd better speed things up. And it turned out perfectly when your pal, Deputy Dog, asked for police surveillance of the house. Of course, I volunteered for duty."

I felt someone watching me from the shadows. Could the Watcher be here in the room with us? I was really beginning to dislike that man or whatever he was. I ignored the feelings and the thoughts about the Watcher.

"So Witchy-woman, you wanted to find me, well here I am. Now, let's get her to the van, shall we?" he said and waved his gun toward the bedroom door.

"You could have just taken her. Why did you come and get me?" I said, still stalling for time.

"Oh, Witchy-woman. I've been planning this ever since I saw you the night my Dad was arrested. I could feel your power. But there was too much attention on you and then you moved out of town so fast. I had to wait. I knew I needed a psychic to make this work better. That psychic is you. Christy being mildly psychic is just an added bonus. A last minute opportunity. This is going to be fan-fucking-tastic. Now, get moving," Robbie demanded.

He ushered us through the house, out the front door, and to the van. I performed similar moves to the ones I had done in the bedroom, and moved Christy onto the back seat that had been partially demolished by Wolf.

"Now get in the van. Front seat." He closed the back door beside Christy's seat, and opened the front door, waving his gun toward the front seat punctuating his intent.

"What about Wolf," I said.

"He stays."

"He goes with us."

Wolf started to growl. Screech, who had been still to this point, started scraping his talons on the roof of the van.

"He stays and so does your bird. And if I hear one more growl from the dog or one more scratch from your bird, they are both dead. I don't need them," Robbie said, and pointed his gun at Wolf.

"You fire that thing out here and everyone will see and hear you."

"Look around. Everyone is asleep, by the time they get up, look out their windows, and figure it out, we'll be gone. Your wolf and bird will be dead. Welcome to the town of Armpit in the county of Nowhere," he said.

"Screech fly. Now. Fast and high," I thought to Screech.

Screech launched himself like a feathered missile. He disappeared into the blackness of the night sky, and thought to me, *"Screech watch Red."*

"What the hell was that?" Robbie asked.

"My eagle is angry because I told him he had to stay behind."

"You can really talk to that bird?" Robbie said relaxing slightly.

"Yah."

"Amazing. Tell the dog to beat it. And you get in the van," Robbie said.

I thought the request to Mother Wolf, and she had already told Wolf, but he had chosen to stand his ground. He bared his teeth and growled louder.

"You're testing my patience Witchy-woman," Robbie said.

"Mother Wolf, would you and Wolf be able to get Tom?" I thought to her.

"We'll get him," Mother Wolf thought to me as Wolf turned and took off up the street at an amazing speed. He could run almost as fast as Screech could fly.

"Screech protect Red," my beloved Screech thought to me, *"Screech follow Red."*

"Stay hidden so Weasel doesn't see you," I thought back to him, *"My beautiful brave, Screech. I love you."*

"Screech hunter. Weasel no see hunter," Screech thought and closed his mind to me.

I got into the van and Robbie got in on the driver's side. I thought for a moment about running, but gave up the idea. I couldn't leave Christy behind.

I wanted to check on Christy but I couldn't see her without turning around. I thought that kind of movement might set Robbie off. He slid into the driver's seat beside me. He uncocked his gun, tucked it between his legs, started the van. We drove away.

I sent a thought out to the Mothers and their Totems to check on Christy's condition. I heard a hissing in my head. It was Mother Diamondback's Totem talking directly to me, *"Sss-she sss-sleepsss. There'sss little venom left in her. Sss-she will wake sss-soon,"* he said.

"Thank you. You are a beautiful and brave Protector," I thought back to him. Now that I could speak directly to the Totems, they responded

with warm feelings that came in wonderful sensations through my dress. Diamondback's embroidered snake tightened and it felt like a giant hug. I needed the hug and was thankful for it.

"You killed those girls eleven years ago," I said to Robbie, hoping that if I could get him to talk, he might reveal something I could use to stop him or to help Christy and me.

"You and the hillbilly-dick Duggan nailed the wrong guy on that one," Robbie sneered.

"And you came back and killed more girls. Why?"

"Those were meant to get you back in town. You had to be here, because I have a special place in the woods for the ride. It's an old native ceremonial ground of some kind, with a circle of stones and in the middle is a stone outline of a turtle. I found it years ago when I was a kid. Special power there, it makes my abilities stronger. That's why you had to be here. I'm taking you there," Robbie said.

"You killed those girls just to get me back to Wheaton? You're a sick bastard," I said, and wondered what kind of ceremonial ground it was. I didn't want to ask the Mothers, I needed to keep Robbie talking. There had to be a way to stop him from killing me and Christy.

"Those girls weren't wasted," Robbie said, "They were good rides. Not as good as this one's going to be, but good anyway," he said.

"Rides?"

"Yeah, death rides. I ride their spirit...soul, as they die. I'm a psychic just like you," Robbie said, there was excitement in his voice. He seemed to think he'd found someone to understand what he was doing.

"I'm not like you. I don't kill children."

"Then you don't get it."

"Explain it to me."

"The death ride is amazing. Best high you'll ever have."

"I've had many kinds of highs and most don't end well. And none of them last," I said.

"This ride's going to last forever. I'm about to prove it with you and this girl. Three psychics will be the ultimate and permanent high." There was childlike excitement in his voice, "I'll be able to cross the bridge and return at will. I know the secret to permanent happiness, love, peace, and joy is on the other side of the bridge."

"Then why don't you just kill yourself and go there? Live there perma-nently," I said, but I knew what he was talking about. I had been seduced by those feelings when I had been in the meadow and at the bridge.

"Kill myself. No. No. It's more complex than that," Robbie said, "You see, when my Dad got all depressed, I...ah...helped him with his ride. And he went to a dark place."

"So you killed your father, too."

"I had to. He was going to chicken out at the end, but I kicked the stool out from under him. When I took hold of his hand, so I could connect with him for the ride, he led me to a dark place filled with sadness and fear. People were moaning, crying, and screaming. It was nothing like the bridge or joy of the meadow."

"The dark place you're talking about is the Between," I said.

"Between...good name for it. Anyway, I'm not going there. Almost got stuck there a couple of times when I was riding with the people who died at the home. Some of them didn't make it to the garden, and ended up in that dark place. If I kill myself, I think I might end up there, too. On a ride I can force myself to let go of the person's hand and I can get back here. By myself, I won't have that kind of control...or choice. Nope, not happening. I'm crossing that bridge and then I'm coming back," he said.

"Coming back. You can't come back. It's a one way trip when you cross the bridge."

"No, it's not. I've always had a feeling I had an ability...a psychic ability, like you have...but different. I always felt I could get to Heaven and return. I tested it with cats and dogs first. They didn't work so well, but I experi-mented with them. That's how I learned to ride. Then I decided to try a girl."

"Why a girl?"

"Because they were easy and I could trick them. I took them out for a picnic, and then gave them some of my dad's tranquilizer in a drink. Once they were asleep, I cut their arms so they would die slowly. As they died, I held their hand. That connected me to them for the ride."

"You killed them," I said, disgust for him filled me.

"Death isn't permanent. I know because on my first ride with that girl, I saw a guy come back off the bridge...he was happy. That's what hooked me."

"Hooked you on the ride," I said.

"No, hooked me to crossing the bridge. The man I saw coming back was so happy he glowed. I mean there was light all around him. He actually glowed. He told me the other side was beautiful and he would hold it with him for the rest of his life. Then he vanished. I knew life was going to be different for him forever. So, I tried to cross the bridge with the girl, but suddenly this darkness came. It scared me because it felt terrible. I let go of the girl's hand."

"So you weren't afraid enough to stop taking rides."

"No, I thought that if I could get the perfect ride, I'd cross the bridge and come back just like the man had done."

"The life after death story," I said.

"Exactly. I figure it can be done on purpose. It's like you did with those girls in the funeral home. You went and came back."

"I didn't cross the bridge and you saw me afterwards. I could have died," I stopped before I told him my eagle protected me. It was better that he didn't know anymore than he did.

"But you didn't die. You came back from the ride. And I believe with you, this girl, and me...at least one of us can cross and come back. I'm going to make sure that person is me," Robbie said, as he bobbed back and forth with excitement.

"Did you know that when you take your '*Death ride*' with these people and they don't cross the bridge, they become lost in the Between? The horrible place with pain and suffering, separated from love and everything that gave them joy," I said.

"That's not true. Those patients in the home crossed the bridge. Some of those bastards ran across the bridge and left me behind."

"All of them crossed?"

"Well...some didn't but most of them did. And some didn't make it to the meadow in the first place. But when I felt the dark place coming, I let them go. Those were really rough rides, bad trips. Sometimes I had a lot of trouble getting back. Just like the ride with my old man. It got too dangerous. So I gave up and came back here for you," Robbie said, paused for a moment, then added, "Best ride is young girls going through puberty with the hormonal thing going on."

I suddenly realized that was what the girls meant when they said '*woman's blood.*' They must have been going through puberty like Christy.

Dorset continued with his rant, "I didn't know what happened to the girls. When I rode with them, it always started to go dark and I let go of them. But this time will be better with the three of us."

"The girls got stuck in the Between. They were frightened and lost," I said.

"I guess it's an acceptable risk for the final goal."

"You're a sick, perverted son-of-a-bitch. I'm not helping you do anything, you stupid asshole." My anger spewed out of my mouth. My rage was getting harder to control.

"Say what you like Witch, but if you really do care about the girl, you'll do what I tell you to do. Hey, maybe you can keep her from going to the Between."

I was furious. My fury was breaking free and driving my thinking. The angry Jessica Seeker part of me roared to the surface. I acted before I thought.

I leaned over and grabbed the steering wheel with my hand-cuffed hands. I pushed and pulled. He lost control of the van. While he tried to recover control, I reached between his legs and managed to find the gun with the tips of my fingers. But I couldn't get a grip on it. He squeezed his legs together, drove the van off the road into a ditch, and slammed on the brakes. I flew forward, and hit my shoulder on the steering wheel. He grabbed my head and pushed me away, smashing me headfirst into the dashboard.

My head hit the dashboard so hard that I saw sparkles flashing in front of my eyes. I felt a warm liquid trickling from my forehead and down my face. I was dizzy. My head instantly began to pound in pain.

He pushed me against the back of the seat, pulled his gun out from between his legs and put it to my head. The look on his face was terrifying. His yellow eyes were thin slits. His lips were pulled back so tight his gums were showing.

"I only need you alive for a short time. You don't have to be in complete working order, bitch," he said.

I felt darkness and coldness radiating from him. I could see that young boy watching me with the yellow eyes the night Mr. Sheffield was arrested. Hatred and anger boiled in me. Those memories had tormented me for all these years. And the horror those girls faced in the Between made me want to rip out his throat.

"Red good hunter. Good kill. Yes." Screech thought to me. And sent back the vision I had of ripping out Robbie's throat and he was beside me helping finish the kill, *"Screech help. Screech protect Red,"* he said.

I realized I'd put us all in greater danger by losing control of my temper and thoughts.

"No. Screech. Stay hidden. Wait," I thought to him as I tried to calm myself, my thoughts, and my anger.

"DO...YOU...UNDERSTAND...ME...WITCH?" Robbie screamed at me.

"I understand," I whispered.

Robbie settled back into his seat. With one hand on the gun and one on the steering wheel, he drove the van out of the shallow ditch, dragging the undercarriage on some hard mounds of debris.

My vision wasn't clear and my head was still pounding. I wanted to wipe the blood from my face but I didn't dare take a chance on moving. I let the blood run down my face and drip off my chin.

Mother Diamondback thought to me, "You have a nasty head wound and a possible concussion Mother Eagle. You may pass out."

"I won't pass out. I won't let this bastard get away with this," I thought to her.

"Red fly. Screech help Red," Screech thought to me.

I gave my mind over to Screech and we flew. I could see our journey on the ground from his eyes in the sky. But his thoughts were hidden from me. We went down back roads, gravel roads, and finally turned down a dirt road that had two tracks where the wheels of other vehicles had driven.

From Screech's vantage point, I could see the road entered into a clearing surrounded by thick forest on three sides and a lake on the other side. An old rotting log cabin with a moss covered roof, sat at the edge of the clearing near the lake.

Robbie jarred me out of my connection with Screech, "This old place has been abandoned ever since I was a kid. Some people still come out here to fish," Robbie said as if nothing had happened and he was an old friend joining me on a road trip.

"Has Mother Wolf and Wolf got Tom, yet," I thought to the Mothers. I knew they were with me. I could feel their presence.

I heard a growling and a grating voice like sandpaper on wood. It was Wolverine. *"They're working on it. They'll be here soon. The Mothers have shown Mother Wolf where you are."*

I thanked Wolverine and complimented him, just as Robbie came around to my door. He opened it and I got out. I was unsteady on my feet from the dizziness, and the headache throbbed more when I moved. Robbie unlocked the handcuffs with one hand and told me to take them off and lift Christy from the back seat. He kept the gun pointed at me through the whole process. She was relatively small but she was still heavy and I was getting weaker. I managed to lift her into my arms.

Robbie forced me down a trail and into the forest. I could feel my moccasins and dress stiffening and flexing as I moved, it gave me the extra strength I needed to carry Christy without stumbling and falling.

It was darker in the woods than it had been by the cabin. I could hear the chirps of crickets and the croaks of frogs from the lake. There were scurrying creatures hidden from sight in the underbrush. It all felt comforting to me.

Mother Badger thought to me, "Our protectors are sending out a call for help."

"Please Mothers, chant for me and Eagle. We will need your strength," I thought to all of them and their Totem protectors. I thought to Screech separately, *"Stay close. Stay hidden."*

I had no strength to make the customary compliments. I was rude but it couldn't be helped. I was getting weaker and dizzier. Christy seemed to be getting heavier. The underbrush was thick and the path was uneven. My moccasins helped, but I knew I wouldn't be able to go much further.

Robbie was behind me pushing me along at the point of his gun.

Finally we came to an area in the forest, where the underbrush had been cleared away. There was a shallow indentation in the ground. The full moon lit up the area and I could make out the circle of stones around it. I could see the shallow indentation was the back of a turtle that had been outlined with stones.

"This was a special place. Used to celebrate and thank Mother Earth. The great Mother's energy will be with us. Trust in her power, child," Mother Spirit Bear thought to me.

"Put the girl there," Robbie said, pointing to the indentation, "And unwrap her."

I tried to bend over and stoop at the same time to put Christy on the ground as gently as I could, but I fell to my knees instead. I leaned forward and dropped Christy. I used my arm with the long sleeve to wipe the blood from my eyes. Then I carefully arranged her on the ground. I took my time unwrapping her, hoping to gain more time to think about how we could escape.

"Screech kill Weasel now," Screech thought to me.

"No. Find a perch in a tree nearby. Be quiet. Wait," I thought back to him, *"Big Bear and others will help soon."*

"Screech. Wait," Screech said, and showed me where he had landed on the top of a tree right behind me.

I began unwrapping Christy. She groaned and moved slightly as I opened the blanket.

"She's waking up," I thought to the Mothers.

For a moment I considered that if she woke up we might be able to run. But I instantly dismissed the idea, I was in no condition to run. Too dizzy and faint. My head was pounding in pain. I worried I might pass out at any second. And at best, Christy would be groggy when she woke. She wouldn't be able to run either. And if she woke up, she would be afraid. We couldn't escape. I had to stall and find a way to protect her, somehow, until Mother Wolf and Tom arrived.

Mother Diamondback thought to me, "I will hum a special sleep song to her. I won't let her wake. There is too much danger here for her. This could create poisonous memories for her."

Christy gave a soft sigh and I knew Mother Diamondback was humming to her. I leaned forward and softly kissed her forehead and whispered, "Sleep."

Robbie watched as I slowly unwrapped Christy, his gun aimed at me the whole time.

"What do you want me to do?" I said noticing my voice was weak and hoarse.

"I want you to sit still like a good little witch," he said as he sat down on the other side of Christy.

He placed the gun in his lap and pulled out a small scalpel from his pocket. He took Christy's arm and started to cut a deep gash in it, the same as I had seen on the girls in the Between and in the pictures of the girls in Duggan's office. I grabbed at his arm to stop him but he slashed my hand,

and I pulled back, shouting, "No. You don't have to do this. No one has to die. I have a better way."

"She has to be dying. That's the only way I can connect with her, and control the death ride," he said, and started to grab her arm again.

My head was throbbing, and I had to keep wiping the blood from my eyes as the wound on my head keep bleeding.

"I have a better idea," I said, "I'll explain."

He picked up the gun from his lap and pointed it at me, "Make it quick," he snapped at me.

"I have a medicine bag around my neck," I said and reached into the neck of my dress to pull it out.

"Don't be stupid," he said.

I could feel Screech getting worried and fidgeting on his perch in the tree. I sent him calming thoughts, and at the same time I thought to Mother Diamondback. Sending her a quick vision of the Vision Quest Mount where Mother Wolf had given me the black vial of liquid.

"It's risky. It could kill her. She's so young," Mother Diamondback thought to me.

"If I don't do this he'll kill her anyway," I thought to her, and said out loud to Robbie, "I have a...a drug...that will take her across, without killing her," I said hoping that was going to be the truth.

Robbie stared at me with his yellow eyes, his tone was sarcastic, "Oh, really."

"One drop on her gums," Mother Diamondback thought to me.

"Really. Please let me show you. You can always cut her if I'm lying," I said.

"And I can always shoot you both. You both need to be dying for me to ride with you."

"I'll take it, too. It'll work," and then I lied, "This is the potion I used in the funeral home to cross over and talk to the girls."

I slowly and carefully removed the black vial from my medicine bag. I removed the cork. My hands were trembling. My head was pounding. My vision was becoming more blurry. I was afraid I was going to drop the vial on the ground.

"Screech. Mothers. Help Red," Screech thought to me.

"Put a drop on your fingertip and wipe it on her gums," Mother Diamondback thought to me.

The Mothers' drumming and chanting increased in pitch and rhythm. I heard Screech in the background making a sound I had never heard him make before. It was a cooing sound that seemed to be coming from deep in his throat. A stillness began to fill my mind and my body. I stopped shaking. I put a drop of the black fluid on my fingertip, slipped my finger between Christy's lips, and rubbed the liquid on her upper gum.

I heard Robbie groan. He was holding Christy's hand. His yellow eyes were staring far into the distance. He quickly refocused his gaze onto me.

"That worked. I'm with her. This is going to be a great ride," he said. I started to put the stopper back in the vial, but Robbie said, "You're next."

Mother Diamondback thought to me, "Mother Eagle, we are all sure that you have a severe concussion. We don't know that you'll survive if you do this."

"I guess we're going to find out," I thought back to her.

"Two drops. No more. No less," Mother Diamondback thought to me and left my mind.

I put two drops in the palm of my hand. I replaced the stopper and put the vial back in my medicine bag. Robbie's yellow-eyed stare was fixed on me.

I licked the black liquid off of my hand as I took Christy's hand with the other. There was the bitter taste of the liquid mixed with the salty iron taste of my own blood.

I thought directly to the Totem Protectors and Mother Earth, "Protect us."

I felt as though I'd been slapped across the back of my head. My mind filled with sadness, anger, and darkness. Utter contempt filled me. I knew it was Robbie's mind. His mind was heavy and dark. It didn't have the light and gentle touch like the minds of the Mothers or the Totem Protectors.

Then like a tiny thread being pulled through the eye of a needle, I could feel Screech entering my mind, **"Weasel taste bad. Screech protect Red. Protect Rabbit. Screech take Weasel. No protect Weasel. Weasel hurt a little,"** Screech said to me.

I could feel Screech's mind filling mine as I saw through his eyes. He was flying down from his perch in the tree behind me. He landed softly in my lap.

"Fly now. Journey well," he thought to me.

In an instant I felt as though I was being sucked through a doorway. It was the same feeling I had on Vision Quest Mount with Mother Wolf. I didn't feel any of the pain or strange sensations I had felt when Screech had taken me to the Between in the funeral home.

I remembered Screech had told me it wasn't as painful when the body was dying. *Was I dying?* The thought of dying no longer pleased me the way it had the night Mother Wolf had found me.

I was happy with my new life as Mother Eagle. I loved my eagle, my family of Mothers, the reserve, and I had grown rather fond of that old rundown cabin-clinic.

Dammit.

I wasn't going to die with this asshole attached to me. Christy and I were coming back. Screw him.

In the distance I could hear a man screaming and yelling colorful expletives.

"Weasel hurt a little. Yes," Screech thought to me, and gave what sounded like an eagle's version of a giggle.

The darkness of Robbie's mind left me. I was standing in the meadow, surrounded by the garden of exotic flowers and their wonderful aromas. The sky was swirling in beautiful shades of amber, gold, and magenta. Tiny colorful creatures scurried about. I heard the Mothers chanting and drumming.

I felt weak but there was no pain. No dizziness. No blood on my hands. No blood dripping down my face.

I was standing in the field of flowers in my white dress with Screech perched on my arm. I felt him shivering but he stood tall and strong. In front of me, Christy was running through the flowers, touching them and smelling them. She was laughing at the little creatures that scurried past.

In a motionless heap beside me was Robbie. I thought he might be dead. I was disappointed when he moved.

"What the hell was that. That never happened before," he said as he stood up.

"Didn't you like the *Death Ride*?" I asked.

"We're here," he said and looked around.

Robbie's lips parted into a big toothy smile. He looked like a child on Christmas morning when he had opened the gift he had wished all year for Santa to bring.

I walked toward Christy and called to her, "It's beautiful isn't it?"

She ran towards me, "It smells nice, too. It's so happy here. Is this a dream? Can we stay?"

I took her hand and we began to walk together. The flowers and the plants moved out of our way as we stepped forward.

"I'm sorry, but we can only visit. We will all go back, soon," I said.

I hoped that was the truth but staying in the meadow was a pleasant thought. I was starting to feel the seduction of the happiness and peace of the meadow.

The bridge appeared on the horizon.

Robbie ran up behind us and grabbed Christy's other hand, "Look. The bridge," he said.

I felt Christy's hand tighten on mine as she whispered up to me, "The man with the yellow eyes."

"Don't worry. He can't hurt you. Eagle and I will protect you," I said loudly, making sure Robbie could hear me. He wasn't in control of this ride. Screech and I were in charge. No more children were going to die.

"I like your eagle. He's so beautiful," Christy said.

I felt Screech stand a little taller on my arm, "And he likes you too," I said.

"Let's get to that bridge. I'm crossing this time," Robbie said, picking up the pace. He broke into a run and was almost dragging Christy and me behind him.

"The hell we are," I said.

Mother Spider appeared in front of us and said, "Mother Eagle, you should mind those colorful expletives of yours. There's a child present."

The other Mothers appeared and surrounded us. They blocked us from the bridge. I noticed Mother Wolf was missing and so were all of the Mother's Totem Protectors. Then I saw the white Spirit Bear ambling up the meadow heading for his Mother. The bear's embroidered figure on my dress moved slightly, as he thought to me in his deep mellow voice, *"Hello, Mother Eagle. The Protectors and Mother Wolf are busy. Eagle and I are here. We will protect you and Rabbit,"* he thought to me as he stepped in beside his Mother and rubbed his gigantic head on her shoulder.

"Who are these women," Robbie said.

"Meet my ancestors, they are respectfully called Our Mothers," I said and pointed to the huge white bear, "The big cuddly guy over there is the brave and courageous Spirit Bear. He is the guardian of crossing souls," I said.

"Spirit Bear is so white and big. I want to hug him," Christy said.

Spirit Bear gave a huge bow of his head to Christy.

"He says he likes you too. And he says he will allow you to hug him, whenever you want," I said translating the thoughts as he sent them to me.

"Yah, yah. So what. Tell these women to move their fat asses out of the way. I want to get to the bridge before it disappears."

"Now you're in trouble. I can tell you from personal experience, they're not fond of disrespectful language or insults," I said.

Mother Spider took one step forward and was instantly standing face to face with Robbie, "Young man, did you ever hear the story about the boy who tickled the belly of the dragon once too often?"

"Afraid, my childhood didn't have a lot of fairytales," Robbie jeered.

"Too bad. Because if you had, you would know that when naughty little boys tickle the bellies of big grumpy dragons too often, the naughty little boys eventually get burned," Mother Spider scolded.

"Fairytales. Schmarytales. Just get your big, fat asses out of my way," Robbie said.

In one swift motion, Mother Spider swept Christy into her arms, and stomped her foot. The sky darkened. The ground shook. The flowers and plants were sucked back into the earth. The colorful creatures disappeared. The entire meadow turned grey. Everything went still and quiet.

The bridge disappeared.

"Eagle and I will take it from here," I thought to the Mothers so Robbie couldn't hear, and sent a separate thought to Screech, *"Can you take Weasel and me Between."*

Screech thought to me, *"Will hurt Weasel. Hurt a lot."*

"Good," I thought back to Screech.

"Mother Spider, we're going Between. I'm going to get the others Robbie has sent there," I thought to her so Robbie wouldn't hear me. I wanted our next ride to be a surprise, "Is Christy safe here with you?"

"Yes. We will protect Christy. Hold us, our home, and our love in your heart. Journey well, Mother Eagle," Mother Spider said.

The blackness engulfed Robbie, Screech, and me. I couldn't hear the Mothers chanting or drumming. Again, I felt no pain and wondered if my body had survived on the other side, but I heard Robbie screaming in pain. I liked the sound of that.

Then feelings of intense sadness, darkness, and a deep sense of loneliness swept through me. I knew we were Between.

I could hear Robbie beside me, screaming and cussing. I hoped the Between wouldn't be the end of our trip, but I certainly didn't have any good feelings about the outcome.

As we settled into the Between, I could feel despair all around me. There were the voices of people shouting, some were weeping, and others were moaning. Pain was everywhere. It was worse than the first time I was Between.

"Many here. Hate Weasel. Screech protect Red. No protect Weasel," Screech thought to me.

I could feel the strain in his mind as he thought to me. His body shivered and his talons dug deeply into my dress. It resisted the pressure and protected my arm. Screech seemed to be heavier on my arm than he had been in the meadow or the last time we were Between.

I looked around in the dim light. I could see Robbie a few feet away. He was surrounded by a large group of people. On a rough count, I could see at least fourteen or fifteen individuals. They were male and female, young and old, and they were all angry.

They were grabbing at his clothing. They pulled his hair, and yanked on his arms. They took turns hitting him and shouting, "Why? Why did you take the bridge away?"

"Screech, we've got to help these poor people," I thought to Screech.

Screech didn't answer right away, but he let me feel what he was feeling. There was so much pain and sorrow around us and in the Ghost Walkers that were attacking Robbie. Pure hatred and revenge filled my mind. I could feel the effort Screech was exerting to protect me. Then the suffering and pain went away.

"Too many... Ghostwalkers. Must leave. No take Weasel. Only Red. Must leave," Screech thought to me in a whisper and I felt him tremble on my arm, *"Spirit Bear help. Red think Spirit Bear."*

I thought about the huge white bear. I felt movement on my dress where the Spirit Bear was. His embroidered pattern on my dress disappeared.

Then out of the darkness strolled the big white Spirit Bear. Screech and Spirit Bear exchanged words in the ancient language. I didn't understand what they said. Screech relaxed slightly.

"Red think. Lost girls," Screech thought to me. I visualized the two girls Robbie had had a death ride with when he was a boy. The girls that had been lost in the Between for over a decade. Then I thought about the girl he had recently killed, she was the most difficult because I had never seen her.

"Think yellow eyes. Think girl lost," Screech whispered in my mind. I could feel he was getting weaker.

From behind me, I heard a chorus of young voices saying, "Yellow-eyes left us here."

I turned and saw three girls. I recognized two of them as the girls who had been killed in Wheaton during Robbie's first killing spree. They were pale and gaunt. Their eyes were sunken into their faces. Lines of tears stained their grey cheeks.

I realized the girl who wasn't familiar to me was Robbie's last victim. She was frightened, pale, and weeping but she was in better condition than the other girls.

In his deep rolling voice Spirit Bear thought to me, *"Eagle and Mother Eagle, thank you. I wouldn't have been able to find these little ones without you and your strong wise Protector's thoughts. They are safe with me. I'll take them across. Journey well, Mother Eagle."*

"Journey well, Spirit Bear," I said, and Screech spoke to him in the ancient language again.

Spirit Bear ambled over to the girls. Two of them threw their arms around his huge neck. The other grabbed onto huge chunks of his thick white fur. Spirit Bear roared at the Ghost Walkers attacking Robbie. He was inviting them to join him, but they ignored him.

In a very faint sad whisper Screech thought to me, *"Ghost Walkers angry. Want revenge. Spirit Bear leave. Take girls. Ghost Walkers stay Between. Weasel stay Between."*

Spirit Bear and the girls transformed into a beautiful white mist that lit up the area around them like a small sun. I could hear the girls laughing and giggling—then they were gone.

A loud piercing scream brought my attention back to Robbie. He was being bitten, beaten, and otherwise abused by the Ghost Walkers around him.

"Screech. Red. Must leave," Screech whispered in my mind. He was losing his grip on my arm and trembling so violently that I could barely balance him. I was also beginning to feel weak. My legs were beginning to tremble.

"Bring Weasel. Yes?" I thought to Screech.

"No Weasel. Only Red and Rabbit. Red think Rabbit. Think home. Remember Mothers. Remember love. Remember Big Bear," Screech said, and for only a split second I could feel his pain. It was deep, physical, and vicious. He was in agony.

Screech slammed his mind shut.

I couldn't feel his thoughts anymore.

I focused my thoughts on Christy and created an image of her in my mind. I willed myself to remember how much I wanted to return to the cabin-clinic. I thought about the Mothers and how much they loved me and I loved them. I thought of flying with Screech. Finally, I thought about Tom and the fragrance of sweetgrass and leather around him. The thought of Tom gave me great pleasure and comfort.

I could hear Robbie screaming. I felt no physical pain, and as I moved out of the Between, the sadness and suffering of the Ghost Walkers faded away.

I awoke to a splitting headache. I was freezing cold. My hand was throbbing. I looked down at my lap and saw my throbbing hand resting on my beloved Screech. It was the hand Robbie had slashed with his scalpel. Screech was covered with the blood from my wound. He was limp and motionless.

A small army of spiders were crawling over my hand. Working together, they were building a web around my wound.

Screech didn't move. I couldn't feel his mind.

"Screech," I thought to him. He didn't answer. He was deadly still. I couldn't feel him breathing. I started to cry. I was afraid that this time I had truly lost my beloved and brave Screech.

I trembled with cold and fear. I was thirsty. My head pounded from the inside out. I was in agony. I tried to sort through the confusion in my mind.

Christy?

The thought of her raced through my head. With great difficulty, I tried to focus my eyes. I saw her blurry form lying in the shallow indentation.

My mind was filled with a cacophony of grunts, squeaks, hisses, and growls. Some of the sounds were in words but I could only make out a few bits of what was being said. I knew that it was Totem Protectors speaking, but they were exchanging information too fast for my mind to translate.

I concentrated trying to process everything that was happening.

In the moonlight, I began to see shapes moving around Christy. As I focused on her, I saw another army of spiders rapidly crawling over Christy's wounded arm. They were building a web around the gash Robbie had cut on her and they had successfully stopped the bleeding.

There was a mother skunk and her young litter of pups cuddled around Christy's body. It was clear from the way they cuddled her that they were trying to keep her warm.

I looked over towards Robbie. He was pinned flat on the ground by an angry wolverine and really pissed off badger. He was struggling to break free when Wolverine clamped his jaw and sharp teeth over Robbie's arm. Robbie screamed in pain.

I saw a small green snake weaving its way over Robbie's chest. It was heading for his face. Robbie saw it and screamed again. I didn't know what kind of snake it was. It might have been poisonous.

"My beautiful Totem Protector's friend won't kill Robbie. It'll hurt a little," Mother Diamondback thought to me as she appeared with her snake wrapped around her neck. The other Mothers and their Totems popped up all around us.

The small bright green snake slithered onto Robbie's face. Wolverine and Badger kept him pinned down. The snake finally arrived at Robbie's nose and bit it.

"That's-sss for Eagle," Diamondback said, and made a couple of short hissing sounds, I think may have been laughter, and added, *"It hurts-sss a lot. It won't kill him. But he can't move."*

"Mother Eagle, you asked for the Totems' protection before you and Eagle left," Mother Diamondback said, "This is what they were up to while you were Between. You may have to refine your requests a little better in the future." Mother Diamondback began chanting and the other Mothers joined her.

As the snake venom took effect, Wolverine released his grip on Robbie's arm, but he remained on guard. Badger repositioned himself, lifted his leg, aimed carefully, and urinated on Robbie's crotch. The urine stank. Badger had marked his territory and signaled his domination of Robbie. Badger's skunk-like odor wasn't going to wash out easily.

I don't remember whether I said it out loud or just thought it, "So, what do you think of the zoo now, asshole?"

My vision started to dissolve into a thick fog. I couldn't see. I heard sirens in the distance.

"Screech. Talk to me, my beautiful brave Screech. Red loves you. Please talk to me," I thought to him.

Screech didn't answer or move. The Mothers chanting faded away into the distance. There was silence, then darkness.

Chapter Nineteen

offee.

I could smell coffee. I opened my eyes. At first my vision was blurry, but as I focused I saw Tom sitting beside my bed, fanning his hand over a steaming mug of coffee. He appeared to be fanning the steam towards my face.

"Ah, see. What did I tell you? I knew she wouldn't be able to resist a cup of coffee," he said to someone on the other side of my bed.

I turned to see who Tom was talking to and saw my beloved Screech perched on the back of a chair that had been moved to my bedside. I was in my hotel room.

"Screech," I thought to him.

He straightened on his roost, cocked his head, and thought to me, ***"Good morning Red. How are you feeling?"***

He didn't sound like Screech. He sounded deliberate and rehearsed.

"I'm feeling well considering. Thank you for asking. How is Screech feeling?" I thought to him, thinking we were having this conversation in a dream.

"Screech is well. And thank you for your...con...concern," Screech was more deliberate and rehearsed than the first time.

"Screech, are you okay? You sound different," I thought to him.

"Mothers and Totem Protectors are...teaching Screech. Talk better. Yes." he thought to me with excitement in his voice. Then he turned his head to look out the open hotel room window, ***"Screech hungry. Go hunt. Yes,"*** he thought to me, sounding more like his old self.

He flutter hopped to the window ledge and then launched into the air.

"Would Red like to fly with her...beloved, brave, and handsome Screech...this morning?" he thought to me with another rehearsed sentence. By the way he had described himself, I was relatively sure this line had been taught to him by the Totem Protectors.

"Thank you for the offer my beautiful, brave, strong, and very smart Screech," I thought to him. *"But I need to talk with Big Bear, and I need to eat."*

"Screech love Red. Red brave and strong," he thought back to me and closed his mind.

I turned my head back to Tom. He had his normal 'she's doing her Shamanic thing' face. Then he smiled. When he wasn't offering his professionally polite smile, his whole face smiled. His eyes seemed to get brighter and his lips drew back to show his white even teeth. He had a handsome face and a special kind of charm when he smiled for real.

He helped me to sit up and put pillows behind my back for me to rest on, and then handed me the cup of coffee. I tried to reach for it with my right hand and was reminded by a sharp stab of pain that it was injured. I could feel a small localized throbbing across my forehead, but the headache was almost gone. A flood of memories came back about the night in the woods.

Those memories quickly passed as Tom put the coffee mug in my other hand and helped me steady it. I liked the warm feel of his hand on mine. I enjoyed his touch. I didn't usually enjoy a man's touch. I'd had too many bad experiences with the men who had drifted through my life in the past. But Tom's touch was different. Gentle, warm, but strong and safe. I trusted his touch and liked it very much.

"Your eagle has been a force to be reckoned with for the last two days. He's been staring at the doc like he wanted to eat him every time he came in to examine you. He was a little better with the nursing assistants the hospital sent to look after you," he paused for a moment, and just gazed at me. His eyes searching mine, then he continued, "Anyway, I had to bring you to the hotel because, as weak as he was, your eagle still wouldn't let anyone but me near you. Then, he wouldn't let me put you in the ambulance."

"He's my Protector," I said.

"And I don't think that anyone doubts it. I almost wish I hadn't given him those white crystals so quickly. We might have had a chance to get you into the ambulance before he woke up," Tom stopped, and looked bashful for a moment. That was even more charming than his smile. Then he continued, "Hope you don't mind. I helped myself to the white crystals. But your eagle was in such bad condition. I thought he might die. I knew the crystals had perked him up in the funeral home after you two had rescued the girls."

"I'm glad you remembered the Golden Foxglove. You saved his life. Thank you," I said.

"You're welcome."

I turned to place my coffee mug on the nightstand beside the bed. I couldn't reach it. Tom stood up, took the mug from me, and placed it on the nightstand. Then he sat down on the edge of my bed.

"You'll have to thank the Mothers for all of us, because I think they did the best they could to keep Eagle settled down."

Ah, that's why they were all teaching Screech how to talk. Keeping him busy. That was clever on all their parts. Then I suddenly thought about Wolf. I hadn't seen him yet.

I looked around the room. I leaned forward to see if he was sleeping at the end of the bed. He wasn't anywhere.

"Where's Wolf?" I asked.

The smile slipped from Tom's face. He looked out the window as he spoke, "When all the chaos settled, I saw Wolf wandering into the woods. I haven't seen him since. But, Mother Wolf sent me a dream last night. I think he's with her."

As Tom was speaking, Mother Wolf appeared at the end of my bed. Wolf was standing beside her. He looked magnificent. His silvery-white fur almost glowed in a halo around him. His blue- green eyes were bright and alert.

"Good morning, Toadstool," Wolf thought to me in a deep silky voice. His mind had a light, pleasant, and somewhat, mischievous touch.

"Good morning, Wolf. You are more handsome now than before. Thank you for your courage and protection," I thought to him.

"You are welcome and it was my pleasure, Mother Eagle," he thought to me.

"Everyone wants to talk to you but I've told them to be patient. You need some time to recover," Mother Wolf paused in her thoughts to me, then she raised her left eyebrow. "You might want give Tom a special thank you for his help and protection, too. The man hasn't left this room in two days," she said. She and Wolf faded away.

I turned my attention back to Tom. He didn't have his usual 'she's talking with the Mothers' look. Instead, he was just gazing at me. His brown eyes were soft and warm, but searching. I was finding it hard to think.

"Ah...yes...ah...Wolf is with his Mother. And, I want to thank you...ah... again, for helping me and Eagle. Mother Wolf told me you've stayed with me for two days."

"You're most welcome, my lady, but I'm a busy man," he took my unin-jured hand in his. "I don't have a lot of time to rescue beautiful red-headed maidens from danger every day. Don't make a habit of this," he said, and gave my hand a gentle, long, and somewhat, gallant kiss.

His lips were soft and warm again my skin. Thinking was now officially impossible. I could feel blood rushing to my checks. I knew he saw me blush. I don't blush. How could this man make me blush...but he did.

As Tom looked at me, his left eyebrow rose. A mischievous smile crossed his face; he patted my hand, released it, and said, "I liked it, too. And you're even more beautiful when you blush, Mother Eagle," he said, and moved back to his chair by the bed, and gave me my cup of coffee back.

Tom just sat in his chair and looked at me. His brown eyes searching mine. I wondered how much my eyes were telling him. Screech was right, I liked this man.

But no. I couldn't do this. I wasn't ready for anything with anyone.

My old fears started to haunt me immediately. No commitments. No expectations. No involvements. I couldn't handle the confusion of feelings. I put them all away. I took a deep breath. Cleared my mind. I could feel the flush in my cheeks leaving me. I would have to be careful with this man and my feelings for him.

When I got my breath back, I asked, "How's Christy?"

"She's fine, and back home with the Blockholds. Which reminds me, you may have a lot of explaining to do when you fill out your statement for the police report," Tom said in his usual casual style, as though nothing had happened.

"Explaining, about what?"

"Everyone was baffled by the spider web bandage around Christy's arm, your hand and forehead. The bite marks on Robbie's arm and the snake bite on his nose. And, he stank like badger pee."

"Oh, that was just friends of the Mothers' Totems helping out," I said as casually as I could.

Tom lifted his left eyebrow again. It must be a family trait. Mother Wolf did the same thing. Then he said, "There weren't any animals around you or the others when we arrived. It just might be better to plead ignorance on this one when you fill out your statement. Shaman business should probably remain Shaman business. Ready to go home?"

"More than ready, but I'd like to see Christy first."

***

The Blockholds were happy to see us when we arrived. Anna and Harold were generous with their hugs. Their overt affection seemed to make Tom uncomfortable, and nearly knocked Screech off my arm.

Christy took me to her room. She went to her bookcase and took a small carving off the shelf and showed it to me. It was an eagle.

"It's not as beautiful as your eagle," she said, "But I wanted it so I could remember him and you."

Screech began to preen his wings. It was difficult for me to hold him steady on my arm with all the fidgeting he was doing. I wished I had my white dress on for the extra strength but I'd put on my 'work clothes' for travelling.

Christy told me about her time on the other side with the Mothers. She clearly enjoyed them. She loved their stories, and she was sad when she had to leave them and the meadow. She told me how they helped her to think about the things she loved at home, and how she missed her foster parents, Mr. and Mrs. Blockhold. By getting her to remember, although she didn't know it, the Mothers were helping Eagle and me to get her back home from the other side.

"I know the Mothers liked you. We will always remember you. You are part of our family," I said.

"I'm going to have two families." Christy was excited.

"Two families?"

"Yours and the Blockholds. They are going to adopt me. We talked about it last night. I would like them to be my mother and father. They said it might take some time, but I'm calling them Mom and Dad anyway. We're going to get a pet, too," she said. "Maybe a puppy."

I congratulated her. Being a foster child, I knew how important this was for her. A real home and family was only a dream for most foster kids.

We talked for a short while longer. I told her a story about how dream catchers protect people when they sleep, and promised to send her one to hang over her bed. But Screech's continued preening and fidgeting was driving me crazy. My arm was getting sore balancing him. I asked him to stop several times but he didn't.

Finally, he pulled a huge feather from his wing, and held it in his beak. He leaned toward Christy and bobbed his head up and down.

I thought to Screech, "*So this is what the fidgeting was all about.*"

"*It hurt a little. Screech can...still fly. The feather...is for...Rabbit,*" he thought to me in his new and improved sentence structure.

I translated as he thought to me, "He wants you to have the feather. Its eagle medicine will protect you from unwanted spirits and dreams. He wishes you a good life journey. We don't say goodbye, we always say. 'Journey well.'" Screech dropped the feather into her outstretched hand.

Christy thanked him, telling him how beautiful and brave he was, and ended with, "Journey well."

Christy and I returned to the living room. There were more hugs, good-byes, and a few tears.

When Tom and I got back into the van, I finally asked him about Robbie.

"He's in lock-up. They're moving him to a psychiatric facility in Hull tomorrow. He's really gone over the edge." Tom gave me a quick glance, "They're going to have him evaluated for his fitness to stand trial."

"I'd like to see him. Does that seem too...strange. I mean after all that's happened."

"You, Mother Eagle, have every right to see him. I think you should. Besides, we have to drop off your statement to Duggan."

Screech had been flying above us, and landed on my arm when we arrived at the station.

We walked through the front door and all heads turned to look. The receptionist greeted us, "Hello, Mother Eagle. Constable Diamondback. Commander Duggan is in his office. He's expecting you."

The officers on duty were silent but stared at us as we walked through the common area on our way to Duggan's office.

When we arrived, Duggan was polite but cool. We exchanged hellos and I gave him my written statement for their report on Robbie's arrest.

I had been careful when I wrote it making sure I left out my journey to the other side and the help the Totems gave me. I also left out Screech's participation. I mentioned that Wolf had tried to help, only because I needed to explain the damage to the seats in the van. But according to my view of the events, Robbie had kidnapped Christy and me. I had struggled with him. He smashed my head on the dashboard of the van, and I had passed out at the site and didn't remember anything until I woke up in the hotel room.

So...it wasn't the whole story, but I agreed with Tom; a Shaman's business should remain a Shaman's business. Besides, who would believe me anyway?

"Well, Mother Eagle, I suppose the town of Wheaton owes you an apology for our treatment of you in the past, and a thank you for your help this time." Duggan twirled his gold lighter between his forefinger and thumb.

"Apology and thanks are appreciated and accepted," I said, "May we see Robbie?"

Duggan lead us down the hall to the lock-up.

There were three cells side by side. Two of the cells had a wooden platform with a mattress, blanket, and pillow for sleeping. But there were no prisoners in them. Robbie's cell had the bare wooden platform. No blanket or pillow. He was wearing a blue paper hospital gown. A constable was seated on a chair outside the cell.

"Robbie is on suicide watch," Duggan explained.

Robbie was pacing in his cell and hitting at the air around him. He shouted, "Leave me alone. Dad, please shut up. Uncle, get away from me. All of you...leave me alone."

He was turning his head and looking around. His yellow eyes were wide and surrounded by dark circles.

"Ghost Walkers," Screech thought to me, and he let me see through his eyes.

There were people all around Robbie. They were punching and pushing him. Men and women shouted at him. They were angry. Robbie's father was also there, and he was shouting at Robbie, asking him why he had kicked the stool away. He kept repeating that he had changed his mind and he hadn't wanted to die. Robbie's Uncle kept asking why Robbie had given him the extra insulin that had killed him.

"Screech did you bring them back?" I thought to him.

"No. Only Red and Rabbit. Screech was weak. Could not bring Weasel back," Screech thought to me. There was sadness mixed in with his thoughts as we watched Robbie battle with the Ghost Walkers.

"How did Weasel and the Ghost Walkers get back here?" I thought back to Screech.

"Screech...not know."

"Is there anything we can do to help them?"

"No."

Robbie was a pitiful sight walking back and forth fighting people no one else could see. I couldn't watch anymore. I turned and walked away. Screech closed his mind to me.

As we walked back to the main offices of the police station Duggan said, "You don't have to pay for the damage your dog and bird did...I mean your wolf and eagle did to the van. You know the ripped up seats and the scratches on the roof."

"Good," Tom said, "There's a damaged chair in the hotel. They'll be sending you the bill for that as well."

"What?" Duggan exclaimed.

"Eagle used it for a perch. The upholstery is a little worse for the wear."

"What the fu...Fine," Duggan said.

***

When we arrived home at the cabin-clinic in Pinewood, it appeared as if half the reserve was there to greet us. Several children were holding up banners with *'Welcome home Mother Eagle'* written across them in black markers and crayons.

Monica, the little girl who had had the twig in her leg was limping toward the car and as I stepped out, she put her arms around me.

"We missed you," she said.

Sky carried her baby on her hip, and hurried over to me and gave me a one-armed hug. She had little blobs of paint in her hair and paint splotches on her clothes.

Swan followed her, took my bright orange backpack off my arm, and said, "We all thought it was about time we did something for you. You do so much for us."

I put out my arm for Screech to land, and said to Swan, "What the he... heck? It's my privilege to be your Medicine Woman. You owe me nothing. But that said, thank you all very much."

Tom walked over to me, carrying my black duffle bag, "They've all been busy, haven't they? See, Mother Eagle, we all love you," he smiled, and gave me a mischievous wink.

Mother Wolf materialized beside me. Wolf was with her. "Seems you've... intrigued my grandson. He's a good man," she thought to me.

"Just friends. Besides he's too much like you. He even has that left-eyebrow lifting thing that you do. Must be a genetic twitch," I thought back to her, trying to avoid revealing any of my feelings. The last thing I wanted was the Mothers meddling in my emotional life.

Mother Wolf lifted her left eyebrow and smiled, "Hmm."

"Mother Wolf. Leave it alone."

"Toadstool, you are a trial," Mother Wolf said, and shrugged.

Swan led me to the house. It looked like new.

"Careful," Swan said, "Some of the paint is still wet."

They had repainted the porch and replaced all the rotten pieces. They had painted the rockers on the porch and made new cushions for them. Inside they had painted, scrubbed, and refurnished the whole cabin. In the kitchen, there was a brand new refrigerator in the corner. All my herbs, medicine bottles, and poultice wrappings were neatly assembled and organized on freshly painted shelves.

Swan led me to the kitchen sink and turned on the hot water tap, and said, "You now have hot water on demand, compliments of a new water heater."

Mother Wolf nodded her approval.

The other Mothers were all busy checking the house and the kitchen. They were impressed with all the work that had been done in so little time.

In the middle of the kitchen, a boy and a girl about Christy's age stood beside a wooden stand that had a pole going up the middle intersecting with a carpet wrapped crossbar. The boy said, "Our class made this perch for Eagle."

The boy's face was awash with pride.

Screech did a flutter hop from my arm to the perch.

"He likes it and thanks your class," I translated Screech's thoughts to the children.

Swan clapped her hands together and announced, "Mother Eagle has had a long day. She would probably like some rest. I think we should leave her to enjoy her home."

Swan guided everyone out and then left. Tom remained with me on the cabin-clinic's porch.

"Swan is right, Mother Eagle. You look tired and a bit beat up." He looked at my bandaged hand and forehead.

"You're both right," I said, feeling the weariness of the past few days settling in on me.

"I'll check in with you tomorrow." He gently took my bandaged hand in his. His eyes searched mine, "Mother Wolf used to tell us kids that a kiss helps all wounds heal faster."

"All wounds?"

"All wounds."

He slowly leaned forward. I closed my eyes. I could smell the wonderful fragrance of leather mixed with sweetgrass. I could feel his warm breath on my face. I felt a hot blush rushing to my cheeks. He gently kissed my bandaged forehead and then tenderly whispered, "Journey well, Mother Eagle."

He slowly released my hand. I opened my eyes. He smiled. His eyes were soft as he searched my face.

"Journey well, Tom." I whispered back to him.

He hesitated for a moment before he turned and strolled off. He waved, got into his car, and drove away.

I stood alone on the porch watching him leave. *Yes. I would definitely have to watch my feelings around this man.* I thought. But I knew that my heart and my body were beginning to disagree with my mind.

Screech thought to me from inside the house. He was going hunting. I could also hear the Mothers checking out the house and arguing over the organization of the medicine shelves.

Home at last. It felt good to be back. I took in a big breath of the fresh, pine scented, moist, air. And relaxed.

I was thinking about sitting in one of the freshly painted rocking chairs, when I felt someone watching me. A slight gust of wind brushed by my arm. I turned and looked.

Mr. Jackson was standing beside me. He still had his cane and sunglasses, but as I looked at him, he began to transform. He became a tall, tawny man.

He was dressed in a raw-hide jacket, blue jeans, and cowboy boots. His short salt and pepper hair turned into a long black braid wrapped with a white leather strap and an eagle feather hung from the end.

He looked at me. He had sharp chiseled features that weren't unpleasant to look at, but made him appear stern. His face was almost too perfect to be real. His eyes were translucent blue with large black pupils.

"Hello, Mother Eagle, I'm Eagle Feather from Two Island Reserve. It's very far away, and I doubt that anyone here has ever heard of it. Thought I'd drop in and say hi," he said, then he displayed his braid to me, "Like the eagle feather? It's a tribute to you and your companion."

I was long past feeling surprised by anything anymore.

The Watcher who now called himself Eagle Feather changed his eyes from translucent blue to brown.

"So, how do you like it? It's my new persona. Much more handsome than Mr. Jackson, don't you think?" he asked.

"What are you doing here? And it's not just to say hi."

"I wanted to tell you that what you and your eagle did in Wheaton was incredibly brave, delightfully stupid, and ridiculously dangerous. The two of you are more powerful than any pairing we've seen. You can act in and affect other dimensions and you don't consider the consequences. Without a great deal of discipline, your talents and powers could be dangerous for your species. We are still not sure that the two of you aren't children playing with matches and gasoline. I want you to know that I'm going to keep a close eye on you two."

"Get to the point."

"Don't you want to know how that Robbie fellow returned with Ghost Walkers attached to him?" Eagle Feather asked.

"I suppose you're going to tell me."

"Your eagle didn't do it. He had to use most of his life force and some of yours to get you and the girl back. Rough trip for him. It came close to killing him. You didn't have any energy gifts for him to use. No crystals, no twine, no feathers, no tobacco. And, then he and you had to be heroes and brought the Spirit Bear to help those girls. He used his life force and yours to make it all happen. That kind of travelling and manifesting takes energy. Lots of energy. You and he seem to have it, but you both need to do a lot more training together. Damn that's a fine eagle you've paired with."

"He's far beyond fine. And I'm too worn out for your bullshit. Who brought Robbie back? You?"

"Jumpin' horny toads. She's smart too," he said and smirked.

"So what do you want? A gold star or something, cause I'm fresh out of gold friggin' stars."

"Ah, Jessica Seeker, nice to see you again," he said, "So, Toadstool, what do you think? Was it a good thing or a bad thing to bring back Robbie with the Ghost Walkers attached? We could have left them there and brought Robbie back. We could have left all of them there."

"It doesn't matter what I think, does it?"

"Hey, you're the one who thinks there's good and bad. Right and wrong. I was just wondering what you thought about this."

"I think it's cruel. He's suffering. The Ghost Walkers are suffering."

"Maybe it's justice. He's made a lot of people suffer. As for the Ghost Walkers, they had a choice. Spirit Bear was willing to take them. They ignored him. Your species is a puzzle to us."

"That still doesn't make it right."

"Doesn't make it wrong, either."

He smiled at me. His eyes flashed a translucent blue and back to brown again.

"And just what does that mean?" I said.

"You certainly are a fountain of questions. Not a lot of answers. That's a good thing."

The Watcher looked up at the sky and pointed to Screech. I looked up to see my beloved Screech soaring above us.

"I suggest you and your eagle start some rigorous training because you're going to need it. We'll be seeing each other again...soon."

There was a soft gust of wind on my face, and I looked to where the Watcher had been standing. He was gone.

"A storm is coming. Yes?" Screech thought to me.

"Yes."

And we both knew we weren't talking about the weather.

CPSIA information can be obtained
at www.ICGtesting.com
Printed in the USA
BVHW07074201122O
594500BV00001B/31